ELMORE LEONAR

CITY PRIMEVAL

HIGH NOON IN DETROIT

"A classic."

Austin American-Statesman

"A certifiable gem . . . Scene after scene . . . rings absolutely true."

Chicago Sun-Times

"A marvelous writer . . . A fast pace, crackling dialogue, and dark ironies [are what] we've come to expect from every Elmore Leonard novel."

New York Times Book Review

"The poet laureate of southeast Michigan's sinister side . . . *City Primeval* is one of his best."

Detroit Free Press

"Elmore Leonard is arguably the best living writer of crime fiction. . . . The true proof of his expertise . . . lies in *City Primeval*."

Roanoke Times & World News

"Elmore Leonard is the Alexander the Great of crime fiction."

Pittsburgh Post-Gazette

CITY
PRIMEVAL

Also by Elmore Leonard

Fiction

Raylan

Djibouti

Comfort to the Enemy and
    Other Carl Webster
    Stories

Road Dogs

Up in Honey's Room

The Hot Kid

The Complete Western
    Stories of Elmore
    Leonard

Mr. Paradise

Fire in the Hole (previously
    titled When the Women
    Come Out to Dance)

Tishomingo Blues

Pagan Babies

Be Cool

The Tonto Woman &
    Other Western Stories

Cuba Libre

Out of Sight

Riding the Rap

Pronto

Rum Punch

Maximum Bob

Get Shorty

Killshot

Freaky Deaky

Touch

Bandits

Glitz

LaBrava

Stick

Cat Chaser

Split Images

Gold Coast

Gunsights

The Switch

The Hunted

Unknown Man No. 89

Swag

Fifty-Two Pickup

Mr. Majestyk

Forty Lashes Less One

Valdez Is Coming

The Moonshine War

The Big Bounce

Hombre

Last Stand at Saber River

Escape from Five Shadows

The Law at Randado

The Bounty Hunters

Nonfiction

Elmore Leonard's 10 Rules of Writing

ELMORE LEONARD

CITY PRIMEVAL

High Noon in Detroit

WILLIAM MORROW
An Imprint of HarperCollinsPublishers

A hardcover edition of this book was published in 1980 by William Morrow.

CITY PRIMEVAL. Copyright © 1980 by Elmore Leonard, Inc. All rights reserved. Printed in the United States of America. No part of this book may be used or reproduced in any manner whatsoever without written permission except in the case of brief quotations embodied in critical articles and reviews. For information address HarperCollins Publishers, 10 East 53rd Street, New York, NY 10022.

HarperCollins books may be purchased for educational, business, or sales promotional use. For information please write: Special Markets Department, HarperCollins Publishers, 10 East 53rd Street, New York, NY 10022.

First HarperCollins trade paperback published 1999.
First HarperTorch paperback published 2002.
First William Morrow paperback edition published 2012.

Library of Congress Cataloging-in-Publication Data is available upon request.

ISBN 978-0-06-219135-9

23 24 25 26 27 LBC 16 15 14 13 12

For Joan

IN THE MATTER OF ALVIN B. GUY, Judge of Recorder's Court, City of Detroit:

The investigation of the Judicial Tenure Commission found the respondent guilty of misconduct in office and conduct clearly prejudicial to the administration of justice. The allegations set forth in the formal complaint were that Judge Guy:

1) Was discourteous and abusive to counsel, litigants, witnesses, court personnel, spectators and news reporters.
2) Used threats of imprisonment or promises of probation to induce pleas of guilty.
3) Abused the power of contempt.
4) Used his office to benefit friends and acquaintances.
5) Bragged of his sexual prowess openly.

6) Was continually guilty of judicial misconduct
   that was not only prejudicial to the administration of justice but destroyed respect for the office
   he holds.

Abridged examples of testimony follow.

On April 26, Judge Guy interceded on behalf of
a twice-convicted narcotics dealer, Tyrone Perry,
who was being questioned as a witness and possible suspect in a murder that had taken place at Mr.
Perry's residence. Judge Guy appeared at Room
527 of police headquarters and told the homicide
detectives questioning Perry that he was "holding
court here and now" and to release the witness.
When Sergeant Gerald Hunter questioned the pro-
priety of this, Judge Guy grabbed him by the arm
and pushed him against a desk. Sgt. Hunter voiced
objection to this treatment and Judge Guy said, before witnesses, "I'll push you around any time I
want. You're in my courtroom and if you open
your mouth I'll hold you in contempt of court."
Judge Guy then left police headquarters with Mr.
Perry.

In testimony describing still another incident the
respondent gave the appearance of judicial impro-
priety by his harrassment of a police officer.

The respondent had presided over a murder case
in which one of the three codefendants was Mar-

cella Bonnie. The charges against Miss Bonnie were dismissed at the preliminary examination.

Judge Guy was talking to Sgt. Wendell Robinson of the Police Homicide Section about the forthcoming trial of the codefendants and revealed how he had met Miss Bonnie in a bar and thereafter spent the night with her. He went on to say that "she was a foxy little thing" and "better than your average piece of ass."

Sgt. Robinson was quite surprised and chagrined to hear a judge boasting of his sexual participation with a former criminal defendant. As a result, Robinson prepared a memorandum about the incident which he forwarded to his superiors.

The respondent learned of this memorandum and exhibited his vindictiveness by improper and heavy-handed efforts to impair Robinson's credibility, referring to Sgt. Robinson before witnesses as "a suck-ass Uncle Tom trying to pass for Caucasian because he's light skinned."

Attorney Carolyn Wilder testified to the events in *People* v. *Cedric Williams*. The charges in this preliminary examination held June 19, were "second-degree criminal sexual conduct and simple assault," and Ms. Wilder, counsel for the defense, had stated clearly that her client would go to trial before entering a reduced plea. However, the respondent, Judge Guy, requested the defendant and his counsel to approach the bench, where he stated that if the defendant pled guilty to the lesser charge of assault and battery—a misdemeanor—he would be placed on probation and that would be the end of it.

"I'm street, just like you are," the judge said to the defendant, "and your attorney either doesn't have her shit together or your best interests at heart." Whereupon he sent the defendant and Ms. Wilder out into the hall to "talk the matter over."

When they returned to the bench and Ms. Wilder still insisted on a trial, Judge Guy said to the defendant, "Look, you better take this plea or your motherfucking ass is dead." When Ms. Wilder informed the bench that her client would, under no circumstances, plead to the lesser charge, Judge Guy berated the defense counsel, threatened her with contempt and stated: "I see now how you operate. You want your own client to be convicted . . . obviously pissed off because a black man got a little white pussy in this case."

Again in testimony Carolyn Wilder told how she attempted to serve a notice of appeal on Judge Guy as a favor to another attorney, Mr. Allan Hayes. The judge berated Ms. Wilder for one half hour calling her "a non-dues, honkie liberal," who had disrupted the orderly process of his courtroom.

Ms. Wilder: "At this time I asked if he was going to hold me in contempt. He did not respond but continued his berating monologue. When Mr. Hayes entered, having learned what was in progress, the judge addressed him at the bench, saying, 'I want you to explain to this honkie bitch who I am and I want her to understand I won't put up with any bullshit ego trips.' "

Sometime thereafter, the respondent, in a mellower mood, asked Ms. Wilder for a date, which she refused. Judge Guy responded to her refusal with a tasteless and insulting inquiry as to whether she was a lesbian. Thereafter, whenever Ms. Wilder came into court, the respondent would seize upon the opportunity to verbally embarrass and harass her.

That Judge Guy abused his contempt of court power was witnessed in an incident which involved Sgt. Raymond Cruz of the Detroit Police Homicide Section.

On this occasion Judge Guy ordered a twelve-year-old student to be locked up in the prisoner's bullpen for causing a disturbance in the courtroom during a school field-trip visit. Sgt. Cruz—testifying at the time in a pre-trial hearing—suggested the judge make the boy stand in a corner instead. At this the judge became enraged, held Sgt. Cruz in contempt of court and ordered him to spend an hour in the bullpen with the boy.

Sometime later, with the court in recess, Judge

Guy said to Sgt. Cruz before witnesses, "I hope you have learned who's boss in this courtroom." Sgt. Cruz made no reply. The judge said then, "You are an easy person to hold in contempt. You had best learn to keep your mouth shut, or I'll shut it for you every time."

Sgt. Cruz said, "Your honor, can I ask a question off the record?" The judge said, "All right, what is it?" Sgt. Cruz said, "Are you ever afraid for your life?" The judge asked, "Are you threatening me?" And Sgt. Cruz said, "No, your honor, I was just wondering if anyone has ever attempted to subject you to great bodily harm."

Judge Guy produced a .32-caliber Smith and Wesson revolver from beneath his robes and said, "I would like to see somebody try."

The record indicates that on several occasions Judge Guy abused members of the media by communicating with them in a manner unbecoming his office. The findings of the Tenure Commission with respect to this allegation state in part:

"Miss Sylvia Marcus is a reporter for *The Detroit News*. In his courtroom and before witnesses, Judge Guy subjected Miss Marcus to discourtesies of a crude nature . . . engaged in an undignified harangue about her newspaper being racist and, further, warned her 'not to fuck around with him.' "

* * *

In summary, the Judicial Tenure Commission warned:

"A cloud of witnesses testify that 'justice must not only be done, it must be seen to be done.' Without the appearance as well as the fact of justice, respect for the law vanishes.

"Judge Guy has demonstrated by his conduct that he is legally, temperamentally and morally unfit to hold any judicial position.

"By reason of the foregoing, it is our recommendation to the Supreme Court that Judge Guy be removed from the office he holds as Recorder's Court Judge of the City of Detroit and further, that he be permanently enjoined from holding any judicial office in the future."

At a press conference following the release of the Tenure Commission opinion, Judge Guy called the investigation a "racist witch-hunt organized by the white-controlled press." In the same statement he accused the Detroit Police Department of trying to kill him, though offered no evidence of specific attempts.

Alvin Guy stated emphatically that if the State Supreme Court suspended him from office he intended to "write a very revealing book, naming names of people with dirty hands and indecent fingers.

"Remember what I'm saying to you if they suspend me," Guy added. "The stuff is going to get put on some people, some names that are going to amaze you."

1

ONE OF THE valet parking attendants at Hazel Park Racecourse would remember the judge leaving sometime after the ninth race, about 1:00 A.M., and fill in the first part of what happened. With the judge's picture in the paper lately and on TV, he was sure it was Alvin Guy in the silver Lincoln Mark VI.

Light skin, about fifty, with a little Xavier Cugat mustache and hair that hung long and stiff over his collar and did not seem to require much straightening.

The other car involved was a Buick, or it might've been an Olds, dark color.

The judge had a young white lady with him, about twenty-seven, around in there. Blond hair, long. Dressed up, wearing something like pink, real loose, lot of gold chains around her neck. Good-looking lady. She had on makeup that made her look pale in the arc lights, dark lipstick. The valet parking attendant said the judge didn't help the lady in. The judge got in on his own side, giving him a dollar tip.

The other car, the dark-colored Buick or Olds—it might've been black—was pretty new. Was a man in it. The man's arm stuck out the window—you know, his elbow did—with the short sleeve rolled up once or twice. The arm looked kind of sunburned and had light kind of reddish-blond-color hair on it.

This other car tried to cut in front of the judge's car, but the judge kept moving and wouldn't let him in. So the other car sped off down toward the head of the exit line, down by the gate, the man in a big hurry. There was a lot of horns blowing. The cars down there wouldn't let the other car in either. People going home after giving their money at the windows, they weren't giving away nothing else.

It looked like the other car tried to edge in again right as the judge's car came to the gate to go out on Dequindre. There was a crash. Bam!

The valet parking attendant, Everett Livingston, said he looked down there, but didn't see anybody get out of the cars. It looked like the judge's car had run into the front fender of the other car as it tried to nose in. Then the judge's car backed up some and went around the other car and out the gate, going south on Dequindre toward Nine Mile. The other car must have stalled. A few more cars went past it. Then the other car made it out and that was the last the valet parking attendant saw or thought of them until he read about the judge in the paper.

Leaving the track, all Clement wanted to do was keep Sandy and the Albanian in sight.

Forget the silver Mark VI.

Follow the black Cadillac, the Albanian stiff-arming the wheel like a student driver taking his road test, hugging the inside lane in the night traffic. It should've been easy.

Except the Mark kept getting in Clement's way.

The ding in the fender didn't bother Clement. It wasn't his car. Realizing the guy in the Mark was a jig with a white girl didn't bother him either, too much. He decided the guy was in numbers or dope and if that's what the girl wanted, some spade with a little fag mustache, fine. Since coming to Detroit, Clement had seen all kinds of jigs with white girls. He didn't stare at them the way he used to.

But this silver Mark was something else, poking along in the center lane with a half block of clear road ahead, holding Clement back while the Cadillac got lost up there among all the red taillights. The jig was driving his big car with his white lady; he didn't care who was behind him or if anybody might be in a hurry. That's what got to Clement, the jig's attitude. Also, the jig's hair.

Clement popped on his brights and could see the

guy clearly through the rear windshield. The guy's hair, when he turned to the girl, looked like a black plastic wig, the twenty-nine-dollar tango-model ducktail. Fucking spook. Clement began thinking of the guy as a Cuban-looking jig. Oily looking. Then, as the chicken-fat jig.

Sandy and the Albanian turned right on Nine Mile. Clement got over into the right lane. When he was almost to the corner the silver Mark cut in front of him and made the turn.

Clement said, You believe it?

He followed the taillights around the corner and gunned it, wanting to run up the guy's silver rear-end. But instinct saved him. Something cautioned Clement to take her easy and, sure enough, there was a dark-blue Hazel Park police car up ahead. The Continental shot past it. The police car kept cruising along and Clement hung back now.

He saw the light at the next intersection, John R, change to green.

The Albanian's Cadillac was already turning left, followed by several cars. Now the Mark was swinging onto John R without blinking, making a wide sweep past the Holiday Inn on the corner. Clement began to accelerate as the police car continued through the intersection. He reached the corner with the light turning red, heard horns blowing and his tires squealing and thought for a second he was going to jump the curb and shoot into the Holiday Inn—a man on the sidewalk was scooping up his little dog to get out of the way—but Clement didn't even hit the curb. As he got straightened out he floored it down John R, beneath an arc of streetlights and past neon signs, came up behind the lumbering Mark and laid on his horn. The chicken-fat jig's head turned to his rear-view mirror. Clement pulled out, glanced over as he passed the Mark and saw the jig's face and his middle finger raised to the side window.

My oh my, Clement thought. I'll play a tune on your head, Mr. Jig, you get smart with me.

Except he had to be alert now. The next light was Eight Mile, the Detroit city limits. Sandy and the Albanian could turn either way or make a little jog and pick up 75 if they were headed downtown. If they made the light Clement would have to make it too. Else he'd lose them and have to start all over setting up the Albanian.

The Eight Mile light showed green. Clement gave the car some gas. He glanced over, surprised, feeling a car passing him on the right—the Mark, the silver boat gliding by, then drifting in front of him as Clement tried to speed up, seeing the light turn to amber. There was still time for both of them to skin through; but the chicken-fat jig braked at the intersection and Clement had to jam his foot down hard, felt his rear-end break loose and heard his tires scream and saw that big silver deck right in front of him as he nailed his car to a stop.

Sandy and the Albanian were gone. Nowhere in sight.

The chicken-fat jig had his head cocked, staring at his rear-view mirror.

Clement said, Well, I got time for you now, Mr. Jig, you want to play . . .

The girl turned half around and had to squint into the bright headlights.

"I think it's the same one."

"Sure it is," Alvin Guy said. "Same wise-ass. You see his license number?"

"He's too close."

"When I start up, take a look. If he follows us pick up the phone, tell the operator it's a nine-eleven."

"I don't think I know how to work it," the girl said. She had lighted a cigarette less than a minute before; now she stubbed it out in the ashtray.

"You don't know how to do much of anything," Alvin Guy said to the rear-view mirror. He saw the light change to green and moved straight ahead at a normal speed, watching the headlights reflected in the mirror as he crossed Eight Mile and entered

John R again, in Detroit now, and said to the headlights, "Out of Hazel Park now, stupid. You don't
know it, but you're going *down*town—assault with
a deadly weapon."

"He hasn't really done anything," the girl said,
holding the phone and looking through the windshield at the empty street that was lighted by a row
of lampposts but seemed dismal, the storefronts
dark. She felt the jolt and the car lurch forward as
she heard metal bang against metal and Alvin Guy
say, "Son of a *bitch*—" She heard the operator's
voice in the telephone receiver. She heard Alvin
Guy yelling at the operator or at her, "Nine eleven,
nine eleven!" And felt the car struck from behind
again and lurch forward, picking up speed.

Clement held his front bumper pressed against the
Mark, accelerating, feeling it as a physical effort, as
though he were using his own strength. The Mark
tried to dig out and run but Clement stayed tight
and kept pushing. The Mark tried to brake, tenta-
tively, and Clement bounced off its bumper a few
times. The Mark edged over into the right lane, the
street empty ahead. Clement was ready, knowing
the guy was about to try something. There was a
cross-street coming up.

But the guy made his move before reaching the

intersection: cut a hard, abrupt left to whip the car off his tail, shot into a parking lot—no doubt to scoot through the alley in some tricky jig move—and Clement said, "You dumb shit," as headlights lit up the cyclone fence and the Mark nosed to a hard, gravel-skidding stop. Clement coasted in past the red sign on the yellow building that said *American La France Fire Equipment*. A spot beamed down from the side of the building, lighting the Lincoln Mark VI like a new model on display.

Or an animal caught in headlight beams, standing dumb. Clement thought of that, easing his car up next to and a little ahead of the Mark—so he could see the chicken-fat jig through his windshield, the jig holding a car telephone, yelling at it like he was pretty sore, while the girl held onto gold chains around her neck.

Clement reached down under the front seat, way under, for the brown-paper grocery bag, opened it and drew out a Walther P.38 automatic. He reached above him then to slide open the sunroof and had to twist out from under the steering wheel before he could pull himself upright. Standing on the seat now, the roof opening catching him at the waist, he had a good view of the Mark's windshield in the flood of light from above. Clement extended the Walther. He shot the chicken-fat jig five times, seeing the man's face, then not seeing it, the windshield taking on a frosted look with the hard, clear hammer of the evenly spaced gunshots, until a chunk fell out of the windshield. He could hear the girl screaming then, giving it all she had.

Clement got out and walked around to the driver's side of the Mark. He had to reach way in to pull the guy upright and then out through the door opening, careful, trying not to touch the blood that was all over the guy's light-blue suit. The guy was a mess. He didn't look Cuban now; he didn't look like anything. The girl was still screaming.

Clement said, "Hey, shut up, will you?"

She stopped to catch her breath, then began making a weird wailing sound, hysterical. Clement said, "Hey!" He saw it wasn't going to do any good to yell at her, so he hunched himself into the Mark with one knee on the seat and punched her hard in the mouth—not with any shoulder or force in it but hard enough to give her a drunk-dazed look as he backed out of the car. Clement stooped down to get the guy's billfold, holding the guy's coat open with the tips of two fingers. There were three one-hundred-dollar bills and two twenties inside, credit cards, a couple of checks, ticket stubs from the track and a thin little 2 by 3 spiral notebook. Clement took the money and notebook. He leaned into the Continental again, bracing his forearm against the steering wheel, pulled the keys from the ignition and said to the girl giving him the dazed look, "Come on. Show me where your boyfriend lives."

They drove over Eight Mile to Woodward and turned south, Clement glancing at the girl sitting rigidly against the door as he gave her a little free advice.

"You take up with colored you become one of them. Don't you know that? Whether it's a white girl with a jig or a white guy with a colored girl, you're with *them*, you go to their places. You don't see the white guy taking the little colored chickie home or the white girl neither. He ever come to your place?"

The girl didn't answer, one hand on her purse, the other still holding onto her gold chains. Hell, he didn't want her chains, even if they were real. You start fooling around trying to fence shit like that . . .

"I asked you a question. He ever come to your place?"

"Sometimes."

"Well, that's unusual. What was he in, numbers, dope? He's too old to be a pimp. He looked like a pimp, though. You know it? I can't say much for your taste, Jesus, a guy like that—Where you from? You live in Detroit all your life?"

She said yes, not sounding too sure about it. Then asked him, "What're you gonna do to me?"

"I ain't gonna do nothing you show me where the man lives. He married?"

"No."

"But he lives in Palmer Woods? Those're big houses."

Clement waited. It was like talking to a child.

They passed the State Fairgrounds off to the left, beyond the headlights moving north to the suburbs, going home. The southbound traffic was thin, almost to nothing this time of night, the taillights of a few cars up ahead; but they were gone by the time Clement stopped for the light at Seven Mile. He said, "This ain't my night. You know it? I believe I've caught every light in town." The girl clung to her door in silence. "We turn right, huh? I know it's just west of Wood'ard some."

He heard the girl's door open and made a grab for her, but she was out of the car, the door swinging wide and coming back at him.

Shit, Clement said.

He waited for the light to change, watching the pale pink figure running across Seven Mile and past the cyclone fence on the corner. All he could see was a dark mass of trees beyond her, darker than the night sky, the girl running awkwardly, past the fence and down the fairway of the public golf course, Palmer Park Municipal—running with her purse, like she had something in it, or running for her life. Dumb broad didn't even know where she was going. A Detroit Police station was just down Seven a ways, toward the other side of the park. He'd been brought in there the time he was picked up for hawking a queer and released when the queer wouldn't identify him. If he remembered correctly it was the 12th Precinct.

Clement jumped the car off the green light so the door would slam closed, turned right, cut across Seven Mile in a jog to the left and came to a stop at the edge of the golf course parking lot. The girl was running down the fairway in his headlight beams, straight down, not even angling for the trees. Clement got out and went after her. He ran about a hundred yards, no more, and stopped, even though he was gaining on her.

He said, What in hell you doing, anyway? Getting your exercise?

Clement extended the Walther, steadied it in the palm of his left hand, squeezed off a round and saw her stumble—Jesus, it was loud—and shot her twice more, he was pretty sure, before she hit the ground.

Anybody standing there, Clement would have bet him the three rounds had done the job. Except he saw the girl, for just a second, sitting in a Frank Murphy courtroom fingering her chains. Better to take an extra twenty seconds to be sure than do twenty years in Jackson. Clement went to have a look. He saw starlight shining in her eyes and thought, That wasn't a bad looking girl. You know it?

Walking back to his car Clement realized something else and said to himself, You dumb shit. Now you can't go to the man's house.

2

"I THINK YOU'RE AFRAID OF WOMEN," the girl from the *News* said. "I think that's the root of the problem."

Raymond Cruz wasn't sure whose problem she was referring to, if it was supposed to be his problem or hers.

She said, "Do you think women are devious?"

"You mean women reporters?"

"Women in general."

Sitting in Carl's Chop House surrounded by an expanse of empty white tablecloths, their waitress off somewhere, Raymond Cruz wondered if it was worth the free drinks and dinner or the effort required to give thoughtful answers.

"No," he said.

"You don't feel intimidated by women?"

"No, I've always liked women."

"At certain times," the girl from the *News* said. "Otherwise, I'd say you're indifferent to women. They don't fit into your male world."

Wherever she was going the girl writer with the

degree from Michigan and four years with *The Detroit News* seemed to be getting there. It was ten past one in the morning. Her face glistened, her wine glass was smudged with prints and lipstick. The edge remained in her tone and she no longer listened to answers. Raymond Cruz was tired. He forgot what he was going to say next—and was rescued by their waitress, smiling through sequined glasses.

"I haven't heard your beeper go off. Must be a slow night."

Raymond touched his napkin to his mustache and gave her a smile. "No, it hasn't, huh?" And said to the girl from the *News*, "One time Milly heard my beeper three tables away. I had it on me and didn't even hear it."

"You weren't feeling no pain either," the waitress said. "I come over to the table. I said isn't that your beeper? He didn't even hear it." She picked up his empty glass. "Can I get you something else?"

The girl from the *News* didn't answer or seem interested. She was lighting another cigarette, leaving a good half of her New York strip sirloin untouched. She already had coffee. Raymond said he'd have another shell of beer and asked Milly if she'd wrap up the piece of steak.

The girl from the *News* said, "I don't want it."

He said, "Well, somebody'll probably take it."

"You have a dog?"

"I'll eat it for breakfast. Here's the thing," Raymond said, trying to show a little interest. "A man wouldn't say to me, 'I think you're afraid of women.' Or ask me if I think women are devious. Women ask questions like that. I don't know why, but they do."

"Your wife said you never talked about your work."

His *wife*—The girl from the *News* kept winging at him, coming in from blind sides.

Raymond said, "I hope you're a psychiatrist along with being a reporter—you're getting into something now. In the first place she's not my wife anymore, we're divorced. Is that what you're writing about, police divorce rate?"

"She feels you didn't say much about anything, but especially your work."

"You talked to Mary Alice?" Sounding almost astonished. "When'd you talk to her?"

"The other day. How come you don't have children?"

"Because we don't, that's all."

"She said you seldom if ever showed any emotion or told her how you felt. Men in other professions, they have a problem at work, they're not getting along with a customer or their boss, they come home and tell their wives about it. Then the wife gives hubby a few sympathetic strokes—poor baby—it's why he tells her."

The waitress with the gray hair and sequined glasses, Milly, placing his shell of beer on the table, said, "Where's your buddy?"

The girl from the *News* jabbed her cigarette out. She sat back and looked off across the field of table-cloths.

"Who, Jerry?"

"The kinda sandy-haired one with the mustache."

"Yeah, Jerry. He was gonna try and make it. You haven't seen him, huh?"

"No, I don't think he's been in. I wouldn't swear to it though. Who gets the doggie bag?"

The girl from the *News* waited.

"Just put it there," Raymond said. "She doesn't take it, I will."

"I have a name," the girl from the *News* said as the waitress walked away. Then hunched toward him and said, "I think your values are totally out of sync with reality."

Raymond sipped his beer, trying to relate her two statements. He saw her nose in sharp focus, the sheen of her skin heightened by tension. She was annoyed and for a moment he felt good about it. But it was a satisfaction he didn't need and he said, "What're you mad at?"

"I think you're still playing a role," the girl said. "You did the Serpico thing in Narcotics. You thought Vice was fun—"

"I said some funny things happened."

"Now you're into another role, the Lieutenant of Homicide."

"Acting Lieutenant. I'm filling in."

"I want to ask you about that. How old are you?"

"Thirty-six."

"Yeah, that's what it said in your file, but you don't look that old. Tell me . . . how do you get along with the guys in your squad?"

"Fine. Why?"

"Do you . . . handle them without any trouble?"

"What do you mean, 'handle them'?"

"You don't seem very forceful to me."

Tell her you have to go to the Men's, Raymond thought.

"Too mild-mannered—" She stopped and then said, with some enthusiasm, making a great discovery, "*That's* it—you're trying to look older, aren't you? The big mustache, conservative navy-blue suit—but you know how you come off?"

"How?"

"Like someone posing in an old tintype photo, old-timey."

Raymond leaned on the table, interested. "No kidding, that's what you see?"

"Like you're trying to look like young Wyatt Earp," the girl from the *News* said, watching him closely. "You relate to that, don't you? The no-bullshit Old West lawman."

"Well," Raymond said, "you know where Holy Trinity is? South of here, not far from Tiger Stadium? That's where I grew up. We played cowboys and Indians over on Belle Isle, shot at each other with B-B guns. I was born in McAllen, Texas, but I don't remember much about living there."

"I thought I heard an accent every once in a while," the girl from the *News* said. "You're Mexican then, not Puerto Rican?"

Raymond sat back again. "You think I was made acting lieutenant as part of Affirmative Action? Get the minorities in?"

"Don't be so sensitive. I asked a simple question. Are you of Mexican descent?"

"What're you, Jewish or Italian?"

"Forget it," the girl from the *News* said.

Raymond raised a finger at her. "See, a man wouldn't say that either. 'Forget it.' "

"Don't point at me." The girl's anger rising that quickly. "Why wouldn't a man say it, because he'd be afraid of you?"

"Or he'd be more polite. I mean why act tough?"

"*I* don't carry a gun," the girl from the *News* said, "and I'm not playing the role, you are. Like John Wayne or somebody. Clint Eastwood. Don't you relate to that type? Want to be like them?"

"Do I want to be an actor?"

"You know what I mean."

"I'm in homicide," Raymond said. "I don't have to make up anything; it's usually dramatic enough the way it is."

"Wow, is that revealing." She stared with a look that said she knew something he didn't. "You're almost in contact with your center. You catch a glimpse of it and the transference is immediate. I have to be this way because of my job—"

"I don't like to look at my center," Raymond said, straight-faced.

"A smart-ass attitude is another defense," the girl said. "I think it's fairly obvious the basic impediment is all this *machismo* bullshit cops are so hung up on—carrying the big gun, that trip. But I don't want to get into male ego or penis symbols if we can help it."

"No, let's keep it clean."

The girl studied him sadly. "I could comment on that, too, the immediate reference to sexuality as something dirty. It's not a question, lieutenant, of keeping it clean, but I guess we should try to keep it simple. Just the facts, ma'm, if you know what I mean."

He wondered if it was safe to speak. Then took a chance. "I'll tell you what influenced me most, once I joined the force. The detective sergeants, the old pros. You had to be in at least twenty years to make detective sergeant. Now, we don't have the rank anymore. You don't wait your turn, you take a test and if you pass you move up."

"Like you did," the girl from the *News* said. "A lieutenant with only fifteen years seniority. Because you went to college?"

"Partly," Raymond said. "If I was black I might even be an inspector by now."

The girl from the *News* perked up. "Do I hear resentment, a little bias, perhaps?"

"No, you don't. I'm telling you how it is. The old pros are still around; but they've been passed up along the way by some who aren't pros yet."

"You sound bitter."

"No, I'm not."

"Then you sound like an old man. In fact you dress like an old man." The girl from the *News* kept punching at him.

Dressing this afternoon, knowing he was going to be interviewed, Raymond had put on the navy-blue summer-weight suit, a white short-sleeved shirt and a dark-blue polka-dot tie. He had bought the suit five months ago, following his appointment to lieutenant. He had grown the mustache, he would have to admit, to look older, letting it grow and liking it more and more as it filled in dark and took a bandit turn down around the corners of his mouth. He felt the mustache made him look serious, maybe a little mean. He was five-ten and a half and weighed one-sixty-four, down fifteen pounds in the past few months. It showed in his face, gave him a gaunt, stringy look and made him appear taller.

The girl from the *News* brought it back to impressions, images, the possible influence of certain screen detective *types*, and Raymond said he thought movie detectives looked like cowboys. A mistake. The girl from the *News* jumped on that, said it was revealing and wrote something in her notebook. Raymond said he didn't mean real working cowboys, he meant, you know, the jeans, the denim outfits some of them wore. He said Detroit Police detectives had to wear coats and ties on duty. The girl from the *News* said she thought that was a drag.

They didn't seem to be getting anywhere. Raymond said, "Well, if that's it . . ."

"You still haven't answered the question," the girl from the *News* said, giving him a weary but patient look.

"Would you mind repeating it?"

"The question is, why can't a cop leave his macho role at headquarters and show a little sensitivity at home? Why can't you separate *self* from your professional role and admit some of your vulnerability, your fears, and not just talk about your triumphs?"

It was the first time he had heard anyone use the word. *Triumphs.*

"You know, like"—lowering her voice to sound masculine—" 'Well, we closed another case, dear. Let's have a drink.' But what about your resentments, all the annoying, picky things that're part of your job?"

Raymond nodded, picturing the scene. "Okay, I come home, my wife says, 'How'd it go today, dear?' I say, 'Oh, not too bad, honey. I got something I want to share with you.' "

The girl from the *News* was staring at him, a little hurt or maybe resigned. "I was hoping we could keep it serious."

"I'm serious. You're the wife. You say, 'Hi, honey. Have anything you'd like to share with me?' And I say, 'As a matter of fact, honey, I want to tell you something I learned today *about* sharing, as a matter of fact.' "

The girl from the *News* was suspicious, but said, "All right, what?"

"Well, a young woman was murdered," Raymond said solemnly. "Cause of death strangulation, asphyxia due to mechanical compression, traces of seminal fluid in mouth, vagina and rectum—"

The girl from the *News* said, "God."

"So today we talk to a couple of suspects and

one of them agrees to cop if we'll trade off with nothing heavier than manslaughter. We dicker around, offer him second degree and finally he says okay. He says actually it was his buddy that killed her. His buddy's fresh out of the joint and very horny. See, what happened, they met the girl in a bar and the guy making the statement says she was all over him. So they take her out in a field and after the first guy's done he lets his buddy have seconds."

"Lieutenant—"

"That's what he said, let his buddy have seconds. Well, the buddy gets in there and won't stop. I mean he just keeps, you know, going. Make a long story short, the girl starts screaming and the buddy panics and strangles her to shut her up. But, he's not sure she's dead. What if she comes to and identifies them in a lineup? So, they find this big chunk of concrete that'd been used to anchor a fence post—weighed about a hundred pounds—and they pick it up and drop it on the girl's face. Pick it up, drop it on her face again."

The girl from the *News* was reaching for her big mail-bag purse.

"Pick it up, drop it. When we found her, we thought maybe a semi had run over her. I mean you wouldn't believe this was a girl's face."

"I don't think you're funny."

"No, it isn't funny at all. But then the guy said in his statement—"

The girl from the *News* was walking away from the table.

"He said, 'This is what I get for playing Mr. Nice Guy and *sharing* my broad with my buddy.' "

He walked across Grand River to Dunleavy's. Jerry Hunter was at the bar with a girl who was resting her arm on Jerry's shoulder, close to him but acting bored. She took time to look Raymond Cruz over while he placed his doggie bag on the bar and ordered a bourbon.

Hunter said, "Where's your girlfriend?"

"They have a new thing," Raymond said. "They invite you to dinner. Then just before the check comes they get mad and walk out. Leave you with a forty-two-dollar tab."

The girl with Hunter said, "Is he one, too? He's kinda cute."

Hunter said, "She's trying to figure out what I do for a living."

"If anything," the girl said, moving slightly to the jukebox disco music. "Don't tell me, okay?" She narrowed green-shadowed eyes as she moved with the beat. "If we were over at Lindell's—who's in town?— you might be ballplayers. Except they never wear ties. Nobody wears ties." She stopped and gave Hunter a shrewd look. "Tie with a sportshirt, suitcoat doesn't match the pants—you teach shop at some high school, right? And your buddy"—looking at Raymond Cruz again—"what's your sign?"

There was an electronic sound close among them, faint but insistent, a mechanical voice saying *beep beep beep beep*—until Raymond opened his coat and shut it off. Going to the payphone he heard the girl saying to Hunter, "Jesus Christ, you're *cops*. I knew it. That's the next thing I was gonna say."

Everybody knows everything, Raymond Cruz thought. How'd everybody get so smart?

3

BECAUSE OF THE LIGHTS Raymond Cruz thought of a movie set. The overhead burglar spot and the headlights illuminating the scene. He thought of an actor in a television commercial saying, "The victim's suit is light blue, the blood dark red and the gravel a grayish white." He thought of a movie running backward in a projector, seeing the uniformed officers sucked into the blue and white Plymouths and the squad cars and the EMS van and the morgue wagon yanked out of the picture. Stop there— leaving the silver Continental and the murder victim. He heard Jerry Hunter say, "Well, somebody finally did in the little fucker."

It was difficult to think of Alvin Guy as victim.

"When I talked to Herzog," Raymond said, "the first thing I thought was how come it hasn't happened before this?" He stood at the edge of the scene with Hunter and his executive sergeant, Norbert Bryl. "Who found him?"

"Car from the 11th," Bryl said. "The judge'd

called nine-eleven on his car phone, but the operator couldn't get the location. Then a few minutes later a woman on the next street over there, 20413 Coventry, she calls at one-thirty-five to report gunshots."

"How about witnesses?"

"Nothing yet. Wendell's talking to the woman. Maureen's around someplace. American La France doesn't have a night number, but I don't think Judge Guy was here buying fire equipment."

"The squad-car guys make him?"

"Yeah. They couldn't tell by looking at him, but his wallet was lying there."

Raymond said, quietly but earnestly, "If they knew it's Guy then why didn't they pick him up and dump him in Hazel Park? It's two blocks away."

"Lieutenants aren't supposed to talk like that," Bryl said. "It's a nice idea though. Their body, their case. The squad-car guys didn't know for sure he's dead, so they call EMS. EMS comes, they take one look, call the meat wagon."

Hunter said, "They don't know he's *dead*? He took about three in the mouth, two more in the chest, through and through, big fucking exit wounds—they don't know he's dead."

Uniformed evidence technicians were taking Polaroid shots of the body and the Mark VI, measuring distances, drawing a plan of the scene, picking up betting ticket stubs, credit cards, cigarette butts;

they would haul the judge's car to the police garage on Jefferson and go over it for prints, poke around in all its crevices. One of the morgue attendants, in khaki shirt and pants, stood watching with a plastic body bag over his shoulder. Bryl began making notes for his Case Assigned Report.

It was 2:50 A.M. Alvin Guy had been dead little more than an hour and Raymond Cruz, the acting lieutenant in the navy-blue suit he had put on because he was meeting the girl from the *News*, felt time running out. He said, "Well, let's knock on some doors. We're not gonna do this one without a witness. We start dipping in the well something like this we'll have people copping to everything but the killing of Jesus. I don't want suspects out of the file. I want a direction we can move on. I want to bust in the door while the guy's still in bed, opens his eyes he can't fucking believe it. Otherwise—we're all retired down in Florida working for the Coconuts Police Department, the case still open. I don't want that to happen."

Norbert Bryl, the executive sergeant of Squad Seven, Detroit Police Homicide Section, had his graying hair razor-cut and styled at "J" Roberts on East Seven Mile once a month. He liked dark shirts and light-colored ties, beige on maroon, wore wire-frame tinted glasses and carried a flashlight that was nearly two feet long. Bryl plotted a course before he moved.

He said, "You don't want to rule out robbery as the only motive."

"Fires through the windshield and hits Guy in the mouth," Raymond said. "I want to meet this robber before he gets into something heavy."

The acting lieutenant left a few minutes later to find a telephone and report to Inspector Herzog. They did not talk about murder over radios.

Wendell Robinson, in a three-piece light-gray suit, came out of the darkness holding a small brown-paper sack. He said, "You doing any good? . . . I talk to the woman on Coventry call the nine-eleven? I say, I believe you heard some gunshots. The woman say yeah, and I saw the man done it. Earlier he was out in the alley and I saw him with this gun. I ask her which man is this and she told me he lives down the street, twenty-two five-eleven. I go down there, get the man out of his bed and ask him about a gun he has. Man frowns and squints like he's trying to get his memory working. Says no, I don't recall no gun. I say well, the lady down the street *saw* you with a gun, out'n the alley. You come on downtown we'll have a witness lineup, see if she can pick you out. The man say oh, *that* gun. Yeah, old thing I was looking to shoot rats with. Yeah, I found that gun yesterday, right in the same alley." Wendell held up the bag. "Little froze-up

Saturday night piece, blow the man's hand off he ever fire it."

"They lie to you," Hunter said. "They fucking lie right to your face."

Another man sitting in a car had been shot to death in front of the Soup Kitchen, corner of Franklin and Orleans, and the shooter—they learned later—had waited around to see the police cars and the EMS van arrive before he hopped on a Jefferson Avenue bus and went home.

There were people here, hanging around the un-marked blue Plymouth sedans, who had thrown on clothes or a bathrobe to come out and watch. Most of them seemed to be black people. Women holding their arms like they were cold. Figures silhouetted by the street light on the corner. It was a clear night, temperature in the mid-60s, warm for October.

Hunter, running a finger beneath his sandy mus-tache, stared openly at the watchers, studying them. When he turned to Bryl he said, "If it's rob-bery, why'd the judge pull in here?"

"To take a leak," Bryl said. "How do I know why he pulled in. But he was robbed and that's all we got so far."

"It was a hit," Hunter said. "Two guys. They set him up—see him at the track, arrange a meet. Maybe sell him some dope. One of 'em gets in the car with the judge, like he's gonna make the deal, the other guy—he's not gonna shoot through the window, his partner's in the line of fire. So he hits him through the windshield. With a .45."

"Now you have the weapon," Bryl said. "Where'd you get the .45?"

"Same place you got the piss he had to take," Hunter said. "Any way you put the judge here, for whatever reason, it's still a hit."

"This other man in the car," Wendell Robinson said, "he sitting there while the judge's calling the nine-eleven?"

"You guys're hung up on details," Hunter said. "We're talking about motive. Did the shooter have a motive other'n robbery?"

"Okay, I'm gonna give you the job, make up the list of suspects," Bryl said, "if you have enough paper and pencils and you have about a month with nothing to do, because you know how many names you're talking about? Every lawyer ever had a case in front of Judge Guy. Every guy he ever sent away. Everybody in the Wayne County Prosecutor's office. Every police officer—I'll be conservative—half the police officers in the city. Put down about twenty-six hundred names right there. Anybody even knew the prick, it's gone through their mind."

Wendell Robinson said to Hunter, "Idea upsets him."

"Yeah, he don't want to think about it," Hunter said, "but it was a fucking hit and he knows it."

Maureen Downey appeared out of the dark now and stood listening, holding a notebook and purse to her breast the way young girls carry school books. When Hunter noticed her she said, "If it was a hit, why'd he drive in here?"

"To go the bathroom," Hunter said. "Maureen, let's get out of here and find a motel."

She said, "Let's see if we can get a positive I.D. on the other car first."

Hunter said, "You think you're gonna impress me with that detective shit, you're crazy. You're a *girl*, Maureen."

"I know I'm a girl," Maureen said. She smiled easily and was never shocked, by words or bullet wounds. She had the healthy look of a brown-haired, 110-pound marathon runner and had been a homicide detective five of her fourteen years with the Detroit Police Department. Hunter would remind Maureen she was a girl. Or Hunter would tell her she was just one of the dicks. Hunter liked to play with Maureen and see her perfect teeth when she smiled.

Bryl used his flashlight to poke her arm and said, "What other car, Maureen?"

*   *   *

They waited as Raymond Cruz walked over to them from the Plymouth. He said, "Who wants another one?" Keeping his voice low. "Twenty-five-to-thirty-year-old white female, no I.D. Well dressed, shot, possibly raped, burn marks—what look like burn marks—on the inside of her thighs. Found her in Palmer Park half hour ago."

"Insect bites," Hunter said. "They can look like burn marks. Remember the guy—what was his name—the GM exec. Looked like he'd been burned, it turned out to be ant bites."

"Somebody lying in the weeds a couple of days, maybe," Raymond said. "This one's fresh. Car from the 12th spotted a guy out on the golf course, two o'clock in the morning. They put a light on him and he runs. Start chasing him and almost trip over the woman's body."

Bryl said, "They get the guy?"

"Not yet, but they think he's still in the park."

Hunter said, "Tell 'em they want to I.D. the lady, go across Woodward—what's the name of that place?—where all the hookers and the fags hang out."

"I asked Herzog, he said no, she doesn't look like a hooker. Probably she was dumped there. So—we can have her if we want. Herzog says how's it look here? I told him I don't know, we could be around all day and still use some help."

Maureen said, "We've got a second car at the

scene. Young guy hanging around—wait'll you hear the story."

Raymond took time to give her a warm look that was almost a smile. "I turn my back a few minutes, Maureen, what do you do? Come up with a witness. Is he any good?"

"I think you're gonna like him," Maureen said, opening her notebook.

In his statement Gary Sovey, twenty-eight, explained how his car had been stolen the previous week and how a friend of his happened to see it this evening in the parking lot of the Intimate Lounge on John R. Gary said he went over there with a baseball bat to wait for whoever stole it to come out of the lounge and get in the car, a '78 VW Scirocco. Gary stated that he waited in the vicinity of Local 771 UAW-CIO headquarters, which is between the Intimate Lounge and the American La France Fire Equipment Company. At approximately 1:30 A.M. he saw the Silver Mark VI traveling at a high rate of speed south on John R with a black Buick like nailed to its tail. He heard tires squeal and thought the two cars had turned the corner onto Remington. He was on the north side of Local 771, in other words away from the American La France parking lot, so he didn't actually see what happened. But he did hear something that sounded like gunshots. Five of them that he could still hear if he concentrated. Pow, pow, pow, pow, pow. About a minute later he thought he heard what sounded like a woman screaming, but he isn't positive about that part. Was he sure the black car was a Buick? Yes. In fact, Gary said, it was an '80 Riviera and he would bet it had red pin-striping on it.

"The part about the woman screaming—" Raymond stopped. "First—did he get the guy who stole his car?"

Maureen said it turned out the car had been there two or three days, abandoned, and the Intimate Lounge owner was about to call the police. So Gary was still mad.

She said, "I like the part about the woman screaming too. We can talk to Gary about it some more."

Raymond said, "If there was a woman with the judge and the guy's gonna shoot her anyway, why didn't he do it here?"

Hunter said, "Took her to the park, fool around a little first."

Bryl said, "I love to listen to you guys. You take the bare possibility a woman was even here and you make her the one found in the park. Two separate shootings with no apparent nexus at all except they were both shot about the same time. The judge here, the woman four, five miles away in Palmer Park."

"Across the street from Palmer Woods," Raymond said, "where the judge lived."

It stopped Bryl for a moment. He said, "Okay, you want to believe it, that's fine. If there's a connection we'll know by this afternoon, but right now I'm not gonna jump up in the air and get all excited. You know why?"

As he spoke they separated, moving aside to let the morgue wagon roll out to the street and Raymond didn't hear the rest of what Bryl said. He didn't have to. Norb Bryl wasn't going to jump up in the air because he was Norb Bryl—who weighed evidence before giving an opinion and kept hunches to himself. He would say, "We don't even know absolutely for sure from the medical examiner the cause of death and you're talking about a nexus." Bryl had established his image.

Raymond Cruz was still working on his.

Thirty-six years old—what do you want to be when you grow up? He wanted to be a police officer. He *was* a police officer. But what kind? (This is where it became gray, hazy.) Uniformed? Precinct Commander? Administrative? Deputy Chief some day with a big office, drapes—shit, why not work for General Motors?

He could be dry-serious like Norbert Bryl, he

could be dry-cool like Wendell Robinson, he could be crude and a little crazy like Jerry Hunter . . . or he could appear quietly unaffected, stand with hands in the pockets of his dark suit, expression solemn beneath the gunfighter mustache . . . and the girl from the *News* would see it as his Dodge City pose: the daguerreotype peace officer, now packing a snub-nosed .38 Smith with rubberbands around the grip instead of a hogleg .44.

How did he explain himself to her? Pictures could jump in his head, as they did right now, clamor for him to tie in the two killings, because he knew beyond any doubt there *was* a nexus and ballistics and lipstick on cigarette butts would prove it . . . Or, tests would prove nothing and that's why there were bored, cynical policemen who seldom ever hoped and were never disappointed . . . if you wanted to get into poses. Tell her there were all different kinds of policemen just as there were all different kinds of priests and baseball players. Why would she tell him he was posing? Playing a role, she said. You had to know you were doing it before you could be accused of posing. The gunship colonel in that Vietnam movie who wore the old-fashioned cavalry hat—what's his name, Robert Duvall—strutting across the beach, taking his shirt off to go surfing while the VC were shooting at him—*that* was posing, for Christ's sake.

Raymond Cruz said to his sergeants, watching

the morgue wagon drive off, "Who wants to go to Palmer Park? . . . Maureen?"

Alone together in the blue Plymouth neither of them said a word until they were almost to the park. Maureen assumed Raymond was going over the case, sorting out evidence, understandably withdrawn. Which was fine. She never felt obliged to talk, make up things, if there was nothing to say.

Maureen Downey wrote a paper in the ninth grade entitled "Why I Want To Be A Policewoman Someday." ("Because it really sounds exciting . . .") She had to leave Nashville, Michigan, to do it, entered the Detroit Police Academy and was assigned, for nine years, to Sex Crimes. Jerry Hunter would ask her why she supposed she was chosen for it and study her through half-closed eyes. He would ask her about deviates with weird fetishes and Maureen would say, "How about a guy who licks honey off of girls' feet?" Hunter would say, "What's wrong with that? . . . Come on, Maureen, give me a really weird one." And Maureen would say, "I'm afraid if I give you a raunchy one you'll try it."

She was comfortable with all the members of the squad, maybe with Raymond a little more than the others; which didn't seem to make sense, because most of the time he was pretty quiet, too. But when he did talk he said unexpected things or asked strange questions that didn't seem to relate to anything.

Like suddenly, after long minutes of silence, asking her if she had seen *Apocalypse Now*.

Yes. She liked it a lot.

"What'd you like about it?"

"Martin Sheen. And the one on the boat, the skinny one that almost died of fright when the tiger jumped out."

"You like Robert Duvall?"

"Yeah, I think he's great."

"You ever see a movie called *The Gunfighter?*"

"I don't think so."

"Gregory Peck. It's pretty old—it was on the other night."

"Not that I remember . . ."

"There's a part in it," Raymond said, "Gregory Peck's sitting at a table in the saloon, his hands are out of sight, like in his lap, and this hotshot two-gun kid comes in and tries to pick a fight, needles Gregory Peck, you know, to go for his gun, so the kid can make a name for himself."

"Did Gregory Peck have a big mustache?"

"Yeah, kinda. Pretty big."

"Yeah, I think I did see it. It was a lot like yours."

"What?"

"His mustache."

"Kind of. Anyway, Gregory Peck doesn't move. He tells the hotshot kid if he wants to draw, go ahead. But, he says, how do you know I don't have a .44 pointing at your belly while you're standing there? The kid almost draws, you can see him trying to make up his mind. Does Gregory Peck have a gun under there or not? Finally the kid backs off. He walks out and Gregory Peck sits back in the saloon chair and you see what he had under there was a pocket knife, paring his fingernails."

"Yeah, I did see it," Maureen said, "but I don't remember much about it."

"That was a good picture," Raymond said, and was silent again.

4

WHEN SANDY STANTON first told Clement about the Albanian, Clement said, "What in the hell's a Albanian?"

Sandy said, "An Albanian is a little fella with black hair and a whole shitpile of money he keeps down in his basement. He says in a safe inside a hidden room. You believe it?"

Clement said, "I still don't know what a Albanian is even. What's he do?"

"His name's Skender Lulgjaraj—" pronouncing it to rhyme with Pull-your-eye.

"Jesus Christ," Clement said.

"And if I spelled it you wouldn't believe it," Sandy said. "He's a little black-eyed doll baby that loves to disco. Owns some Coney Island hot dog places and tells me about all this money he's got every time I see him."

"How many times is that?"

"I been seeing him at discos for months. Dresses nice; I think he's doing all right."

"Well, let's go over and have us one with everything," Clement said.

"Wait till I find out if he's for real," Sandy said. "Skender wants to take me to the race track."

That had sounded pretty good. See what kind of a spender the Albanian was. Clement would tag along in Sandy's other boyfriend's car and Sandy would introduce him later that night—like they just happened to run into each other.

Except Clement ran into something else.

Del Weems wasn't exactly Sandy's other boyfriend, but she was staying in his apartment while he was out of town giving management seminars. Clement was staying with her.

Clement had never met Del Weems. He prowled around the man's apartment learning about him: studying weird prints and pottery and metal sculptures the man had acquired as a member of the Fine-Art-of-the-Month Club and trying on the man's Brooks Brothers clothes, size 42 suits, size 36 pants, the length not too bad but the bulk of the garments obscuring Clement's wiry 160-pound frame. Sandy said he looked like he was playing dress-up, trying on his dad's clothes. She said a boy with his build and his tattoos ought to stick to Duck Head bib overalls. They'd laugh and Clement would come out of the bedroom wearing yellow

slacks and a flowery Lily Pulitzer sports jacket
Clement said looked like a camouflage outfit in the
war of the fairies and they'd laugh some more: the
thirty-four-year-old boy from Lawton, Oklahoma,
and the twenty-three-year-old girl from French
Lick, Indiana, making it in the big city.

Sandy had met Del Weems when she was a cocktail waitress at Nemo's in the Renaissance Center
(and had quit after six months because she could
never find her way out of the complex with all its
different walks and levels and elevators you weren't
supposed to use—like being in Mammoth Cave—
you looked way up about one hundred feet to the
ceiling, except the RenCen was all rough cement,
escalators, expensive shops and ficus trees). Del
Weems was a good tipper. She started going out
with him and staying over at his apartment, at first
thinking Clement would love Del's specs: forty-
seven, divorced management consultant, lived on
the twenty-fifth floor of 1300 Lafayette, drove a
black Buick Riviera with red pin-striping, owned
twelve suits and eight sportcoats; she hadn't
counted the pants.

Clement had asked what a management consultant was. Sandy said he like put deals together for
big companies and told corporate executives—the
way she understood it—how to run their business
and not fuck up. Clement was skeptical because he
couldn't picture in his mind what Del Weems actu-

ally did. So when the man went off on this latest seminar and Clement came to stay, he pulled the man's bills and bank statements out of the teak-wood desk in the living room, studied them a few minutes and said shit, the man didn't have money, he had credit cards. Clement said, You stick a .38 in the man's mouth—all right, partner, give me all the money you been raking in off these fools, and what does the chicken fat do? Hands you his VISA card. Shit no, it had to be cash and carry. Ethnics were the ones, Clement said. Ethnics, niggers, anybody that didn't trust banks, had a piss-poor regard for the IRS and kept their money underneath the bed or in a lard can. Ethnics and dentists.

That's why the Coney Island Albanian sounded good—if Clement could ever get close enough to check him out. In the meantime, cross off the chicken-fat consultant as a score, but use his place to rest up and get acquainted with the finer things in life. Drink the man's Chivas, watch some TV and look out at the twenty-fifth-floor view of Motor City. Man oh man.

The Detroit River looked like any big-city river with worn-out industrial works and warehouses lining the frontage, ore boats and ocean freighters passing by, a view of Windsor across the way that looked about as much fun as Moline, Illinois, except for the giant illuminated Canadian Club sign over the distillery.

But then all of a sudden—as Clement edged his gaze to the right a little—there were the massive dark-glass tubes of the Renaissance Center, five towers, the tallest one seven hundred feet high, standing like a Buck Rogers monument over downtown. From here on, the riverfront was being purified with plain lines in clean cement, modern structures that reminded Clement a little of Kansas City or Cincinnati—everybody putting their new convention centers and sports arenas out where you could see them. (They had even been building a modernistic new shopping center in Lawton just before the terrible spring twister hit, the same one that picked Clement's mom right out of the yard, running from the house to the storm cellar, and carried her off without leaving a trace.) Clement would swivel his gaze then over downtown and come around north—looking at all the parking lots that were like fallow fields among stands of old 1920s office buildings and patches of new cement—past Greektown tucked in down there— he could almost smell the garlic—past the nine-story Detroit Police headquarters, big and ugly, a glimpse of the top floors of the Wayne County jail beyond the police building, and on to the slender rise of the Frank Murphy Hall of Justice, where they had tried to nail Clement's ass one time and failed. Clement liked views from high places after years in the flatlands of Oklahoma and feeling the sky pressing down on him. It was the same sky when you could see it, when it wasn't thick with dampness, but it seemed a lot higher in Detroit. He would look up there and wonder if his mom was floating around somewhere in space.

Sandy stayed with the Albanian all night and came home to the high-rise apartment about noon with a tale of wonders—a secret door, a room hidden away in the basement—aching to tell Clement about it.

And what was Clement doing? Reading the paper. Something he never did. Sitting on the couch in his Hanes briefs, scratching the reddish hair on his chest, idly tugging at his crotch, hunched over and staring at the newspaper spread open next to him, his mouth moving silently as he read.

"You reading the *paper?*"

Clement didn't even look up. Now he was scratching the bright new blue and red tattoo of a gravestone on his right forearm that said *In Memory of Mother*.

"Hey!"

Hell with him. Sandy went into the bedroom and changed from her silk shirt and slacks to green satin jogging shorts and a T-shirt that said, *Cedar Point, Sandusky, Ohio*. She looked about seventeen, a freckled, reddish-blond 95-pounder with perky little breasts. Sort of a girl version of Clement, though a lot better looking. Not the type, at first glance, some management consultant would keep in his stylish apartment. But look again and see the fun in her eyes. It gave a man the feeling that if he turned her little motor on she'd whirl him back to his youth and take him places he'd never been.

Back in the living room she tried again. "You still reading the paper?"

You bet he was, every word for the second time, wondering how in the world he hadn't recognized the judge last night—the face with the little tango-dancer mustache staring up at him from the front page. He had shot and killed Judge Alvin Guy and didn't have a thing to show for it. Not even peace of mind now. If there wasn't a reward for shooting the little dinge he ought to get a medal, *some*thing.

Sandy Stanton said, "Well, I saw the secret room and I saw this little safe he's so proud of. I think me and you could pick it up without any fear of getting a hernia. But it was weird. I mean the room, with all these cots folded up and a fridge, one tiny room like full of canned goods . . . Hey, you listening or what?"

Clement sat back on the couch, exposing the pair of bluebirds tattooed above his pure-white breasts. When they had first met three and a half years ago at a disco, Clement had said, "You want to see my birds?" and opened his shirt to show her. Then he'd said, "You want to see my chicken?" When Sandy said yes he pulled his shirt out of his pants and showed her his navel in the center of his hard belly. Sandy said, "I don't see any chicken." And Clement said, "It's faded out; all that's left is its asshole."

He nodded toward the picture in the paper. "You know who that is?"

"I saw it," Sandy said. She looked from the bold headline, JUDGE GUY MURDERED, and the grinning photograph to Clement's solemn face. Her mind said, Uh-oh, what does he care? And edged toward the answer, saying, "He couldn'ta been a friend of yours. Why you taking it so hard?"

Silence.

Uh-oh.

Sandy said, "Hey, quit biting your nails. You want to tell me something or's it better I don't know?"

Clement said, "Wouldn't you think they'd be a bounty on the little fucker? A reward you could claim?"

"*Who* could claim?" Sandy waited while Clement bit on the cuticle of his middle finger, left hand, like a little boy watching his dad read his report card.

"You know how many people," Clement said, "would pay money—I mean real money—to have this done? Jesus."

"Maybe somebody did pay."

"Nuh-uh, it was done free of charge. God *damn* it."

"Oh, shit," Sandy said, with a sigh of weariness. "Don't tell me no more, okay?"

She was in the kitchen, Clement was still scratching, biting his nails, staring at the grinning ex-judge, when the security man in the lobby called. He was an older colored man that Sandy liked to kid with, calling him Carlton the doorman. They didn't kid around today, though. Sandy came out to the living room.

"Maybe they come to give you the medal."

Clement hadn't even heard the buzzer. He looked up now. "Who's that?"

"The police," Sandy said.

5

RAYMOND SAID TO WENDELL ROBINSON, "You want to be the good guy?"

"No, you be the good guy," Wendell said. "I'm tired and grouchy enough to be a natural heavy, we need to get into that shit."

Raymond said, "What're you tired from?" But didn't get an answer. The door opened and a girl in a Cedar Point T-shirt and satin shorts was looking at them with innocent eyes. Raymond held up his I.D.

"How you doing? I'm Lieutenant Raymond Cruz, Detroit Police. This is Sergeant Robinson. We understand—the man downstairs says your name's Sandy Stanton?" Very friendly, almost smiling.

The girl gave them a nod, guarded.

"He said Mr. Weems is out of town." Raymond watched the girl's wide-eyed expression come to life.

"Oh, you're looking for Del."

Raymond said, "Is that right, Sandy, he's out of town?"

"Yeah, on business. I think he went out to California or someplace."

"You mind if we come inside?"

"I know it sounds corny," Sandy said, as though she hated to have to bring it up, "but have you got a warrant?"

Raymond said, "A *warrant*—for what? We're not looking for anything. We just want to ask you about Mr. Weems."

Sandy sighed, stepping out of the way. She watched the two cops, the white one in the dark suit and the black one in the light-gray suit, glance down the short hallway at the closed doors as they went into the living room: the white cop looking around, the black cop going straight to the windows—which is what almost everyone did—to look out at the river and the city. The view was sharply defined this afternoon, the sun backlighting the Renaissance Center, giving the glass towers the look of black marble.

Raymond didn't care too much for the colors in the room: green, gray and black with a lot of chrome. It reminded him of a lawyer's office. He said, "I understand you drove Mr. Weems to the airport."

"The day before yesterday," Sandy said. "What is it you want him for?"

"You drive him out in his car?"

"Yeah . . . why?"

"Buick Riviera, license PYX-546?"

"I don't know the license number."

"What do you do for a living, Sandy?"

"You mean when I work? I tend bar, wait tables if I have to."

"You use the car last night?"

"What car?"

"The Buick."

"No, as a matter of fact, I didn't," Sandy said. "I went to the race track with somebody."

"What one, over in Windsor?"

"No, out to Hazel Park."

She saw the black cop turn from the window. He looked like a suit salesman or a professional athlete. A colored guy who spent money on clothes.

The other one was smiling somewhat. "You win?"

Sandy gave him a bored look. "You kidding?"

"I know what you mean," Raymond said. "Who'd you go with?"

"Fella I know. Skender Lulgjaraj."

Amazing. The white cop didn't blink or make a face or say, Lul-what?

"What time'd you get home?"

"It was pretty late."

"Skender drive?"

There, again, like he was familiar with the name. "Yeah, he picked me up."

Raymond frowned, like he was a little confused. "Then who used Mr. Weems' car last night?"

He had a little-boy look about him, even with the droopy mustache. The dark hair down on his forehead . . .

"Nobody did," Sandy said.

She watched them give her the old silent treatment, waiting for her to say too much if she tried to fake it or tried to act innocent or amazed—when all she had to do was hang tough and not act at all. It was hard, though; too hard and finally she said, "What's wrong?"

Raymond said, "Did you loan the car to somebody?"

"Uh-unh."

"Did Mr. Weems, before he left?"

"Not that I know of. Hey, maybe it was stolen."

"It's downstairs," Raymond said. "You have the keys, don't you?"

"Yeah, someplace."

"Why don't you check, just to make sure."

Oh shit, Sandy thought, feeling exposed now in her shorts and T-shirt and barefeet, wanting to walk over to the desk and pick up the keys, but having no idea in the world what Clement did with them—trying to picture him coming in then. No, *she* had come in and he was sitting on the couch reading the paper—the paper still lying there pulled apart. She said, "Gee, I never know what I do with keys," and got away from them, starting to move about the room.

Raymond said, "Maybe we can help you," and began looking around.

"That's okay," Sandy said, "I think I know where they are. You all sit down and take it easy." She made herself *walk* down the short hallway, dark with the doors closed, went into the master bedroom and shut the door behind her.

Clement was stretched out on the king-size bed. He put his hands behind his curly head as Sandy entered and wiggled his toes, showing her how cool he was.

"They gone?"

"No, they're not gone. They want the keys."

"What keys?"

"The fucking car keys, what do you think what keys?" Her whisper came out hoarse, as though from a bigger, huskier woman.

"Shit," Clement said. He thought a moment, watching her feel the top of the dresser. "They got a search warrant?" She didn't answer him. "Hey, you don't have to give 'em no keys."

"You go out and tell 'em that," Sandy said. She had the ring of keys in her hand now, moving toward the door.

"Well, it's up to you," Clement said. "You want to give 'em the keys, go ahead."

Sandy stopped at the door. "What else'm I supposed to do?" Her whisper a hiss now.

"Give 'em the keys," Clement said. "It don't matter."

"What if they find your prints in the car?"

"Ain't no prints to find." Clement's arms were reddish-tan, his body pure white, his bluebirds and ribs resting against the green and gray swirls of Del Weems' designer bedspread. Sandy started to open the door and he said, "Hon? I had sort of an accident parking the car when I come back."

"I love the time you pick to tell me." Sandy took time herself to raise her eyes to the ceiling, giving her words a dramatic effect. "What'd you hit?"

"You know those cement pillars?" Clement said. "I scraped one of 'em parking, took a little paint off the fender—if they was to ask you how it happened." He paused, letting her stare at him. "Why don't we keep it simple, say you did it. How's that sound to you?"

Raymond Cruz looked at the desk, wanting to open the drawers. He looked at the metallic stick figures on the glass coffeetable. He looked at the newspaper lying open on the couch and then over to the dark hallway. What if he walked in there and started opening doors? . . .

Sandy Stanton. He could see the name in a type-written report, a statement. He tried the name in his mind. Sandy Stanton. He tried it with Norb Bryl saying the name, Sandy Stanton, and then with Jerry Hunter's voice, Sandy Stanton. The name, just the name, was registered in his mind from a time in the past. He walked to the window and looked out. Then turned again, abruptly, and was facing the room as Wendell came out through the dining-L from the kitchen, Wendell shaking his head.

Raymond motioned to the window. "You can see 1300 from here."

"I noticed," Wendell said. "You can see the window of the squad room."

Past the Blue Cross building and beyond the dome of old St. Mary's to the granite nine-story municipal building, police headquarters—1300 Beaubien—to a window on the fifth floor, above the police garage.

"You notice," Raymond said, "that's 1300 and this is 1300?"

"No shit," Wendell said. "I notice something else, too, while I'm busy noticing. You got hold of something in your head you're playing with."

Raymond frowned at him, amazed. What was going on? Everybody, all of a sudden, reading him.

"You're laying back, savoring it," Wendell said. "You gonna share it with me or keep it a secret?"

Amazing. It was spooky. Raymond thought of the girl from the *News* and said, "You tell your wife what you do?"

Now Wendell was frowning. "What I *do?* You mean tell her everything? Do I look like I want to get shot with my own gun?"

"How do you know what I'm thinking?" Raymond said.

"I don't. That's why I'm asking."

"But you said—like I was onto something."

"Some kind of scheme," Wendell said. "When you lay back and don't move around you understand?—but look like you want to be *do*ing something? It means you ready to spring. Am I right?"

"Sandy Stanton," Raymond said.

"Cute little lady."

"Where've you heard the name?"

"I don't have the recall you do," Wendell said, "but it's familiar, like a movie star or a name you see in the paper."

"Or in a case file."

"Now we moving," Wendell said.

"Albert RaCosta," Raymond said.

Wendell nodded. "Keep going."

"Louis Nix . . . Victor Reddick. And one more."

"Yeah, the Wrecking Crew." Wendell was still nodding. "I know the names but they were a little before my time."

"Three years ago," Raymond said. "I'd just come over to Seven."

"Yeah, and I came like six months after you," Wendell said. "I read the file, all the newspaper stuff, but I don't recall any Sandy Stanton."

Coming into the living room Sandy said, "What're you doing, talking about me?" She held up the ring of keys. "I found 'em. But if you want to take the car—I don't think I can let you. I mean you haven't even told me why you want it."

Raymond said, "You're sure, Sandy, those're the keys to the Buick?"

"Yeah." She held them up again. "GM keys. He's only got one car."

"When's the last time you drove it?"

"I told you—when I took him to the airport."

"The car was in good shape?"

"Yeah, I guess so."

"No dings in it or anything?"

"Oh," Sandy said and made a face, an expression of pain. "Yeah, I guess I scraped the fender, you know, on the cement down where you park. Del's gonna kill me."

"Getting into a tight place, huh?"

"Yeah, I misjudged a little."

"Which fender was it you scraped, Sandy?"

She held her hands up in front of her and looked at them, trying to remember if shitbird, lying on the bed in his bikinis, had told her. "It was . . . this one, the left one." She looked from the white cop to the black cop and back to the white cop, wanting to say, Am I right?

"You're sure?" Raymond asked her.

Shit, Sandy thought. "Well, I'm pretty sure. But I get mixed up with left and right."

"You live here, Sandy?"

God, it was hard to keep up with him. "No, I'm just staying here while Del's gone, like apartment-sitting."

"Anybody staying with you?"

She hesitated—which she knew she shouldn't do. "No, just me."

"Is anybody else here right now?"

Christ. She hesitated again. "You mean besides us?"

"Uh-huh, besides us," Raymond said.

"No, there isn't anybody here."

"I thought I heard you talking to somebody— you went out to the bedroom."

Sandy said, "I don't think you're being fair at all. If you aren't gonna tell me what you want, then I'm gonna ask you to please leave. Okay?"

"You were at the Hazel Park track last night?"

"I already told you I was."

"You see, Sandy, a car that sounds like Mr. Weems' Buick—maybe the same license number—was involved in an accident out there. About one o'clock."

Sandy said, "You're *traffic* cops? Jesus, I thought this was something more important than *that*."

"Like what?" Raymond asked.

"I don't know. I just thought . . . two of you come up here, it has to be, you know, something important." Sandy began to feel herself relax. The white cop was saying, well, they have to check out the car first, see if it might be the one, before they get into anything else. Probably—Sandy was thinking at the same time—it was a car that looked like Del's and had almost the same license numbers. That *could* be what happened, a coincidence, and shitbird in the bedroom had nothing to do with it. There were all kinds of black Buicks, it was a very popular color this year . . . she told the white cop that, too, and the white cop agreed, nodding, and then he was saying, "Oh, by the way . . .

"You seen Clement Mansell lately?"

Like a total stranger coming up to you and saying your name—she couldn't be*lieve* it because she could look right at the white cop and was positive she had never seen him before in her life; he *couldn't* know anything about her. She felt exposed and vulnerable again standing there barefoot with no place to hide, no way to play it over again and be ready for the question. Still, she said, "Who?"

"Clement Mansell," Raymond said. "Isn't he an old friend of yours?"

Sandy said, "Oh . . . you know him? Yeah, I recall the name, sure."

Raymond took a business card out of his suit-coat pocket. Handing it to her he said, "You see him, have him give me a call, okay?" The white cop and the black cop both thanked her as they left.

In the elevator Wendell said, "Clement Mansell. You name the Wrecking Crew and save the best one. I don't know how I forgot him."

Raymond was watching the floor numbers light up in descending order. "I probably shouldn't have done that."

"What, ask her about him? We all stunt a little bit."

"If it's Mansell I want him to know. I don't want him to run, but I want him to think about it. You understand what I mean?"

"Man could be back in Oklahoma, nowhere around here."

"Yeah, he could be in Oklahoma," Raymond said. His gaze came down from the numbers to the elevator door as it opened. They walked out of the alcove, across the lobby to the desk where the door-man sat with a wall of television monitors behind him. Raymond waited for him to look up at them.

"You didn't tell us somebody was with her, Miss Stanton, twenty-five oh-four."

"I don't believe you ask me," the doorman said.

Wendell said, "How long he been staying with her, uncle?"

The middle-aged black man in the porter's coat looked at the younger, well-built black man in the three-piece light-gray suit. "How long is *who* been staying with her?"

"Shit," Wendell said. "Here we go."

6

ONE TIME CLEMENT WAS RUN OVER by a train and lived. It was a thirty-three-car Chesapeake & Ohio freight train with two engines and a caboose.

Clement was with a girl. They were waiting at a street crossing in Redford Township about eleven at night, the red lights flashing and the striped barrier across the road, when Clement got out of the car and went out to stand on the tracks, his back to the engine's spotlight coming toward him at forty miles an hour. Yes, he was a little high, though not too high. He was going to jump out of the way at the last second, turned with his *back* to the approaching train, looking over at the girl's face in the car windshield, the girl's eyes about to come out of her head. Instead of jumping out of the way Clement changed his mind and laid down between the tracks. The train engineer saw Clement and slammed on the emergency brake, but not in time. Twenty-one cars passed over Clement before the train was brought to a stop and he crawled out from beneath the twenty-second one. The train engineer, Harold Howell of Grand Rapids, said, "There was just no excuse for it." Clement was taken to Garden City Hospital where he was treated for a bruised back and released. When questioned by the Redford Township Police Clement said, "Did I break a law? Show me where it says I can't lay down in front of a train if I want?"

Clement said it was like conditioning, preparing for the ball-clutching moments of life while building your sphincter muscle. After lying in front of a freight train you can lie in bed in your underwear while two cops are visiting, asking about a certain black Buick—and while a mean-looking Walther P.38 automatic is hidden nearby at that very moment—and not worry about making doo-doo in the bed.

See, just as he knew he could easily have jumped out of the train's way—as he explained it to Sandy—he knew he had time to skin through this present situation and get rid of the gun—though he hated to do it—before the cops came back with a warrant to search or impound the car. He admired the cops' restraint these days in not opening bedroom doors or looking inside cars without a warrant. Cops had to go by the rules or have their evidence thrown out of court. It gave Clement, he felt, an edge: he could grin at the ball yankers, antagonize them some, knowing they had to respect his rights as a citizen.

But who in the hell was Lieutenant Raymond Cruz? Clement studied the business card, then looked out the bedroom window and squinted toward the police headquarters building.

"I don't know any Lieutenant Raymond Cruz."

"Well, he knows you."

"What's he look like? Regular old beer-gut dick?"

"No, he's skinny almost."

"Raymond Cruz," Clement said thoughtfully. "He's a greaser, huh?"

"Well, he's sort of dark, but not real. He seems quiet . . . Except, it's funny, I get the feeling there's some meanness in him," Sandy said. "Otherwise he's kinda cute."

Clement turned from the windows to look at her, idly scratching himself. "He's cute, huh? I got to see a De-troit homicide dick that's cute; that'll be one of my goals in life." He said then, "I guess you better get dressed."

"Where we going?"

"Want you to drive over to Belle Isle for me."

"Now wait a sec—"

"I'll tell you where the gun's hid down the garage. Up over one of them beams? Put it in your purse—it's in a paper sack so it won't get your purse oily or nothing—go on over to Belle Isle and park and come walking back across the bridge part way. When there's no cars around—'specially any blue Plymouths—take the sack out of your purse and drop it in the river."

"Do I have to?" Sandy turned on her pained expression. Clement just looked at her, patiently, and she said, "I ought to least have a joint first. Half a one?"

"I want you clear-headed, hon bun."

There wasn't any grass in the apartment anyway. Down to seeds and stems. She'd have to stop at the store on the way and pick up a baggie.

Clement tucked Raymond Cruz's business card into the elastic of his briefs and took hold of Sandy's arms, sliding his hands up under the satiny sleeves and tugging her gently against him. He said, "What're you nervous about, huh? You never been nervous before. You need one of Dr. Mansell's treatments? That it, hon bun, get you relaxed? Well, we can fix you up."

"Mmmmm, that feels good," Sandy said, closing her eyes. She could feel him breathing close to her ear. After a moment she said, "I have to do it, huh?"

"You want us to be friends, don't you?" Clement said. "Don't friends help each other?"

"I think I feel another little friend—"

"See, Homer don't pout or wimp out on you.

He's always there when you need him. 'Specially when I'm hung over some, huh? You can hit him with a stick and he won't go 'way."

"Does it have to be in the river?"

"Can you think of a better place? You get back, sugar, we'll go see your Albanian. How's that sound?"

Tell 'em anything long as you tell 'em something.

Women were fun, but you had to treat them like little kids, play with them, promise them things; especially Sandy, who was a good girl and never let him down. Clement kissed her goodbye and looked at his situation as he got dressed.

He'd have to leave here in the next day or so. He'd miss the view, but there was no sense in being easy to reach. Man, they were swift this time. Or lucky. He couldn't recall a Lieutenant Raymond Cruz. Maybe if he saw the man's face. Get rid of anything incriminating, like the gun. Which was a shame; he loved that P.38.

Clement picked up his pants from the floor and dug out what he'd scored off the judge. The money, three hundred forty bucks, was clean, no problem with it. He'd left the checks in the wallet; he couldn't see himself peddling a dead man's checks. The little 2 by 3 spiral notebook—it was thin, like pages had been torn out—had names and phone numbers in it, also columns of figures and dates, impressive amounts up in the thousands with a lot of dollar signs, but meaningless to him . . . until he came to a right-hand page—the second to last one in the notebook—and a phone number jumped out at him.

W.S.F. 644-5905.

The initials and numbers gone over several times with a ballpoint and then underlined and enclosed within a heavily drawn square.

To make it special, Clement thought. He didn't recognize the initials, but the number was sure familiar, one he had seen not too long ago. But where?

Two officers from the Major Crime Mobile Unit—in street clothes, in a black unmarked Ford sedan—were assigned the surveillance of the Buick Riviera, license number PYX-546, located in the lower-level parking area at 1300 Lafayette East. They were given mug-shot photos of Clement Mansell, 373-8411, full face and profile, the photos bearing a '78 date. If he got in the car, Mansell was to be approached with caution and taken into custody for questioning. If he refused, resisted or tried to drive off, the officers were to arrest him, but under no circumstances search the car. If a woman got in the car they were to follow, keep her under close surveillance and call in.

Which is what the MCMU officers did when Sandy drove off in the Buick, took Jefferson to East Grand Boulevard, turned left—going away from the Belle Isle bridge—and proceeded to a bar named Sweety's Lounge, located at 2921 Kercheval. The subject went inside, came out again in approximately ten minutes with a middle-aged black male and accompanied him next door, to 2925 Kercheval, where they entered the lower household of a two-family flat.

MCMU called Homicide, Squad Seven, and requested instructions.

7

TECHNICALLY, SQUAD SEVEN of the Detroit Police Homicide Section specialized in the investigation of "homicides committed during the commission of a felony," most often an armed robbery, a rape, sometimes a breaking and entering, as opposed to barroom shootings and Saturday night mom and pop murders that were emotionally stimulated and not considered who-done-its.

The squad's home was in Room 527 of Police Headquarters, a colorless, high-ceilinged office roughly twenty-four-by-twenty that contained an assortment of ageless metal desks and wooden tables butted together, file cabinets, seven telephones, a Norelco coffeemaker, a GE battery-charge box for PREP radios, a locked cabinet where squad members sometimes stored their handguns, two banks of flickering fluorescent lights, a wall display of 263 mug shots of accused murderers, a coatrack next to the door and a sign that read:

Do something—
either lead, follow
or get the hell
out of the way!

A very old poster, peeling from the column that
stood in the middle of the squadroom and left over
from another time, stated: *I will give up my gun*
when they pry my cold fingers from around it.

It was 2:30 in the afternoon when Raymond Cruz
returned to the squadroom. The investigations into
the deaths of Alvin Guy and the young woman
found in Palmer Park were less than thirteen hours
old.

Raymond hung up the suitcoat he'd been wearing for the past twenty-four hours, crossed to the
unofficial lieutenant's desk in the corner—the desk
facing out to the squadroom, beneath the room's
only window and the air-conditioning unit that
didn't work—and listened.

Norb Bryl's desk faced the lieutenant's. Bryl was
on the phone—taking notes and saying, ". . . key-
hole defectment, bullet found in anterior cranial
fossa . . ."—talking to someone at the Wayne
County morgue.

Hunter, also on the phone, had a young black
guy sitting at his desk who was the suspect/witness

in the Palmer Park murder. They sat almost knee to knee, the young black guy slouched low, wearing a white T-shirt and a plaid golf hat with a narrow brim that he fooled with as he waited for Hunter, who was waiting for someone to come back on the line. No one else was in the squadroom.

Still waiting, Hunter said to the young black guy, "Twenty-five years old and all you got are some *traffic* tickets? You must've been in the army a while."

Raymond watched the young black guy give a slow shrug without saying anything.

Hunter said, "Let's see your hair."

The young black guy raised his hat above his head and held it there.

"We'll call it nappy," Hunter said and made a notation on the DPD Interrogation Record lying on his desk.

"It's Afro," the young black guy said.

Hunter said, "An *Afro?* It's a shitty looking Afro. We'll call it a nappy 'fro." He straightened then and said into the phone, "Yeah? . . . *Darrold* Woods? . . . Okay, give me what you got." Hunter nodded and said yeah, uh-huh, as he made notes on a yellow legal pad. When he finished, Hunter picked up a *Constitutional Rights Certificate of Notification* form and said to the young black guy, "How come you signed this Donald Woods? You lied to me, Darrold"—sounding a little hurt—"try to tell me you're cherry and they got a sheet on you, man. First thing, I'm gonna erase this zero cause it's a bunch of shit."

Darrold Woods was saying, "Two larceny from a person reduced from larceny not armed and a little bitty assault thing . . ."

And Hunter was saying, "Little *bitty* . . . little bitty fucking tire iron you used on the guy . . ."

Bryl put his hand over the phone and said to Raymond, "Cause of death multiple gunshots . . . two slugs, one with copper jacket recovered intact within the spinal canal, the other one in his head . . ."

Raymond said, "Judge Guy?"

Bryl nodded and said into the phone, "Okay, how many holes in the girl, Adele Simpson? . . . You sure? . . . Can't find any more, uh?" He put his hand over the phone and said to Raymond, "It's looking good. Maureen's already taken the slugs over to the lab."

Hunter was saying to the young black guy, "How well did you know Adele Simpson?"

"I never seen her before right then."

"You took her purse—what else?"

"What purse you talking about?"

"Darrold, you had Adele Simpson's credit cards on you."

"I found 'em."

Hunter said, "You gonna start shucking me

again, Darrold? We're talking about murder, man, not a little half-assed assault. You understand me, mandatory life . . ."

Raymond got up from his desk. He walked over to the young black guy in the plaid golf hat and touched him on the shoulder.

"Let me ask you something, okay?"

The young black guy didn't answer, but looked up at the lieutenant.

"The woman's lying there dead—is that right?"

"What I been trying to tell him."

"What did you burn her with?"

The young black guy didn't answer.

"Shit," Hunter said, "let's put him upstairs."

"I just touch her a little," the young black guy said then, "see if she's alive."

Hunter said, "What'd you touch her with, your dick?"

"No, man, nothing like that."

"They're doing an autopsy on her," Hunter said. "Now they find any semen in her and it matches your blood type—then we got to ask you, Darrold, you rape her before or after you shot her?"

"I *didn't* shoot her. You find a gun on me? Shit no."

"Where'd you touch her?" Raymond asked.

After a moment the young black guy said, "Like around her legs."

"Just touched her a little?"

"Yeah, just, you know, a little bit."

"You touch her with a cigarette?" Raymond asked.

"Yeah, I believe was a cigarette."

"Lit cigarette?"

"Yeah, was smoked down though, you know, like a butt."

"Why'd you touch her with a cigarette?"

"I told you," the young black guy said, "see if she's alive, tha's all."

Raymond went over to the coffeemaker, picked up the glass pitcher and walked out.

Maureen Downey, coming along the hall, raised a file folder she was carrying. She looked eager, pleased.

Raymond waited for her.

"Pathologist reports," Maureen said.

"How about the lab?"

"They're still comparing, but as far as they're concerned the slugs're identical."

"What kind of gun?"

"They got frags from the woman and two good ones from Guy, the casing intact . . ."

"Norb told me."

"Nine-millimeter or a .38. You know what they're leaning toward and looking into now?" Maureen was beaming.

"Walther P.38," Raymond said.

Maureen's grin dissolved. "How'd you know?"

"November, seventy-eight," Raymond said, "the shooting in the drug house on St. Mary's—"

Maureen's eyes came alive again.

"Remember? Two slugs were taken out of the woodwork, from a P.38."

"My God," Maureen said. "You don't suppose—"

"I sure do," Raymond said. "Go on back to the lab, get 'em to do a comparison, the slugs out of the wall with the slugs from Judge Guy and Adele Simpson."

"It sounds too good to be true," Maureen said.

"If they compare," Raymond said and continued down the hall and around the corner to the sink in the janitor's closet where he rinsed out the glass percolator and filled it with fresh water—aware of the good feeling, the rush of excitement he would have to contain, the feeling telling him—without any doubt or pauses or maybes—that all the slugs would compare. He saw Clement Mansell in a green-red-and-yellow Hawaiian sportshirt standing before the judge's bench. He saw Clement Mansell turn and walk out of the courtroom, grinning at everybody.

8

THEY WERE QUIET MEN who discussed murder in normal tones.

Robert Herzog, Inspector of the Homicide Section, seated at a glass-topped desk in his glass-walled office: twenty-nine years a policeman, a large man with a sad face, a full head of gray hair. And Raymond Cruz, whose gaze came away from the window when Herzog asked him if the glare bothered him.

"No, it's fine."

"You look like you were squinting."

The window, directly behind Herzog, facing south toward the river, framed late afternoon sunlight and the top half of a highrise in the near distance.

"So what do we know about Adele Simpson?"

"Worked for a real estate company, divorced, no children. Lived alone, apartment over near Westland, dated a couple of guys from the office. One of them married."

"Can you tie in either of the guys to Judge Guy?"

"I don't know yet, but I doubt it."

"You're gonna need help on this one. I'll see what I can do."

"I don't know . . ." Raymond said, easing into it, wanting to hear his own theory out loud and not rush it or leave anything out. Herzog was looking at him expectantly now; but he knew Herzog would ask the right questions and let him take his time.

"Maybe it was luck you gave us both cases," Raymond said. "I mean the two investigations might've never been related, but the first thing we did was look for a nexus and there it was. Same gun was used on Guy and Adele Simpson."

"So," Herzog said, "you assume the same guy did 'em both, but you don't know if it was revenge or jealousy or what."

"Actually," Raymond said, "I'm not too anxious about motive right now. Take the most obvious approach, you'd say it's a hit and the girl, it's too bad, happened to be with the judge."

"How do you know the girl was there?"

"Witness heard five shots, exactly five. Then a woman scream, though he's not positive about it. Three slugs in Guy plus two exit wounds, two slugs found in the car upholstery, in the backrest of the seat. Two matching slugs were taken from Adele Simpson's body. They caught her in the back, shattered her spine and were deflected into her lung. A third gunshot was through and through."

"But the scream," Herzog said, "didn't necessarily come from Adele Simpson."

"No, I wouldn't want to offer it in court," Raymond said, "but we've got a valet parking attendant at Hazel Park by the name of Everett Livingston who tells us Guy left there in his silver Mark VI with a blond lady wearing like a pink dress, gold chains and dark lipstick. Which matches Adele Simpson."

Herzog said, "What's Everett doing parking cars?"

"Everett remembers the judge because he knows him by sight. And, because the judge was involved in a little bumper tag with a black car that was either a Buick or an Olds."

"He describe the driver?"

"He described the driver's left arm—sort of sunburned with reddish hair, sleeve turned up. Which brings us to Gary Sovey—white, twenty-eight years old, he saw a black Buick Riviera pushing or racing the judge's car down John R."

Herzog said, "Where do you find witnesses like that?"

"It gets better," Raymond said. "A guy was standing on the corner of Nine Mile and John R, one-thirty this morning, when a black late-model GM car, possibly a Buick, nearly jumped the curb and almost ran over his dog taking a leak. License number, the guy says, PVX-five something. Lansing doesn't have a Buick with a PVX five-something number, but they sure have a PYX-546 . . . Buick Riviera registered to a Del Weems who lives right over there in that building."

"What building?"

Raymond nodded toward the window. "Thirteen hundred Lafayette East."

Herzog swiveled to look over his shoulder at the highrise and came back to the desk again. "Del Weems have red hair on his arms?"

"I don't know what color hair he's got. He was out of town last night."

"Then why're you telling me about Del Weems?"

"He's got a dinged front left fender," Raymond said.

"That's interesting," Herzog said.

"And he's got a young lady living in his apartment who was out at Hazel Park last night."

"The lady have red hair?"

"Sort of, but more blond than red. No, the young lady wasn't in the Buick, she was in a Cadillac with—you ready?—Skender Lulgjaraj."

Herzog said, "That's kind of a familiar name."

"Skender's Toma's cousin."

"Ah, Toma," Herzog said, "the Albanian. We haven't heard from him in a while, have we?"

"No, at the moment the Albanians are quiet," Raymond said. "We talked to Skender and he said yes, he was at the track with a young lady, but wouldn't give her name."

"Why not?"

"It's the way they are, a very private group. But it doesn't matter," Raymond said, "we know it's the same young lady who's living in Del Weems' apartment, the guy who owns the Buick Riviera, and the young lady's name is Sandy Stanton." Raymond waited.

Herzog waited. He said, "I give up. Who's Sandy Stanton?"

Raymond said, "Let me take you back to November, seventy-eight, to a little house on St. Marys Street . . ."

"Ah, yes," Herzog said.

". . . where you could get top-grade smack when everybody else was dealing that Mexican brown—an evening in November and three white dudes walk in off the street a little past eleven . . ."

Herzog said, "Albert RaCosta, Victor Reddick . . . let's see if I can remember. Louis Nix . . ."

"He was the driver," Raymond said. "You're saving the best for last, aren't you? Everybody does that."

Herzog seemed to smile. "And Clement Mansell."

"And Clement Mansell, yes sir," Raymond said, "with the reddish hair on his arms and the bluebirds. Remember the bluebirds? Well, Clement's address at the time was also Sandy Stanton's. Somebody, I think Norb, talked to her. I didn't, but I remember seeing her in court . . . then this afternoon."

Herzog was moving ahead, thinking of something else. "Louis Nix was killed with a P.38, wasn't he?"

"We *think* he was," Raymond said, "but we only got a frag for the test—remember? Not enough to say conclusively it was from a Walther. But—you remember something else? The woodwork in the house on St. Marys?"

"The woodwork . . ." Herzog said.

"The frame around the opening between the living room and the dining room," Raymond said. "Two slugs from a Walther were dug out of the woodwork, but the gun wasn't found on the scene. We found *vic*tims, three of 'em. Guy by the name of Champ, who ran the house. Guy by the name of Short Dog, eighteen years old, he was the doorman. And Champ's little girl, seven years old, asleep in the bedroom at the time, killed by one shot that went through the door."

"I remember the little girl," Herzog said. "And the same gun did all three of 'em?"

"Yes sir, but not the Walther, a Beretta .22-

caliber Parabellum. The gun was found in the back alley, no prints, if you recall. But when Louis Nix copped he identified the Beretta as belonging to Clement Mansell."

Herzog said, "I vaguely remember that part. Is it important?"

"I don't want to leave anything out that might be," Raymond said. "What happened—somebody in the neighborhood heard the shots, called in, a squad car arrives and Louis is sitting out front in a van with the engine running. By this time, Clement and RaCosta and Reddick had gone out the back, leaving Louis sitting there not knowing what's going on. So, we offer Louis a deal and he gives us his three buddies. Reddick and RaCosta were convicted, got mandatory life. Clement Mansell was also convicted, but he appealed on that federal detainer statute—you remember that?"

"Yeah, sort of. Go on."

"Court of Appeals reversed his conviction and Clement walked."

"Something about another charge against him," Herzog said, trying to remember.

"I think the prosecutor blew it," Raymond said. "At the time Clement was arrested the feds wanted him on some shitty little charge, auto theft, transporting across a state line—he was taking a Seville down to Florida—so Clement's lawyer gets him to plead guilty to the federal indictment and they send him to Milan for nine months. While he's there, he's brought back to stand trial on the triple and he's convicted. Louis Nix took the stand, told how they planned the whole thing, how Clement had the Parabellum, everything, and off they go to Jackson, mandatory life. All three of them appealed, naturally. Reddick and RaCosta are turned down; but Clement gets his appeal and wins and you know why?"

Herzog said, "This is the detainer part."

"Right—because when a prisoner is serving time and he's got another indictment pending in another court, he has to be brought to trial within a hundred and eighty days, otherwise"—Raymond paused, getting the thought clearly in his mind—"if he has to wait any longer it could produce uncertainties in the mind of the prisoner and fuck up his rehabilitation."

"That's how the statute reads?"

"Words to that effect," Raymond said. "If you recall, about that time Recorder's Court was in a mess, the docket overloaded. Well, the trial that convicted Clement Mansell and the Wrecking Crew didn't come up until the hundred and eighty-*sixth* day after they were arraigned. Clement's lawyer filed on the grounds of the detainer statute and he walked . . . after being convicted without any doubt . . . even after Reddick and RaCosta testified the murder weapon, the Parabellum, was Clement's and that it was Clement who killed the two guys and the little seven-year-old girl . . . The guy walks because he was brought to trial six days later while being held in federal detention . . . which fucked up his peace of mind and rehabilitation."

"Who was his lawyer?"

"Carolyn Wilder."

Herzog said, "Ahhh—" and nodded and seemed to smile. "That's a very smart woman. I've watched her and I can say I've always enjoyed it. Clement's got the mandatory hanging over him, nothing to lose. She knows the Recorder's Court docket's all fucked up, so she hands him to the feds hoping six months'll go by before he's brought back for the triple."

"And makes it by six days."

"Figuring the prosecutor's office isn't counting or might not even be thinking of a detainer," Herzog said. "Yes, that's a very smart woman."

"Clement walks," Raymond said, "and a couple weeks later Louis Nix is found shot in the head. *Up* through the head with a gun that was stuck in his mouth . . . very, *very* likely the same gun that put the slugs in the woodwork on St. Marys Street and the same gun, I like to believe, that killed the judge and Adele Simpson. A Walther P.38."

"I'd like to believe it too," Herzog said.

"Well, the lab's fairly sure, but they want to test the gun before they'll say absolutely."

"Where'd the gun come from?"

"Champ, the guy that was running the house," Raymond said, "his wife said Champ carried a Luger. Only it didn't turn up at the scene."

"A P.38 isn't a Luger," Herzog said, "but I see what you mean."

"Right, it looks like one and the woman wouldn't know the difference. So we place a P.38 at the scene of the triple three years ago. Say Clement lifted it off the guy. We find the same gun used in a double that went down this morning. The victims were at the race track, so was Clement's girlfriend, Sandy Stanton. The car she's driving around in right now—as a matter of fact—it's possible we can place it at the race track last night and at the scene where the judge was killed."

"So why didn't you impound the car?"

"We will, soon as Sandy gets done riding around. She just went over to a house on Kercheval."

"Grosse Pointe?" Herzog sounded surprised.

"No, no, way this side, twenty-nine twenty-five, off East Grand, next to a place called Sweety's Lounge. Maybe she's a junkie, but I don't think so. We'll check the place out."

"If Mansell did use the car last night," Herzog said, "she could be riding around with the gun."

"It's a judgment call," Raymond said. "Do you pick up the car, go over it, or follow Sandy around and do the car later? If Clement used it I assume he's wiped it down. But anything he might've missed'll still be there for the evidence techs."

Herzog nodded; yes, it was a matter of judgment.

"MCMU's doing the surveillance," Raymond said. "If it's apparent, I mean Sandy drives down to the river or stops by a trash barrel, they'll jump her. But I don't want to panic anybody right at the moment, including myself. I don't want to go bust in the wrong door and have Clement take off on us."

"He could've already," Herzog said.

"That's right," Raymond said, "or he could be in that highrise over there, twenty-five-oh-four. If you remember Clement, he's got very large balls. The papers at the time called him the Oklahoma Wildman, but he's more like a daredevil, a death-defier . . ."

"Evel Knievel with a gun," Herzog said.

"That's right, he likes to live dangerously and he likes to kill people."

Herzog said, "Well, if you don't get him with the gun, the Walther, what do you get him with?"

"That's it," Raymond said, "we got an arm with reddish hair sticking out a car window, but I never heard of a lineup of just arms. No, we got to get him with the gun in his possession, I know that."

"You seem very calm about it," Herzog said. "It can't be lack of desire."

"No, I'm trying to hold back from kicking in doors," Raymond said. "I don't want to blow it and see him walk like he did the last time."

Herzog said, "Why'd he shoot Guy?"

"I'm gonna ask him that," Raymond said, "soon as I get him sitting in the corner. He never appeared before Guy, so I don't think it's something personal. He saw him at the track, maybe Guy was winning, and Clement set something up. Maybe. Or, the way I'm inclined to lean, somebody paid Clement to do him.

"Or," Raymond said then, "he was out at the track because Sandy was there with Skender and they're setting up the Albanian. Same kind of thing Clement used to work with the Wrecking Crew. Find some ethnic storeowner, guy who might be taking his money home . . . the Wrecking Crew pays a visit, beats the shit out of the guy after they turn his place upside-down and walk out with his savings. I think Clement's still at it."

Herzog said, "How about arrests since the triple?"

"Nothing. Clement's been a suspect—shit, he's always a suspect, but nothing new on the computer. Less you want to count a drunk-driving charge. He got it in Lawton, Oklahoma last spring. Oklahoma sent it to Lansing and Lansing revoked his license."

"Well, if you catch him driving without it . . ."
Herzog said. "I'm gonna be off next week, drive up
to Leland with Sally."

"Taking her kids?"

"No, that's the whole idea, get away alone. If we
can work it."

"What do you need, a sitter?"

"No, her kids're old enough. It's the mothers.
Sally's mother asks her who she's going with, she
says me. Alone? Yeah, just the two of us. Her mother'd have a fit."

"Why?"

"Why?" The large man behind the desk who had
been a policeman twenty-nine years seemed self-
conscious, vulnerable.

"Because we're not married. Last winter, trying
to get to Florida for a week? The same thing. I tell
my mother I'm going with Sally, my mother says,
'Oh, are you married now?' Sally's forty-nine, I'm
fifty-four, both of us divorced. Our kids have traveled all over the country with their boyfriend, their
girlfriend . . . see, it's the grandchildren and they
accept that. But if Sally and I tried to do it—"

"You're kidding," Raymond said.

"Is your mother still living?" Herzog asked him.

"Yeah, in Daytona."

"Okay, try it. Tell her you're coming down with
a woman you're very fond of but you're not married to, see what she says. 'You mean the two of

you're traveling *alone* together?' Shocked, can't believe it. I know you're not as old as I am," the Inspector of Homicide said, "but I'll tell you
something, we're in the wrong fucking genera-
tion."

9

MARY ALICE, Raymond's former wife, called at 6:20. It was dark outside. He had come home to his apartment in bright fall sunlight, stepped into the shower . . . and now the sun had vanished from the living room window. He could see his reflection, the white towel wrapped around his middle. Mary Alice told him the roof was leaking again in the family room. She described what the water was doing to the walls and the carpeting, how it was impossible to dry the carpeting completely and take out the stain.

He wanted to say, "Mary Alice, I don't give a fuck about the carpeting . . ." But he didn't. He said, "What do you want me to do about it?" Knowing what she was going to say.

She told him she wanted him to pay to have the roof repaired and the carpeting replaced, speaking to him without using his name. Also, she needed a new clothes dryer.

His first-floor apartment was on the south edge

of Palmer Park, across from a heavily wooded area, about three-quarters of a mile from where Adele Simpson's body was found and a mile from Judge Guy's residence. He said, "Mary Alice, I don't think you understand. We're not married any more. You have the house, I don't have anything to do with it now." She started to speak again, using her quiet, almost lifeless tone, and he said, "It hasn't even rained lately."

She said he shouldn't have given her the house in the condition it was in—getting an edge to her tone now. She always had the edge ready for when she needed it. A pouty edge. She could tell him what they were having for dinner and sound defensive, conspired against. She said she would get some estimates—not having heard a word he said—and let him know. Raymond said fine and hung up.

He sliced the leftover New York strip sirloin into thin pieces and fried them in a hot skillet, watching the pieces sizzle and curl, thinking of the girl from the *News*, picturing her face the way it had appeared, soft, pleasant, before taking on a sheen and her features became sharply defined. He had looked at her as a possibility, a very attractive girl. But with acid-etched opinions that came out and changed her looks. She could be right, though.

You know it? Raymond thought.

And then thought, No, there was no way in the world he could have talked to his wife and told her how he felt. In the first place she didn't like the idea of being a policeman's wife. She wanted him to sell the life insurance like her dad and join her dad's Masonic lodge and go deer hunting with her dad and remodel the back porch into a family room with an acoustical tile ceiling and use some of her mom and dad's maple furniture. The marriage counselor they visited six times said, "Have you considered having children?" Mary Alice told him she'd had two early miscarriages. She did not tell him she refused to even consider trying again and would begin love-making with reluctance and remain detached while Raymond slowly, gently, tried to involve her to the point of losing herself. (Which had nothing to do with not wanting to have children.) In her detachment, in the automatic, monotonous movement of her hips, she would remain wherever she was, alone.

The marriage counselor asked Raymond if he had always wanted to be a police officer. Raymond said no, he had wanted to be a fireman, but didn't pass the test. The marriage counselor asked him if he had ever had a homosexual experience. Raymond said, "Well—" The marriage counselor said, "Tell me about it." Raymond said, "Well, when I was working Vice I'd go into the Men's room of a gay bar; I'd stand at the urinal and when a guy would come up next to me I'd take out a salt shaker and shake some of it, you know, down like right in front of me. And if the guy rolled his eyes and rubbed his tummy I knew I had a collar." The marriage counselor stared at him and said, "Are you serious?" Raymond said, "Look, I like girls. I just don't like *her*. Don't you see that?"

He ate the fried steak with sliced tomatoes and onions and a can of Strohs. He wasn't tired. He hadn't slept since yesterday morning, but he wasn't tired. He thought about going out. The prospect still gave him a strange feeling after twelve years of married life. He thought about the girl from the *News*. He thought about Sandy Stanton and wondered how he might run into her somewhere. He thought of girls he had met at Pipers Alley on St. Antoine, the Friday after-work place, girls who came with toothbrushes in their purses. He thought of girls and saw glimpses of pleasure in strange apartments, chrome lamps turned down, macrame and fringed pillows made of wool, drinking wine, performing the ritual to the girl playing coy or seductive, giving him dreamy eyes, saying undress me and getting down to the patterned bikini panties, wondering why none of these girls wore plain white ones, most of them big girls, bigger than the girls he remembered in college sixteen years ago, the girls acting coy all the way to bed then accepting the decorator-patterned sheets as a release point and turning on with moans like death-throes and dirty words that took some getting used to, though girls in bars said fuck all the time now and when the girl would say do-it-to-me, do-it-to-me, he would think, What do you think I'm doing? Never ever completely caught up in it, but aware and observing, giving it about seventy percent . . . He remembered the girl from the *News* saying he was old-fashioned—no, old-timey; but it probably meant the same thing. The girl who knew everything . . .

The phone rang.

The woman's voice, quiet, unhurried, said, "Lieutenant, this is Carolyn Wilder. I understand you're looking for a client of mine, Clement Mansell."

Raymond saw her in a courtroom, slim in something beige, light-brown hair—and had recognized her voice—the goodlooking lady with the quiet manner who defended criminals. He said, "How about if you bring him in tomorrow morning, eight o'clock."

"If you don't have a warrant, why bother?"

"I'd like to talk to him," Raymond said.

There was a pause, silence.

"All right, you can talk to him in my office, in my presence," Carolyn Wilder said. "If that doesn't suit you, get a warrant and I'll see you at the arraignment."

He asked her where her office was. She told him

the 555 Building in Birmingham and asked him to please come within an hour.

Raymond said, "Wait, where'd you get my number?"

But Carolyn Wilder had hung up.

10

"SEE, A BLACKJACK'S THE BEST," Hunter said. "Put it in your pants pocket, you know, right against your thigh. You don't have a blackjack then you move your gun around, stick it in front by your belt buckle. You start dancing close with the broad, watch the look on her face."

Raymond said, "You horny tonight?"

Hunter said, "What do you mean, tonight? I've always wanted to try one of these broads out here. Husband's a vice-president with General Motors, bores the shit out of her . . . Look-it that one, fucking outfit on her."

They were in Archibald's on the ground floor of the 555 Building—shoulder to shoulder with the after-work cocktail crowd, the young lawyers and salesmen from around the north end and the girls that came from everywhere—Hunter with visions of restless suburban ladies looking for action, waiting to be dazzled by the homicide dick with the nickel-plated 9-mm Colt strapped to his belt.

Raymond said, "You know how old the bored wife of a GM vice-president would be?" He finished his bourbon and placed the glass on the bar. "I'm going up. Clement parked across the street. Tan Chevy Impala, TFB seven-eighty-one."

"Probably stole it," Hunter said.

"The phone's over there by the men's room."

"I saw it when I came in."

"Clement leaves before I do, I'll call you."

Raymond walked out of the bar, edging past the secretaries and young executives and took an elevator up to seven, to Wilder, Sultan and Fine, celebrity names around Detroit Recorder's Court, criminal lawyers venturing into the corporate world now, out seventeen miles from downtown, into contracts and tax shelters and a brown leather lobby with copies of *Fortune* and *Forbes* on glass tables.

He went in past the row of clean secretary desks and covered typewriters to an office softly lighted where Carolyn Wilder and Clement Mansell were waiting—Clement watching him, beginning to grin, Carolyn Wilder saying, "Why don't you sit down."

He concentrated on observing, noticing Clement's shiny blue and red tattoo on his right forearm, Clement in a sport shirt sitting at one end of the couch with his elbows drawn back, limp hands in his lap, a faded denim jacket on the couch, next to him. Raymond saw a file folder on the coffee table, a pair of glasses with thin dark frames. He noticed the line of Carolyn Wilder's thigh beneath a deep red material, one leg crossed over the other, the criminal lawyer and her client sitting away from the desk at the other end of the room, the lawyer relaxed but poised in a leather director's chair, open white blouse with the dark maroon suit, tailored, soft brown hair with light streaks almost to her shoulders . . . brown eyes, saying nothing now . . . somewhere in her mid-thirties, better looking, much better looking, than he remembered her.

She said, "You don't seem especially interested, Lieutenant. Are you bored?"

It was in his mind: Pick Clement up and throw him against the wall, hard enough to put him out, then cuff him and say to her, No, I'm not bored.

Get it done.

Raymond didn't say anything. He looked from Carolyn Wilder to Clement, who was staring, squinting his eyes at him.

Clement said, "I don't recall your face."

"I remember yours," Raymond said and stared back at him, looking at a point between Clement's half-closed eyes.

"I should know you, huh?"

Raymond didn't say anything. He heard Carolyn

Wilder sigh and murmur a sound and then say, "This is in connection with the Guy murder?"

Raymond nodded, turning his head to her. "That's right."

"What have you got?"

"Witnesses."

"I don't believe you."

"A car."

Clement said, "Shit, he ain't got any witnesses. He's blowing smoke at us."

"The racetrack and the scene," Raymond said.

Carolyn Wilder turned to Clement. "Don't say anything unless I ask you a question, all right?" And to Raymond, "Are you going to read his rights?"

"I hadn't planned on it," Raymond said.

Carolyn Wilder looked at him a moment and then shrugged. "He's not going to say anything anyway."

"Can I ask him a question?"

"What is it?"

"Was he driving around in a Buick Riviera last night, license number PYX-5-4-6?"

"No, he's not going to answer that."

Clement looked from his attorney to Raymond, enjoying himself.

"Can I ask if he's seen Sandy Stanton lately?"

"Is it her car?" Carolyn Wilder asked.

"A friend of hers."

"I don't think you can put together even circum-stantial evidence," Carolyn Wilder said. "And he's not going to say anything, so why bother?"

Raymond looked directly at Clement now. "How you doing otherwise?"

"Can't complain," Clement said. "I'm still trying to place you. You have a mustache that time—what was it, three years ago?"

"I just grew it," Raymond said and was aware of Carolyn Wilder staring at him.

"You were heavier then." Clement began to nod. "I remember you, the quiet fella, didn't say much."

"It wasn't my case. I don't think I ever spoke to you directly."

"Yeah, I remember you now," Clement said. "What was that reddish-haired fella's name? Not reddish, kinda sandy."

"Hunter," Raymond said. "Sergeant Hunter."

Clement was grinning again. "He tried every which way get me to say I pulled the trigger. Was in that little room with all the old files?"

Raymond nodded, feeling a strange rapport with the man that excluded the woman lawyer, made her an outsider.

"He had me in there, I thought he was gonna punch me through the wall. He never laid a hand on me, but he come close, I know he did. You ask him."

Raymond said, "You been anywhere since Milan?"

"I think we should all go home," Carolyn Wilder said, stirring in the director's chair, about to get up.

"Milan wasn't too bad," Clement said. "You know, there was some famous people there one time. Frank Costello—some others, I can't think of the names right off."

Raymond said, "You been staying out of trouble?"

"Long as I got this lady here," Clement said. He squirmed, getting comfortable. "I'd like to hear how you think you're gonna lay the judge on me."

Carolyn Wilder said, "That's all."

Clement looked at her. "He can't use anything I say. He hasn't read me my rights." Smirky, having a good time.

"You can say anything you want," Raymond said, "I won't hold it against you." And gave Clement a friendly grin.

Carolyn Wilder stood up, brushing a hand down to smooth her skirt.

"He's dying," Clement said. "Got this idea of what happened to the judge and can't get nobody to—what's the word, corab . . . corobate it?"

"Corroborate," Raymond said. "You hang around courtrooms and county jails you learn some words, don't you?"

"Become a jailhouse lawyer," Clement said. "I met a few of them here'n there."

Carolyn Wilder said, "Lieutenant . . . good night."

Raymond got up. "Can I use your phone?"

She nodded toward her desk, a massive dark-wood dining room table set against Levelor blinds and chrome-framed graphics.

Raymond walked across the room, picked up the phone and dialed a number. He waited and then said, "Jerry? You gonna meet me downtown? . . . I'll see you." And hung up, wondering as he turned from the desk if they heard Hunter's voice, Hunter saying, "Fuck you, I'm not leaving here, man, this is the *place*."

Clement was saying something to Carolyn Wilder, both standing now, Clement with his hand on her arm, and Carolyn frowning as she stared at him, as though trying to understand what he was telling her—twenty feet from Raymond Cruz—and now she pulled her arm away abruptly, amazed or shocked, and said, "What!" and Clement was shrugging, saying a few parting words as he turned and walked out of the office.

There was a silence. Raymond moved toward her. He said, "What's the matter?"

But she was still in her mind and didn't answer. She was not the woman lawyer he had watched in court, but a woman caught off balance, a girl now, vulnerable, a girl who had just been grossly insulted or told a terrible secret. Raymond wanted to touch her and the words came out easily.

"Can I help you, Carolyn?"

It surprised him, using her first name, and yet it sounded natural and seemed to touch an awareness in her. She looked at him in a different way now, not with suspicion as much as caution, wanting to be sure of his tone, his intention.

"Did you happen to hear what he said?"

Raymond shook his head. "No."

"Any part of it?"

"No, I didn't."

He watched her pick up the file from the coffeetable and come past him to her desk, saying, "He's a beauty." Sounding tired.

"He kills people," Raymond said.

She looked at him now. "Tell me about it. You've been a downtown cop long enough—I know I've seen you around—so you know what my job is and I know what yours is."

"But can I help you?" Raymond said.

She hesitated, staring at him again and seemed about to tell him something. But she hesitated too long. He saw her gaze move and come back and move again and now she was sitting down at her desk, looking up at him with a bland expression.

"I think you mean well . . ."

"But it's none of my business," Raymond said. He picked a Squad Seven card out of his coat pocket and laid it on her desk. "Unless he scares you again, huh? And you admit it."

"Good night, lieutenant."

He said, "Good night, Carolyn," and left, feeling pretty good that he hadn't said too much, but then wondering if he shouldn't have insisted on helping and maybe said a lot more.

Hunter used the phone next to the men's room, staring at the slim girl in the fur vest and wide leather belt as he called MCMU directly, the Major Crime Mobile Unit. He told them a tan '79 Chevy Impala, Tango Fox Baker 781, was heading south on Woodward and would cross the overpass at Eight Mile in about twelve minutes. He told them to check the sheet on the car, apprehend the driver and take him down to 1300, Room 527. MCMU asked Hunter on what charge and Hunter said, "Driving without an operator's license."

He returned to the bar, worked his way in next to the stylish girl in the fur vest and said to her up-raised profile, "If we can't fall in love in the next twelve minutes, you want to give me your number and we'll try later?"

The girl looked over her shoulder to stare at him

with a mildly wistful expression. She said, "I'm not against falling in love, sport; but I'm sure as hell not gonna hustle a cop. I mean even if I thought you'd pay."

11

THEY LET CLEMENT SIT ALONE in the interrogation/file room for about forty minutes before Wendell Robinson went in to talk to him.

It was close to 10:00 P.M. Raymond Cruz crossed his feet on the corner of his desk and closed his eyes to the fluorescent lights . . . while Hunter made coffee and told about Pamela and the rough time Pamela was having trying to make it with all the goddamn amateurs out there giving it away, selling themselves for Amaretto on the rocks, Kahlua and cream . . . Raymond half listening, catching glimpses of the Carolyn Wilder he had never seen before this evening, wondering what Clement had said to her, wondering if—at another time, the right time—she'd be easy to talk to.

The windowless file room, about seven-by-eleven, held three folding chairs, an old office table and a wall of built-in shelves where closed case-records were stored. On the wall directly behind Clement was a stain, a formless smudge, where several thousand heads had rested, off and on, during interrogations.

Wendell said, "How well you know Edison?"

Clement grinned. "Detroit Edison?"

"Thomas Edison."

"I never did understand nigger humor," Clement said.

"Man whose car you were driving this evening."

"That's his name? I just call him Tom. Only nigger I ever knew owned a Chevy. He loaned it to me."

"He a friend of yours?"

"Friend of a friend."

"I understand he's a doorman. Works over at 1300 Lafayette. That where your friend live?"

"I forget which friend it was's a friend of old Tom's."

"Sandy Stanton lives over there," Wendell said. "She's a pretty good friend, isn't she?"

"You know everything, what're you asking me for?"

"She a friend of yours?"

"I know her."

"She loan you the Buick last night?"

"It tickles me," Clement said, "you people trying

to act like you know something. You don't have shit, else I'd be over'n the Wayne County jail waiting on my exam."

"We want to be ugly, we could get you some time over there right now," Wendell said. "Driving after your license was revoked on a D.U.I.L., that's a pretty heavy charge."

"What, the drunk-driving thing? Jesus Christ," Clement said, "you trying to threaten me with a fucking *traffic* violation?"

"No, the violation's nothing to a man of your experience," Wendell said. "I was thinking of how you'd be over there with all them niggers."

"Why is that?" Clement said. "Are niggers the only ones fuck up in this town? Or they picking on you? I was a nigger I wouldn't put up with it."

"Yeah, what would you do?"

"Move. All this town is is one big Niggerville with a few whites sprinkled in, some of 'em going with each other. You'd think you'd see more mongrelization, except I guess they're just fucking each other and not making any kids like they did back in the plantation days . . . You want to know something?"

"What's that?"

"One of my best friend's a nigger."

"Yeah, what's his name?"

"You don't know him."

"I might. You know us niggers sticks together."

"Bullshit. Saturday night you kill each other."

"I'm curious. What's the man's name?"

"Alvin Guy." Clement grinned.

"Is that right? You knew him?"

Clement said, "Shit, I could tell you anything, couldn't I?"

"There was a window in there I'd have thought seriously about throwing him out," Wendell said, and Raymond nodded.

"I know what you mean."

"Man doesn't give you anything to hook onto. You understand what I'm saying? He jive you around with all this bullshit, you don't know who's asking who the question. See, he does the judge, then goes home to his bed. We been up two days and a night."

"Go on home," Raymond said.

"I'll stay on it, you want me to."

"We'll let the old pro take a shot," Raymond said, looking over at Hunter. "The old reddish-gray wolf. What do you say? If we can't shake him tonight we'll turn him loose, try some other time."

Hunter got up from his desk. He said, "You want to watch, see how it's done?"

* * *

There was no clear reason why Hunter was the squad's star interrogator: why suspects so often confided in him and why the confessions he elicited almost always stood up in court. Maureen said it was because the bad guys got the feeling he was one of them. Hunter said it was because he was patient, understanding, sympathetic, alert, never raised his voice . . . and would cite as an example the time last winter he questioned the suspect, young guy, who admitted "sort of strangling" two women while "overcome with cocaine." The young guy said he thought this belt one of them had was a snake and wanted to see what it would look like around their necks; that's how the whole thing had come about, while they were sitting on the floor tooting and having a few drinks. But he refused to tell what he did with their bodies. Hunter said, well, the bodies would show up by spring, when the snow melted, and added, "Unless you're some kind of animal and you stored them away for the winter." Hunter noticed the suspect appeared visibly agitated by this off-hand remark and quickly followed up on it, asking the suspect if he liked animals or if he was afraid of them or if he related to animals in some way. The suspect insisted he hated animals, rats especially, and that when he went out to the abandoned farmhouse a few days after and saw that rats had been "nibbling" on the two women he immediately took measures to prevent them from being "all eaten up." He cut the bodies up with a hacksaw and burned them in the coal furnace. He was no animal . . .

"What you do," Hunter said, "you see your opening and you step in. You don't let the guy out until he's told you something."

"Remember this room?" Hunter asked Clement.

"Yeah, I remember it. I remember you, too."

"Still put grease on your hair?"

"No, I like the dry look now," Clement said.

"Good," Hunter said. "You messed up the wall the last time—all that guck you slicked your hair down with."

Clement looked over his shoulder at the wall. "Don't you ever clean this place up?"

"We hose it out once a week," Hunter said, "like at the zoo. Get rid of the stink."

"What're you," Clement said, "the heavy? First the nigger and then you. When's the good guy come in?"

"I'm the good guy," Hunter said. "I'm as good as it's gonna get."

"You haven't read me my rights."

"I figured you know it by heart. You want me to read 'em to you? Sure, I'll read 'em."

Hunter went out into the squad room. Raymond Cruz sat at his desk with his eyes closed. Hunter poured himself a mug of coffee, picked up a *Constitutional Rights* form and went back into the file room, sat down and read the first paragraph of the document to Clement.

"You know your rights now? Okay, sign here." Hunter pushed the document over to Clement with a ballpoint pen.

"What if I don't want to sign?"

"I don't give a shit if you sign or you don't sign. I'll put down you refused, give us a hard time."

"But why do I need to sign it?"

"I just told you, asshole, you don't."

"I'm in here for questioning as . . . what?"

"You were arrested."

"For not having a driver's license? What's this got to do with it?"

"While in custody the defendant's record was examined with reason to believe he might be involved in a homicide under investigation and was detained for questioning."

"Detained—I can hear you," Clement said. "And then my lawyer stands up and says, 'Your Honor, this poor boy was held against his will, without any complaint being filed and was not read his rights as a citizen.' Buddy, I don't even know why I'm here. I mean, nobody's told me nothing yet."

"You're in here, Clement, because you're in some deep shit, that's why."

"Yeah? Friend of mine was in this room one time, he refused to sign and nothing happened to him."

Hunter said, "Look at it from the court's point of view, Clement, all right? . . . Which looks better, we get a warrant and arrest you for first degree murder, which carries mandatory life? Or, we report you came to us voluntarily to make a statement. Under no duress or apprehension you describe the circumstances—"

Clement began to smile.

"—under which a man lost his life, telling it in your own words, putting in whatever mitigating factors there may be, such as your mental or emotional state at the time, whether there was some form of incitement or threat to your well being . . . what're you grinning at?"

"You must think I went to about the fifth grade," Clement said, "buy that load of shit. I don't have to say a word to you. On the other hand I can say anything I want and you can't use it because I ain't signed your piece of paper. So what're we sitting here for?"

"It's a formality," Hunter said. "I got to give you the opportunity to make a statement. You don't, then I take you down the garage, stand you against the wall and beat the shit out of you with the front end of a squad car."

* * *

Hunter said to Raymond Cruz, "Fuck—we don't get him with the piece, we don't get him."

"He sign the sheet?"

"No, but what difference does it make? He's not gonna say anything. He knows the routine better'n we do."

"I'll give it a try," Raymond said. "Go on home."

"No, I'll stick around."

"Go on. What're we doing, we're just chatting with the guy."

"Clement . . . how you doing?"

"You're in trouble," Clement said. "Carolyn told you, you guys don't talk to me without her."

Raymond said, "You spend the night here, she might be a little mad when she finds out, stamp her feet maybe. But she knows it's part of the business. We see a shot, we have to take it. Listen . . . let's go in the other room. You want some coffee?"

Clement said, "I wondered who the good guy was gonna be."

He sat at Hunter's desk swivelling around in the chair, unimpressed, until he spotted the mug-shot display, the 263 color shots mounted on the wall and extending from Norb Bryl's desk—where Raymond sat—to the coatrack by the door. Raymond sat sideways to the desk facing Mansell, ten feet away, who was turned sideways to Hunter's desk.

"Poor fuckers," Clement said. "You put all those people away?"

"About ninety-eight percent of 'em," Raymond said. "That's this year's graduates, so far."

"About ninety-eight percent niggers," Clement said. "The fuck am I doing sitting here?"

"You want me to tell you?" Raymond said.

"I wish somebody would," Clement said. "I can guess what your heart's desire is, but I *know* you don't have nothing good else I'd be across the street."

"I might've jumped the gun a little."

"I believe you jumped the hell out of her."

"You know how you get anxious."

"Got to stay cool," Clement said. "Evidently you got somebody made a car somewhere—"

"At the scene, for one."

"Yeah?" Non-committal.

"And at the Hazel Park track," Raymond said. "The car belongs to Del Weems, a friend of Sandy Stanton."

"Yeah?"

"She's staying at Del Weems' apartment, using his car sometimes."

"Yeah?"

"So are you. I know I can place you over at 1300

Lafayette if I talk to enough people. And there's a good chance I can put you in the car at Hazel Park, the same time the judge was there, same night he was killed." Raymond looked at the wall clock. "About twenty-two hours ago . . . What did you think when we got on you this fast?"

"You got a tape recorder going some place?"

Raymond raised his hands, helpless. "For what?"

"Won't do you any good if you have." Clement looked up at the ceiling and raised his voice as he said, "You can't use anything I'm saying, so fuck you!"

"I can hear you fine," Raymond said pleasantly. "I'm not trying to pull anything, legal or otherwise. I just thought you and I might save some time if we know where we stand."

"That sounds like it makes sense," Clement said, "except I think it's pure bullshit. There's no way I can be doing myself any good sitting here. This is a miserable fucking place, you know it?"

"You never went before Guy, did you?"

"No, I was never in his court."

"So it couldn't be anything personal."

"Jesus, you got your mind made up, haven't you?"

"The only other reason I can think of, somebody must've paid you." Raymond waited. Clement didn't say anything. Raymond smiled slightly.

"That person finds out you're in custody I think it would clutch him up some . . . the kind of situation you get into when two or more people are involved in a murder. Like the guy that was shot in front of the Soup Kitchen, the promoter. You remember him? This past summer. Who was convicted? The shooter. Not the guy that arranged it. He copped and we gave him immunity."

"Jesus Christ," Clement said, "you're starting to sound like that other chicken-fat dick, giving me this scary story like I got grits or something for brains."

"I guess I ought to come right out with it," Raymond said.

Clement nodded. "I think you'd feel better."

"Okay," Raymond said, "what's gonna happen as soon as we put you in the Buick—we already have the Buick at the scene—you'll want to start talking deal. You'll give us something if we'll ease up a little. Except by then it will probably be too late. We settle for Clement Mansell, he gets the mandatory, that's it. Did somebody pay him? Who knows? Or more to the point, who cares? See, there isn't that much wrath, you might say, or righteous indignation involved. Some people think the guy who did the judge ought to get a medal instead of a prison term. But it's a capital crime, so we have to go through the motions. I want you to understand now we *will* nail you down, there isn't any doubt about that . . . *unless*, before we put in all these hours and get pissed off and cranky and unreasonable . . . you say okay, here's what happened, here's the name of the guy that put up the fee . . . *then* we could probably do something for you. Talk to the prosecutor about second degree, maybe even get it down to manslaughter and put the mandatory on the guy that hired you. You see what I mean?"

Clement leaned his right forearm on the desk and stared across the ten feet at Raymond Cruz.

"You got a nice, polite way about you. But underneath all that shit, you really want my ass, don't you?"

"I don't have a choice," Raymond said.

"You feel this as something personal? I mean this particular case?"

Raymond thought a moment; he shrugged.

"Shit no," Clement said. "What's bothering you, three years ago you guys blew it. You had me convicted on a triple, air-tight with witnesses, and I walked. That's been bothering the shit out of you. So now you're gonna try and get me on this one to make up for it. See, now it *does* get personal. Right? You don't care who hit the judge, you just want *me*. Am I right or wrong?"

Raymond took his time. He said, "See, we're finding out where we stand."

"Am I right or wrong?"

"Well, I have to admit there's some truth in what you say."

"I knew it," Clement said. "You got no higher motive'n I do, you talk about laying things on the table, see where we stand. You don't set out to uphold the law any more'n I set out to break it. What happens, we get in a situation like this and then me and you start playing a game. You try and catch me and I try and keep from getting caught and still make a living. You follow me? We're over here in this life playing and we don't even give a shit if anybody's watching us or not or if anybody gets hurt. We got our own rules and words we use and everything else. You got numbers, all these chicken-fat dicks that'd rather play the game than work; but I got the law to protect me and all I got to do is keep my mouth shut, don't associate with stupid people and there's no way in hell you're gonna lay this one on me . . . or any of the others."

Raymond nodded, thoughtful but at ease, alert but not showing it. He said, "You know what, Clement? I think you're right." There was a silence. "What others?"

And again, a silence.

Clement leaned on his arm that rested along the edge of the desk, as if to draw a little closer to Raymond Cruz.

"You know how many people I've killed?"

"Five," Raymond said.

"Nine," Clement said.

"In Detroit?"

"Not all in De-troit. One in Oklahoma, one in Kansas."

"Seven in Detroit?"

"That's right. But five—no, six of 'em was niggers."

"Counting Judge Guy."

"Count who you want. I ain't giving you a score-card lineup."

"When you were with the Wrecking Crew, huh?"

"Most by myself. Well, kind of by myself. Other fella didn't do shit."

"Going into dope houses, huh?"

Clement didn't answer.

"Like the one on St. Marys, the triple?"

Clement didn't say anything.

"I don't mean to pry," Raymond said. "You arouse my curiosity." He sat back in Norb Bryl's stiff swivel chair and placed his legs on the corner of the desk. "It's interesting what you said, like it's a game. Cops and robbers. A different life that's got nothing to do with anybody else."

"Less we need 'em," Clement said. "Then you get into victims and witnesses. Use who you can."

"But what it comes down to," Raymond said,

"what it's all about, I mean, is just you and me, huh?"

"That's it, partner."

"Some other time—I mean a long time ago, we might have settled this between us. I mean if we each took the situation personally."

"Or if we thought it'd be fun," Clement said. "You married?"

It took Raymond by surprise. "I was."

"You got a family? Kids?"

"No."

"So you get bored, don't have nothing to do and you put more time in on the job."

Raymond didn't say anything. He waited, looking at the wall clock. It was 11:15.

Clement said, "You ever shoot anybody?"

"Well . . . not lately."

"Come on, how many?"

"Two," Raymond said.

"Niggers?"

He felt self-conscious. "When I was in Robbery."

"Use that little dick gun? . . . I been meaning to ask why you put the rubber bands around the grip."

"Keep it from slipping down."

"Cheap fuck, get a holster. Shit, get a regular size weapon first, 'stead of that little parlor gun."

"It does the job," Raymond said. It sounded familiar: a table of cops at the Athens Bar drinking beer.

Clement said, "Yeah?" and let his gaze move around the squad room before returning to Raymond Cruz, sitting with his feet on the desk. "Say you're pretty good with it, huh?"

Raymond shrugged. "I qualify every year."

"Yeah?" Clement paused, staring at Raymond now. "Be something we had us a shooting match, wouldn't it?"

"I know a range out in Royal Oak," Raymond said. "It's in the basement of a hardware store."

"I'm not talking about any range," Clement said, staring at Raymond. "I was thinking out on the street." He paused for effect. "Like when you least expect."

"I'll ask my inspector," Raymond said, "see if it's okay."

"You won't do nothing of the kind," Clement said, "cause you know I'm not kidding."

They stared at each other in silence and Raymond wondered if this was part of the game: who would look away first. A little kids' game except it was real, it was happening.

He said, "Can I ask you a question?"

"Like what?"

"Why'd you shoot Guy?"

"Jesus Christ," Clement said, "we been talking

all this time, I think we're getting some place—
what difference does it make why? Me and you,
we're sitting here looking at each other, sizing each
other up—aren't we? What's it got to do with Guy,
or anything else?"

12

SOME MONTHS BEFORE, a story in *The Detroit News Magazine*, part of the Sunday edition, had featured eight "Women At Work" in which they described, beneath on-the-job photos in color, exactly what they did for a living. The women were a crane operator, automotive engineer, realty executive, homemaker, attorney, waitress, interior decorator and city assessor.

The attorney was Carolyn Wilder, photographed in an ultra-suede jacket leaning against her dining-table desk. Framed on the wall behind her and almost out of focus was an enlarged printed quotation that read:

*"Whatever women do, they
must do twice as well as men*

to be thought half as good.
Luckily, this is not difficult."

CHARLOTTE WILTON
Mayor of Ottawa, 1963

Set in two columns beneath the photo, the text read:

CAROLYN WILDER, Attorney, Senior Partner of Wilder, Sultan and Fine, Birmingham.

"At one time I thought I was an artist. In fact I attended The Center for Creative Studies three years, believed I could draw, paint adequately, set out with my portfolio and found work in the art department of a well-known automotive ad agency where the word 'creative' was heard constantly but appeared exiguously, if at all, in their advertising; married a 'creative' director and was both fired and divorced within fifteen months on two counts of insubordination. (No children, a few samples.) The switch to law is an involved tale; though I did have clear visions, goals, that saw me through the University of Detroit Law School and two years with the Legal Aid and Defender Association. The latter prepared me for criminal law as it is served in the Frank Murphy Hall of Justice on a daily basis. My

clients, for the most part, are charged with serious
felonies: varying degrees of murder, rape, armed
robbery and assault. Seventy-nine percent of them
are acquitted, placed on probation, or, their charges
are dismissed. Implicit in the question I'm most fre-
quently asked—why am I in criminal law?—is the
notion that women by nature abhor violence and
would never, under any circumstances, help violent
criminals remain at large. The truth is: criminals are a
police problem; individuals accused of crime are
mine."

Another notion, that life can be simple, if you
base it on a fairly black and white attitude about
behavior, appealed to Carolyn in providing answers to dumb questions. It made her sound at
least curt when not profound and helped develop
her courtroom image as an incisive defense counsel. Wayne County prosecuting attorneys referred
to her, not altogether disparagingly, as the Iron
Cunt. She might say hello on an elevator; she
might not. She would never, under any condition,
give her view of the weather. When facing her in
court the prosecutor had better have his case docu-
mented far beyond implications or dramatic effects or Carolyn would counterpunch him to a
decision with pure knowledge of law. Recorder's
Court judges were known to sit up straighter, listen

more attentively, when Carolyn was working their courtrooms.

Raymond Cruz ran into her on the fifth floor, where two of the Frank Murphy courtrooms were holding pretrial examinations and witnesses and families of defendants were waiting in the corridor.

It was 11:00 A.M. Raymond was coming out of an exam, having identified the photograph of a woman, bound and gagged with a pantyhose and shot twice in the back of the head, as Liselle Taylor, and testified that upon showing the photo to Alfonso Goddard, Mr. Goddard denied knowing the deceased until, after several hours of questioning, he stated: "Oh, yeah, I *know* her. See, you asked me if she was my girlfriend and I said no to *that*, because she wasn't my girlfriend, we was only living together, you understand?" . . . There were two more exams scheduled this week . . . five cases in the squad's "open" file . . . when Carolyn Wilder stopped him, taking him by the arm in the crowded corridor.

She said, "Don't ever do that to me again. I don't care if you just wanted to buy him a drink, when I say you can only talk to a client in my presence it means exactly that."

Raymond touched her hand on his arm, covering

it with his own in the moment before she drew it away.

"What did he tell you?"

"He was arrested—how you used that drunk-driving charge—"

"We let him go, didn't we? Listen, I don't even know how he got home. But if he keeps driving without a license he's gonna get in serious trouble."

Carolyn didn't smile. She seemed genuinely disturbed, her esteem damaged. Raymond stepped quickly, quietly, inside her guard. He said, "What did Clement tell you last night? In your office."

And there was the vulnerable look again, a glimpse of the girl who could be uncertain, afraid.

"If he scared *you*, and I mean that as a compliment, then he said something pretty bad."

"You're out of line. Whatever my client says to me, if you don't know, is privileged information—"

"Yeah, but it wasn't like that. He didn't confide something, he scared you. The look on your face—you could have filed a complaint for assault. Or improper advances, lewd suggestions . . . Let me tell you something if you don't already know it." Raymond looked around. He took Carolyn by the arm then and guided her through the waiting people, held doors open and followed her into an empty courtroom.

"You want to sit down?"

She went into one of the spectator rows that

were like widely spaced church pews, sat down, crossed her legs beneath a gray skirt, smoothing it, and turned on the contoured bench to face him or to keep some distance between them.

"What?"

"Clement Mansell killed the judge and Adele Simpson. We know he did."

"All you have to do is prove it," Carolyn said.

Raymond took time to gaze all around the courtroom before looking at Carolyn again. He said, "Just quit being the lawyer for a minute, all right? Clement Mansell has *killed* nine people. Four more than we know of and seven more than he'll ever be convicted for. He isn't a misguided boy, somebody you can defend, feel sorry for. He's a fucking killer. He likes it. He actually *likes* killing people. Do you understand that?"

Carolyn Wilder said quietly, "Even a fucking killer has rights under the law. You said last night, 'He kills people.' And I believe I said, 'Tell me about it.' We both know the purpose of this room. If you feel you have a case against Mansell, let's bring him in and find out. Until then, leave him alone . . . All right?"

The lady lawyer rose from the bench.

Raymond was dismissed.

He had felt this way standing before judges who had the final word and would pound a gavel and that was it. He had felt the urge to punch several judges. He had once felt the urge to punch Alvin Guy just as he felt the urge now to punch Carolyn Wilder. It seemed a natural reaction. The strange part was—he realized now, in the same moment— he did not have the urge to punch Clement Mansell.

He could see himself killing Mansell, but not hitting him with a fist, for there was no emotion involved.

It stopped him, brought him back to where he could say something and not be afraid of his tone, of an edge getting in the way. She had moved past him and was almost to the door.

"Carolyn? Let me ask you something."

She waited, half-turned, giving him a deadpan look. No person inside. Let him try to get through if he could.

"How come in the hall before, you said, 'Don't ever do that to me again'? About picking Clement up and bringing him in. How come you didn't say don't ever do that to *him* again?"

Carolyn Wilder turned without a word and walked out.

Raymond felt better, but not a whole lot.

13

NORBERT BRYL SAID, "You didn't question him in the room?"

"Nobody was here by then. I sat right where you're sitting, he was over at Jerry's desk."

Hunter said, "Jesus, I better check the drawers."

Bryl said, "What've you got that he'd want?" And swivelled back to Raymond Cruz. "So how'd you get to the nine people?"

The phone rang. Hunter said, "Take that, will you, Maureen? Act like you're the secretary."

Maureen, at her desk next to the file-room door, said, "Sure," and picked up the phone. "Squad Seven, Sergeant Downey—"

Wendell Robinson entered with a young black male wearing a T-shirt and a wool watchcap, motioned him into the file room to wait and closed the door. "Another boyfriend of Liselle Taylor. Says he believes Alfonso killed her, and if we can get his traffic tickets tore up—like three hundred dollars' worth and a suspended license—he'll tell us things so we'll believe it too."

"Tell him what the food's like across the street," Hunter said.

"He's been there. Probably likes the food."

Raymond said, "Before you go in—what'd Clement say to you, something about having a black friend?"

"He said one of my *best* friends," Wendell answered. "I said what's his name? He wouldn't tell me."

"Yeah—" Raymond, thoughtful, looked from his desk to Hunter. "He mention a friend to you?"

Hunter said, "How could that asshole have a friend?" But then squinted, closing one eye. "Wait a minute. He *did* say something. He wouldn't sign the rights sheet and he said, yeah, he said he had a friend who wouldn't sign it either and nothing happened to him."

"The Wrecking Crew," Raymond said, "they ever use a black driver?"

No one answered him.

"Then before the Wrecking Crew. You see what I'm getting at? He knows a black guy who was brought in here. The black guy wouldn't say anything about whatever it was. Which could be the reason Mansell thinks of him as a friend. Why, because the black guy wouldn't talk? A matter of principle? No, because the black guy wouldn't talk about Mansell. How's that sound?"

"That's not bad," Bryl said. "Let me go consult the great computer, see what it says."

Raymond said, "Check with Art Blaney in Robbery. He's got a memory better than a computer. Ask him if he recalls a black guy that ever ran with Mansell."

Bryl went out. A uniformed officer stood holding the door open. He said, "Judge Guy was shot four times with a .38, right?"

Hunter looked up. "Five times."

"Shit," the uniformed officer said, "I went and played four-three-eight."

The door swung closed.

Hunter said, "Probably boxed it, too, the dumb shit."

Raymond said, "He tells me he's killed nine people. I say, oh, in Detroit?"

The door swung open. A black officer in shirtsleeves, wearing a .44 magnum revolver in a white shoulder rig, came in with a stack of papers, licked his thumb, took off the top sheet and said, "Who wants it? Schedule for the play-offs, nine-thirty, Softball City. Homicide versus Sex Crimes."

The door swung closed.

Maureen hung up the phone. "MCMU. Mansell and Sandy Stanton just left 1300 Lafayette in a cab."

*   *   *

Inspector Herzog listened with his hands clasped as though in prayer, fingers pressed together, pointing straight up.

"He's telling me he's killed nine people," Raymond said, "without going into detail, two there, seven here, and I'm trying to get him to be a little more specific. With the Wrecking Crew? He says no. Well, we know he performed the triple on St. Marys and that was with the Crew. So what he meant was none of the others. But he was with *some*body. He said the guy was along but didn't do anything."

"This is the black guy?" Herzog asked.

"He didn't say he was black," Raymond said. "He only told me another guy was along. But he told Wendell he had a black friend. See, first he keeps throwing 'nigger' in Wendell's face, then he tells him, 'One of my best friends is a nigger.' He tells Jerry he's got a friend who was questioned here and refused to say a word or even sign the rights sheet. He tells me a guy was with him when he killed some people and now we put the pieces together and Norb consults the computer, checking out Mansell in depth, all his arrests for whatever, all the times he was picked up on suspicion, brought in for questioning, to see if he's got a black guy in his past anywhere."

Raymond's gaze moved to the window framing Herzog's mane of gray hair. He could see the top floors of the highrise in the near distance.

"Incidentally, Clement and Sandy, about an hour ago they took a cab out to the Tel-Twelve Mall. They went inside, MCMU lost them."

"They're not using the Buick," Herzog said. "How come?"

"I think he cleaned it up," Raymond said, "doesn't want to touch it again."

"Maybe you should've picked it up yesterday."

"Well, as I mentioned to you," Raymond said, "it was a judgment call. MCMU followed Sandy around, they're pretty sure she didn't dump anything. And if they *hadn't* followed her, then Mr. Sweety wouldn't be the important man he is today."

"Who's Mr. Sweety?"

"You remember yesterday Sandy went to a place on Kercheval, Sweety's Lounge?"

Herzog nodded. "Came out with a guy and went in the house next door."

"Came out with Mr. Sweety and went to *his* house," Raymond said. "It's where he lives."

"I think you said yesterday the guy's black."

"Yes, and according to the sheets on Mansell, so is a guy by the name of Marcus Sweeton who did some work with Clement back when he first came here and before he joined the Wrecking Crew.

Sweeton's had two convictions—one probation, two years on a gun charge and I guess he's not looking forward to that third fall, because he's been pure ever since, now operates Sweety's Lounge."

"How'd he get a liquor license?"

"It's in his brother's name. Sweeton says he's only a bartender; but he runs the place and lives next door with his girlfriend, Anita. The brother works out at Chrysler Mound Road. So we know Marcus is the original Mr. Sweety of Sweety's Lounge. Art Blaney remembers him—"

"What do we need a computer for with Blaney?" Herzog said.

"That's what I said to Norb. Art looks up at the ceiling, it's like he wrote some notes up there. What do you want to know? Marcus Sweeton, a.k.a. the Dark Mark, Sweetwater, a couple more and Mr. Sweety. He makes about fifteen grand a year from the bar and another twenty-five or thirty from drugs, nothing worth busting, little neighborhood store."

"This is how he stays pure," Herzog said.

"Well, it's relative," Raymond said. "Pure compared to going in someplace with a gun. Art says Mansell used him as a bird dog. Mr. Sweety would go in a dope house—very friendly type of guy—sit around and chat a while, pass out some angel dust, tell a few jokes—that's the way they worked. Get 'em laid back on the dust, then Clement comes in and takes 'em off easy—all these clowns sitting around grinning at him."

"How many times can you do that?" Herzog said.

"In *this* town?" Raymond said. "You put all the dope stores on a computer the printout would reach down the hall, down the stairs, out onto Beaubien—"

"I get the picture," Herzog said. "So now you've got a possible witness to one or more of these nine killings Mansell claims he did. Are you trying to tie in Mr. Sweety to Judge Guy and Adele Simpson?"

"Not necessarily," Raymond said. "See, the original idea, find out who this old buddy is, tie him in to Mansell as an accessory and get him to cop on one of the earlier murders. Just in case we don't get Mansell on the current one, the judge and Adele. I thought, ah, use a lead Mansell himself gave us and doesn't even know it. Bring him in and watch his mouth fall open."

"I'm not gonna hold up my vacation on that happening," Herzog said.

"No, I said that was the original idea," Raymond said. "But now—what *is* this? Mansell shoots the judge and Adele and the next *day* Sandy Stanton goes to see the old buddy, Mr. Sweety. What's going on here?"

"So you *are* trying to tie him in."

"Yeah, but not necessarily in the way I think you mean."

"I'm not sure I know what I mean," Herzog said.

"Look at it this way," Raymond said. "If Mansell was hired to do the judge and then he hired Mr. Sweety to drive for him—"

"Then why didn't Sweety get a car?"

"That's the first question. The next one—since Mansell knows we've made the Buick, would he tell Sandy to drive over to Mr. Sweety's house in it the next day?"

"I don't know," Herzog said, "would he?"

"Or—did Sandy go over there on her own?"

"For what?"

"I don't know."

"Why don't you ask her."

"I'm going to," Raymond said, "soon as she gets home."

"But then she tells Mansell and he'll know you're onto Mr. Sweety. How do you get around that?"

"It's a game, isn't it?" Raymond said. "Nothing but a game . . . Why don't I just go find Clement and shoot him?"

Herzog said, "That's the best idea I've heard yet."

14

CLEMENT BOUGHT A TEN-SHOT .22 Ruger automatic rifle, a regular $87.50 value for $69.95, and a box of .22 longs at K-mart in the Tel-Twelve Mall. He went over to the typewriter counter and asked the girl if he could try one. She said sure and gave him a sheet of notepaper. Clement pecked away for a minute, using his index fingers, pulled the notepaper out of the Smith-Corona and took it with him. He saw a black cowboy hat he liked, put it on and walked out with it . . . down a block to Red Bowers Chevrolet where Sandy Stanton was wandering around the used car lot in her high-heel boots and tight jeans.

She saw him coming with the black hat on, carrying the long cardboard box sticking out of the K-mart sack and said, "Oh, my Lord, what have you got now?"

He told her it was a surprise and Sandy brightened. "For me?" Clement said no, for somebody else. He looked around at the rows of "Fall Clean-up Specials" and asked her if she'd picked one out.

Sandy led him to a Pontiac Firebird with a big air scoop and the hood flamed in red and gold, sunlight flashing on the windshield.

"Isn't it a honey? Looks like it eats other cars right up."

Clement said, "Sugar, I told you I want a regular car. I ain't gonna street race, I ain't gonna hang out at the Big Boy; I just need me some wheels in your name till things get a little better. Now here's seven one-hundred-dollar bills, all the grocery money till we get some more. You buy a nice car and pick me up over there—if I can make it across Telegraph without getting killed—where you see that sign? Ramada Inn? I'll be in there having a cocktail."

Sandy got him a '76 Mercury Montego, sky blue over rust, with only forty thousand miles on it for six-fifty plus tax and Clement said, "Now you're talking."

A boy who was born on an oil lease and traveled in the beds of pickup trucks till he was twelve years old would be likely to have dreams of Mark VIs and Eldorados. Not Clement. He had driven, had in his possession for varying periods of time in his life, an estimated 268 automobiles, all makes and models, counting the used '56 Chevy four-barrel he'd bought when he was seventeen and the used

TR-3 he'd bought one time when he was feeling sporty; all the rest he stole. Clement said cars were to get you from here to there or a way of picking up spending money. If you wanted to impress somebody, open their eyes, shit, stick a nickel-plate .45 in their mouth and ear back the hammer.

Clement drove back downtown and over to Lafayette East, but didn't go to the apartment. Sandy said she wanted to get some Vernor's. So while she was in the supermarket down the street from the apartment building, Clement found a telephone booth with a directory and looked up Cruz . . .

Cruz, Cruz, Cruz . . . no Raymond Cruz, which he didn't expect to find anyway, but there was an M. Cruz—the kind of initial-only listing women thought would prevent dirty phone calls—and Clement bet twenty cents, dialing the number, that M. Cruz was Raymond Cruz's former wife.

MCMU called Raymond Cruz. Sandy Stanton was back, crossing the street toward 1300 Lafayette with a bag of groceries. Alone. A 1st Precinct squad car got him over there, up the circular drive to the entrance, in less than four minutes. Sandy was in the lobby, pulling Del Weems' credit-card bills out of the mailbox, when Raymond walked in.

"Well, hi there." Sandy gave him a nice smile.

Raymond smiled too, appreciating her, close to believing she was glad to see him.

"What brings you around, may I ask? Del isn't back yet, if you're looking for him."

Raymond said, "No, I'm looking for you, Sandy." And she said, oh, losing some of her sparkle. They went up to 2504. Raymond walked over to the skyline view while Sandy ran to the bathroom. She was in there a long time. It was quiet. Raymond listened, wondering if she was flushing something down the toilet. She came out wearing her satin running shorts, a white T-shirt with a portrait on it, barefoot, saying she had to get out of those tight designer jeans. Saying she wished uncomfortable outfits weren't so fashionable, but what were you supposed to do? You had to keep up. Like with cowboy boots now. Back home she'd worked at a riding stable at Spring Mills State Park and wore cowboy boots all the time, never dreaming they'd be the fashion one day and you'd even wear 'em to shopping centers . . . Sandy talking fast to keep Raymond from talking and maybe he'd forget why he came. It did give him time to identify the portrait on her T-shirt and read the words SAVE BERT PARKS.

She hesitated too long and he said, "Where's Clement?"

"Well, so much for the world of fashion," Sandy said. "I don't know where he is."

"You drop him off someplace?"

"You think I'm dumb or something? I'm not gonna tell you a thing. If I didn't have a kind heart, I wouldn't even be talking to you . . . You want a drink?"

Raymond was ready to say no, but paused and said sure and went with her into the kitchen that was like a narrow passageway between the front hall and the dining-L. She asked him if Scotch was all right. He said fine and watched her get out the ice and pour the Chivas. Sandy opened a can of Vernor's 1-Cal ginger ale for herself. She said, "Ouuuuuu, it sure tickles your nose, but I like it. You can't buy it most other places but here."

Raymond said, "You have any grass?"

"Boy—" Sandy said. "You never know anymore who's into what."

"You have trouble getting it?"

"What do you want, my source?"

"No, a guy in the prosecutor's office I know has a pretty good source. I was thinking maybe I could help you out, I mean if Mr. Sweety isn't coming through."

"Man oh man," Sandy said. "I think I better go sit down. You're scary, you know it?"

"Looks like Mr. Sweety's in some trouble."

"Jesus, who isn't?"

"Have to be careful who you associate with."

"*That* is the truth," Sandy said. "I think I might be running around with the wrong crowd. Let's go in the other room; I feel cornered in here."

"I just wanted to ask you something," Raymond said. "See, we're gonna be talking to Mr. Sweety. He was supposed to be working the night the judge was killed. Maybe he was. But we do know you have something going with him—"

Sandy said, "Have something *going?*"

"You went to his house yesterday—"

"To get some dope. You already said—you *know* he's a source I use. You just said so."

"Yeah, but why would Clement send you over there?"

"He *didn't*. He didn't even know I went." Sandy paused. "Wait a sec, you're confusing me. I did go over there yesterday to score some grass. Period. It's got nothing to do with anything else."

"Clement let you use the car?"

"It isn't *his* car, it's Del Weems'."

"I know, but I wondered why he'd let you go there."

"He didn't *know* I went. I already told you that."

Twice, Raymond thought. He believed her because he wanted to, because it was reasonable. He didn't like to come onto facts that appeared unreasonable and have to change his course.

He liked it that she was upset and he kept going now. "I mean considering everything," Raymond said. "Here we've got a car that was identified at a murder scene, Del's Buick . . ."

Sandy rolled her eyes—little girl standing there in her satin running shorts, nipples poking out at Bert Parks on her T-shirt. Skinny little thing—he felt sorry for her too.

"What's the matter?" Raymond asked.

"Oh, nothing . . . Jesus."

"We don't have Clement in the car yet, but we know Clement did both the judge and the girl, Adele Simpson."

"Now it's starting to snow," Sandy said, "and we're hardly into October."

"Ask him," Raymond said. "But here's the thing. Would Clement like to know you were over there in the car, the Buick, seeing a man who used to work with him and could be a suspect in Guy's murder? You understand what I'm saying?"

"Do I under*stand*? Are you kidding?"

"So it isn't so much Clement doesn't know you went over there," Raymond said. "You don't *want* him to know."

"If you say so."

"Why don't you want him to know, Sandy?"

"He don't like it when I smoke too much grass."

"Like when you get nervous or upset?"

"Yeah, usually."

"Well, the way things're going, Sandy," Raymond said, "I think you better hit on a couple pounds of good Colombian."

15

CLEMENT HAD NEVER ICE-SKATED, but he could see the Palmer Park lagoon would be a good place. It wasn't a big open rink, like most. It was a pond, several acres in size, with wooded islands in it to skate around. A good place to dump the Ruger when he was finished with it. He parked by the refreshment pavilion and cut through the woods along Merrill Plaisance Drive to where he had hidden the rifle in some bushes a few minutes before.

It was almost six o'clock; getting dark in a hurry. He picked up the rifle and moved up to the edge of the trees where he could look directly across Merrill Plaisance, across the narrow island separating the drive from the residential street and the front of the four-story, L-shaped apartment building that was 913 Covington, the home of Lt. Raymond chicken-fat Cruz—with the sad mustache and the quiet way about him, which could be politeness or just empty-headed dumbness.

Clement had said to the woman's voice on the phone, the cop's former wife, "What's Ray's address again? I lost it . . . And the apartment number? . . . Oh, that's right on the first floor, huh?" Then had got the name of the building manager off her mailbox and called her saying this was Sgt. Hunter: they were planning a surprise party for Lt. Cruz; the guys were gonna drop in and then, when he wasn't looking, reach out the window and haul in this present as a surprise, a stereo outfit, and he wanted to know which window to put it outside of. The landlady said in this neighborhood they better put a policeman with it or they would be the ones surprised when they reached out to get it.

There were three windows: one with an air-conditioning unit, one with a plant, one with raised venetian blinds, close to the sidewalk on Covington.

Ten past six.

The landlady had said he was usually home by six-thirty the latest, unless he didn't come home. Her apartment was next to his and if she was in the kitchen she'd hear his door slam and then sometimes she'd hear him playing music . . . Didn't he already have a victrola? . . . A little cheap one, Clement told her, which was probably the truth.

Look for a medium-blue four-door Plymouth. Clement had heard cops didn't use their own cars on the job because no one would insure them.

Twenty after. There was a last trace of red in the sky. The front of the building was without definition now, a few lights showing in apartments. Clement practice-sighted on Raymond Cruz's dark windows. Range, about fifty yards. But a tough shot with the cars going by in front of him, on the park drive.

Maybe this Raymond Cruz did use his own car. Or lieutenants got a different color than that shitty medium blue. Clement didn't worry about odds or luck. Something happened or it didn't. The man would come home or he wouldn't. If not tonight, tomorrow. Clement didn't plan on waiting around forever; but a little patience was good and more often than not got rewarded.

That's why Clement wasn't too surprised or especially elated when he saw the light go on in Raymond Cruz's apartment. Sooner or later it was supposed to. Clement put the Ruger against a tree and lined up his sights on the figure moving inside the apartment, Clement waiting for a lull in the traffic . . .

Raymond had come into the apartment building from the alley, walked through to the foyer and got his mail: *Newsweek*, a VISA bill, a bank statement, a thick window-envelope from Oral Roberts, Tulsa, Oklahoma, addressed to Mr. M. Cruz, and a folded piece of notepaper.

In his apartment Raymond dropped the mail on

the coffeetable, went into the kitchen with
Newsweek and got a can of Strohs out of the refrigerator. He drank from the can as he glanced
through the magazine on the counter, learning that
beer was now discovered to cause cancer along
with everything else. In the living room again he sat
down at the end of the couch by the floor lamp he'd
bought at Goodwill Industries. He picked up the
mail from the coffeetable, threw back the bill from
VISA and the bank statement, laid the Oral Roberts
envelope on his lap and opened the piece of notepaper that was folded three times. The typewritten
message said:

SURPRISE
CHICKEN FAT!!!

Raymond would replay the scene, what happened next, and at first believe the guy was right
outside because the timing was that good . . . sitting there looking at the typed words, wondering . . .

And the front window and the lamp exploded,
the glass shattering and he was in darkness, instinc-
tively rolling off the couch, catching a knee on the
coffeetable, trying to yank the snub-nosed .38 out
of his waistband that was tight on his hip, crawling
toward the window now, the flat sound of reports
reaching him, erupting through fragments of glass,

thudding into the wall, six, seven shots—he got his legs under him, turned and ran for the door . . . down the hall, out the front entrance. Cars were going by on the park drive, headlights on, making faint humming sounds. He crossed Covington to the island, kept going, heard a car horn and brakes squeal and he was into the trees, in darkness, with no sense of purpose or direction now, no sounds except for the cars going past on the park drive.

In the apartment again he picked up the phone, began to punch buttons. He stopped, replaced the receiver. If Sandy was home with the Buick, what was Clement driving? Could it have been someone else? No. He sat in semidarkness, a light showing in the open doorway to the hall.

Raymond picked up the phone again and punched a number.

"Mary Alice, I just want to ask you a question, okay? . . . No, I don't have time to get into that. Somebody called and you gave him my address. Did the guy have kind of a southern accent? . . . I know you didn't know who it was. Mary Alice, that's why you're not supposed to give out . . . No, you just tell them you don't know. Last night, did a lady call? . . ."

Jesus Christ, Raymond said. He put the phone, in both of his hands, in his lap and could hear her talking. He saw streetlight reflections in the jagged pieces of windowpane. Raising the phone again he heard her pause and said, quickly, "Mary Alice? Nice talking to you."

He called Squad Seven. Maureen answered and he asked her to look in his book and give him Carolyn Wilder's phone number. Maureen came back and said, "Six-four-five . . ."

And Raymond said, "No, that's her office. Give me her home number. And the address." He got out his pen and wrote on the back of the Oral Roberts envelope as Maureen dictated. Maureen said, "Why would she have an office in Birmingham if she lives on the east side?"

Raymond said, "You want me to I'll ask her. But I got a few other questions first."

He dialed Carolyn Wilder's home number. Following the first ring her voice came on. "Yes?"

"You were waiting for me to call," Raymond said.

"Who is this?"

He told her and said, "I'd like to talk to the Oklahoma Wildman, but I don't know where he is."

"He isn't here."

It stopped Raymond. "I didn't expect him to be."

There was a pause. "He *was* here," Carolyn Wilder said. "He left a few minutes ago."

Raymond said, "Carolyn, don't move. You just stepped in a deep pile of something."

16

CAROLYN WILDER'S HOME on Van Dyke Place, off Jefferson, had been built in 1912 along the formal lines of a Paris townhouse. During the 1920s and '30s it had changed from residence to speakeasy to restaurant and was serving a limited but selective menu—for the most part to Grosse Pointe residents who knew about the place and were willing to reserve one of ten tables a week in advance—when Carolyn Wilder bought it as an investment, hired a decorator and, in the midst of restoring a past splendor, decided to move in and make it her home.

Standing in the front hall, facing the rose-carpeted stairway that turned twice on its way to the second-floor hall, Raymond said, "It looks familiar."

The young black woman didn't say anything. She stood with arms folded in an off-white housedress, letting him look around, the lamplight from side fixtures reflecting on mirrored walls and giving a yellow cast to the massive chandelier that hung above them.

"You look familiar too," Raymond said. "You're not Angela Davis."

"No, I'm not."

"You're . . . Marcie Coleman. About two years ago?"

"Two years in January."

"And Mrs. Wilder defended you."

"That's right."

"We offered you, I believe, manslaughter and you turned it down. Stood trial for first degree."

"That's right."

"I'll tell you something. I'm glad you got off."

"Thank you."

"How long ago was Clement Mansell here?"

There was a pause, silence. "Ms. Wilder's waiting for you upstairs."

"I was just telling Marcie," Raymond said, "your house seems familiar, the downstairs part." Though not this room with its look of a century later, plexiglass tables, strange shapes and colors on the wall, small areas softly illuminated by track lighting. "You do these?"

"Some of them."

The room was like a dim gallery. He was sure

that most of the paintings, not just some, were hers. "What's this one?"

"Whatever you want it to be."

"Were you mad when you painted it?"

Carolyn Wilder stared at him with a look that was curious but guarded.

"Why?"

"I don't know. I get the feeling you were upset."

"I think I was when I started."

She sat in a bamboo chair with deep cushions of some dark silky material, a wall of books next to her, Carolyn half in, half out of a dimmed beam of light. She had not asked him to sit down; she had not offered him a drink, though a cordial glass of clear liquid sat on the glass table close to her chair and a tea-table bar of whiskeys and liqueurs stood only a few feet from Raymond.

"Marcie married again?"

"She's thinking about it."

"I bet the guy's giving it some serious thought too. She live here?"

"Downstairs. She has rooms. Most of it's closed off though."

He turned from the abstract painting over the fireplace to look at her: legs crossed in a brown caftan—some kind of loose cover—her feet hidden by a hassock that matched the chair.

"Are you somebody else when you're home?"

"I'm not sure I know what you mean."

"You go out much?"

"When I want to."

"I have a hard question coming up."

"Why don't you ask it?"

"Are you working at being a mystery woman?"

"Is that the question?"

"No." He paused.

He was aware that he had no trouble talking to her, saying whatever came to mind without wondering what her reaction would be or even caring. He felt a small hook of irritation, standing before the woman in shadow, but the irritation was all right because he could control it. He didn't want to rush the reason he was here. He would hit her with it in time; but first he wanted to jab a little. She intrigued him. Or she challenged him. One or the other, or both.

He said, "Do you still paint?"

"Not really. Once in a while."

"You switch from fine art to law . . . On impulse?"

"I suppose," Carolyn said. "But it wasn't that difficult."

"You were divorced first—is that where the impulse comes in? The way the divorce was handled?"

She continued to stare at him, but with something more in her eyes, creeping in now, something more than ordinary interest. She said, "You don't seem old enough to be a lieutenant; unless you have an M.B.A. and you're somewhere in administration. But you're homicide."

"I'm older than you are," Raymond said. He walked toward her chair, moved the hassock with his foot and sat down on it, somewhat half-turned from her but with their legs almost touching. She seemed to draw back against the cushion as he made the move, but he wasn't sure. He could see her face clearly now, her eyes staring, expectant.

"I'm almost a year older. You want to know what my sign is?" She didn't answer. He picked up the cordial glass and raised it to his face. "What is it?"

"Aquavit. Help yourself . . . but it's not very cold."

He took a sip, put the glass down. "You watched this lawyer handle your divorce, thinking, I can do better than that . . . Huh?"

"He agreed to their settlement offer," Carolyn said, "practically everything, let my husband have the house, a place in Harbor Springs, charged ten thousand and billed me for half."

Raymond said, "And treated you like a little kid who wouldn't understand anything even if he explained it."

Her eyes held. "You know the feeling?"

"I know lawyers," Raymond said. "I'm in court about twice a week."

"He was so condescending—he was oily. I couldn't get through to him."

"You could've fired him."

"I was different then. But at least it turned me around. I actually made up my mind to get a law degree—listen to this—and specialize in divorce and represent poor, defenseless, cast-off wives."

"I can't see you doing that."

"I didn't, for very long. I decided if I wanted to work with children I should work with real children. I even felt a tinge of sympathy for that jerk who represented me; he'd probably become conditioned to vacuous outbursts and treated all his women clients exactly the same. Eventually I found my way into the Defender's office and Recorder's Court."

She was more relaxed now, not making a pretense of it.

"I've always liked to watch you," Raymond said. "You never seem to get upset. You're always prepared . . . full of surprises for the prosecutor." He placed a hand on the brown cotton material covering her knee.

Her eyes, still calm, raised from his hand to his face.

"But you're fucking up, Carolyn, and it isn't like you, is it?"

"If I tell you Mansell was here this evening," Carolyn said, "it means I'm not going to discuss his involvement in *any*thing until you produce a warrant and he's placed under arrest."

"No, it means you're telling me a story," Raymond said. "Clement wasn't here." He watched her expression; it didn't begin to change until he said, "He was outside my window at 6:30 P.M. trying to blow my head off with an automatic rifle. Otherwise—if he was here at the same time, then Clement's into bilocation. And I'm getting off the case."

Carolyn took her time, as if studying him before she said, "You saw him?"

"No."

"How many people, do you think, you're directly responsible for sending to prison? In round numbers."

"I don't know—five hundred?"

"Then count their friends, relatives—"

"Lot of people."

"You have the gun whoever it was used?"

Raymond shook his head.

"Do you have the gun that killed Guy and the woman?"

Raymond almost smiled. He said, "Why?"

"You know you're not going to get Mansell unless you can produce the murder weapon and prove it's his and even then you're going to have a tough time. On this new allegation, a suspicion of an attempt—what have you got? Did anyone see him? At 6:30 it's already dark. Where are you going to even look for a witness?"

"Carolyn," Raymond said, getting used to saying the name. "Clement wasn't here."

"What I said to you on the phone," Carolyn said, with a hint of irritation now, in eye movement more than tone, "is not something you can enter as evidence, even if you recorded the conversation. You know that, don't you?"

"You lied," Raymond said.

"God *damn* it—" She seemed to come up from the cushion, but in the next moment she was composed again. "If I don't care to admit I made a statement, whether to protect my client or because of the particular interpretation I believe you might give the statement, then I'll rephrase it to the best of my ability and memory."

"Why did you lie?" Raymond said.

"Jesus Christ, are you dense or something?" Finally with a bite to her tone, "If you intend to use whatever I said then I'll flatly deny it."

Raymond got up, giving her a chance to breathe, maybe bring her guard down a little. He went over to the tea-table bar, found a cordial glass and concentrated on pouring aquavit into it, up past a crisscross design in the crystal.

"I'm not threatening to use what you said in court. I'm not threatening, period." He sipped the clear liqueur from the rim of the glass and came back to the hassock, watching the glass carefully as he sat down again. "All I'm trying to do"—looking at her now—"see, I have a feeling that Clement, that time in your office, scared you to death . . . holding something over your head. He called you this evening and did it again. Scared you to the point of covering for him. Then you have a couple of these and calm down and you're the lawyer again and you start using words on me, try and dazzle me with your footwork. But it doesn't change Clement, does it?"

She said quietly, "I can handle Clement."

He wanted to grab her by the arms and shake her and tell her to wake up. Fucking lawyers and judges who used words and a certain irritating tone and there wasn't a thing you could do about it . . .

Holding the cordial glass helped. He took a sip and placed it on the table next to hers. It was hard, but he was going to play this with her. He said, "A man by the name of Champ who packed a Walther P.38 thought he could handle Clement and Clement took him out. Remember? Three years ago. I'll bet Judge Guy, calling the nine-eleven in his car, the judge thought he could handle him too. Clement's holding something over your head, he's threatening you or extorting you and you're letting him do it."

Carolyn picked up her glass and he knew she was going to dodge him.

"He did tell me something interesting," Carolyn said. "That you want to meet him somewhere and have it out. Just the two of you."

"He said that?"

"How else would I know?"

"There are stories," Raymond said, "the cop takes off his badge and they settle it man to man in the alley. If you think it's like that—no, this is Clement's idea. You look at my living room window you'll see he's already started."

"You're saying, what, he challenged you to—what amounts to a duel?"

"He didn't give me his card or slap my face or anything, or give me a choice of weapons; but it looks like he leans toward automatic rifles. This is your client I'm talking about. The one you can handle."

Carolyn said, "What're you going to do about it?" Quietly but with new interest.

"I'm gonna keep looking over my shoulder, for one thing," Raymond said. "I'm not gonna turn a light on with the shades up."

"What does the department say about it?"

"The police department?"

"Your inspector, commander, whoever you report to."

"I haven't told anybody yet. It just happened."

"Are you going to?"

"I'm gonna report the shooting, yes."

"You know what I mean. Are you going to tell them Clement challenged you?"

Raymond paused. "I haven't thought about it."

"What's the difference in the way you look at Clement Mansell and the way I do?" Carolyn said. "I tell you I can handle him. You imply to me, in effect, the same thing, that it's a personal matter."

"There's one big difference," Raymond said. "I've got a gun."

"I know. That's why I think the idea appeals to you," Carolyn said. "Mano a mano. No—more like High Noon. Gunfight at the O.K. Corral. You have to go back a hundred years and out west to find an analogy. But there it is."

He thought of the girl from the *News*.

He said, "I don't know—" and paused. In his mind the allusion to a western scene, the street, men with guns approaching, dissolved and now he saw kids playing guns in a vacant lot near Holy Trinity, before the places where they played disappeared beneath a freeway, seeing the same kids in school then, a little blond-haired girl named Carmel something, on a dismal fall afternoon in the fifth grade, dropping a note on his desk that said *I Love You* on ruled paper, like an exercise in Palmer Method—kids sharing secrets—a long time ago but still clear in his mind, part of him now as he sat in dimmed light with someone else who had a secret. He wondered if she had close friends or someone she spoke to intimately.

She said, "What don't you know?"

"I thought of that, it's strange, what you said. When I was talking to Clement he kept making the point that I wasn't any more interested in upholding the law than he was in breaking it—"

"*He* said that?"

"Yes, that it was a personal thing between us that didn't have anything to do with other people."

"Did you agree?"

"I said, 'A long time ago we might've settled this between us.' And he said . . . 'Or if we thought it might be fun.'"

Staring intently she said, "You haven't told this to the people you work with. But you've told me."

She came up from the silky cushion, close to him now but closed in on herself, arms against her body, hands clasped on her knees.

"You said the other night in my office, 'Can I help you?' You said it twice. Both times, the way you said it, I came so close to telling you, I *wanted* to—"

Her eyes were brown, the pupils dilated in the

dim light, making her eyes appear dark and clearly
defined, like eyes in a drawing that were accentu-
ated, inked in except for a small pale square to in-
dicate reflected light, a soft sparkle.

"Everybody," Raymond said, "has to have
somebody to tell secrets to." He liked the delicate
line of her nose, the shape of her mouth and saw
where he would go in and take part of her lower
lip, biting it very gently.

She said, "I make assumptions—I think I know
you, but I don't. You say, 'fine art.' You say, 'if he's
into bilocation . . . ' "

Raymond said, "But he isn't, is he?"

She didn't answer.

"Let me help you."

She continued to look into his eyes, into the deep
end of a pool, gathering courage—

"Carolyn, I give you my word . . ."

She said, "Hold me . . . please."

17

THEY MADE LOVE IN A BED with white sheets and a dark oak headboard that towered to the ceiling. They made love almost at once, as though they missed each other so much they couldn't wait, hands moving, learning quickly, and when he entered her she breathed a sound of relief he had never heard before—even in the beds with decorator pillows and designer sheets, with the girls who would groan dramatic obscenities—none of them came out of themselves the way Carolyn did. Raymond moved with her, involved, but aware of himself too, because he couldn't believe it was happening, he couldn't believe it was Carolyn Wilder moving and making the sounds, thrusting, arching up with her head back, straining in faint light that let him see her face in a way she would never see it or recognize herself, Raymond seeing a secret Carolyn and then, for a moment, seeing her eyes open, seeing her awareness. He wanted to say something to her. He said, "I know you." The moment became a brief silence that was gone as her eyes closed again and then became something that had happened a long time ago.

They remained in darkness, in silence for several minutes, Raymond holding her, seeing the faint outside light against window shades across the bedroom. He heard her say, very quietly, close to him, "God, that was good." He thought of ways to reply but said nothing. She would feel him holding her, his hands moving gently, stroking; she would know what he felt.

Finally she said, in a voice that was a murmur but clear in the silence, "In my office the other night, when you were on the phone—" She paused. "He said, as he started to leave he said, 'When do I get the money?' I looked at him, I didn't know what he was talking about. He said, 'The hundred-thousand you promised me for killing the judge.' I said 'What?' I couldn't believe it. He said, 'Don't try and act dumb to get out of paying me. I have proof the judge was putting the stuff on you.' I said, 'What do you mean?' But that was all. He said something else like 'I'll be in touch,' and left."

"Then tonight," Raymond said, "he called you—"

"He called this morning, too. Tonight he called just a few minutes before you did. He said, 'I've been at your place the past hour if anybody wants to know.' I didn't say a word to him; I hung up the phone. He called back within a minute and said, 'Look, if I take a fall on the Guy thing, you're going with me.' This time I told him if he was worried about it he'd better get a lawyer, because I was no longer representing him. He said . . . 'Oh, yes you are.' He said if it even looked like he might be convicted he'd sign a statement that I had paid him to kill Guy and he'd—words to the effect that he'd produce enough evidence to substantiate it or at least give credence to a motive."

"How can he do that?"

"That's what's interesting about it, that he thinks he can implicate me." Carolyn turned enough to see his face in the darkness. "This is in confidence, right?" Raymond didn't say anything. "I'm not telling you something you can use anyway."

He was aware of a strange feeling—even with her breast against his arm and their naked thighs touching—that the lawyer was returning, that the woman who had let go was pulling in again, regrouping, perhaps not even aware of it herself as she lay in his arms.

Carolyn said, "I mean if I filed a complaint against him, say on the grounds of extortion, it would be my word against his. Which would be considerable, but not nearly enough to convict him.

He'll put on his dumb-hillbilly act and say I misunderstood him. Clement is very good at playing dumb."

Raymond said, "Let's go back a little bit. First, he wants a hundred thousand or he'll cop, swear you paid him to kill Guy."

"I think," Carolyn said, "considering he's an opportunist, Clement's first thought is to capitalize on Guy's death." She paused. "Whether he killed him or not."

Raymond told himself to wait, be patient. Ignore, for the time being, the warning trying to tighten up his insides.

"But now he's a suspect and he's telling me to use every effort to keep him out of jail—I presume free of charge—or else he'll take me with him."

"When did he tell you this?"

"This morning, he called me at the office."

"What'd he say exactly?"

"He said he knows and can prove I had some kind of bribe scheme going with Guy, that I paid him off for acquittals or reduced sentences. *But*, because I testified against Guy before the Tenure Commission, helped to get him thrown off the bench in fact, I'm supposedly one of the ones Guy threatened to expose. He was going to write a book, 'name names of people,' Guy said in the paper, 'with dirty hands and indecent fingers.'

Clement will say I had Guy killed to keep him from writing the book."

"Clement thought up all this?"

"Everybody misjudges him," Carolyn said. "That's how he gets away with what he does, why he's . . . fascinating, really." She stirred, bringing her arm out from beneath Raymond. "Would you like a drink?"

Carolyn left the bed naked and came back wearing the brown caftan. She handed Raymond a glass of aquavit and turned on the night table lamp before getting into bed again to rest against the headboard. When Raymond placed his hand on her thigh she raised her glass and sipped the clear liqueur. He had never thought of women using men other than to get carpeting and appliances. He had said to her, "I know you," and she had said nothing in return. He wondered what he felt about her beyond the fact he liked her eyes and her nose and her body. He wondered if he had been genuinely moved or if he had only wanted to mount and subdue the dignified, distinguished lady lawyer, or if it had been the other way around and it was Raymond Cruz who had been seduced.

"Is he *saying* he has proof you were involved with Guy," Raymond said, "or does he have something?"

She turned, leaning against the headboard, to look at him, holding her glass in two hands. "Are you asking *was* I actually involved, and could there be some valid bit of evidence?"

"I'm asking what he's holding over you."

Carolyn paused. "Well . . . if, for example, you found my name in Guy's address book . . . name, phone number and figures that could be interpreted to represent amounts of money, perhaps, by some stretch of the imagination, a list of payments made to him, Guy—and you were looking for a suspect, someone who might have contracted for Guy's murder—would you consider that evidence?"

Raymond shook his head. "Not by itself . . . Did you see the address book?"

"What address book?"

"The one Clement, I assume, lifted off the judge."

Carolyn was still looking at him, at ease against the headboard. "I said what if you found my name in his book. I didn't say Clement took it, did I?"

"We've come a long way," Raymond said, "but I get the feeling we're back where we started. You were scared to death of him a little while ago—"

"I'm still reasonably afraid," Carolyn said, "enough to know that I have to be very careful with Clement. But that doesn't mean I can't handle him."

"You don't have to *handle* him. All you have to do is make a statement, Clement admitted to you he shot the judge."

"Because he's trying to capitalize on it," Carolyn said. "I told you before, that doesn't mean he actually did it."

"But he *did!*" Raymond spilled some of the aquavit, pushing himself up on the pillow to get to Carolyn's level. She watched him brush at the wet spot on the sheet.

"Don't worry about it," she said quietly, "the bed's going to be changed." She lounged against the dark wood of the headboard while Raymond sat erect, stiffly, bare above the sheet around his waist. She said, "Look, we've confided in each other because sometimes we feel the need. You said before, everybody has to have somebody to tell secrets to. I've told you things I wouldn't tell my partners and you've told me things, you've indicated, you aren't going to tell your people. You have your game with Clement and I have mine. We both will admit he's an unusual study, a pretty fascinating character, or neither of us would be quite so uniquely involved. Isn't that true?"

"You told him to find another lawyer," Raymond said.

"Yes, but he won't. He not only needs me, he likes me . . ."

Raymond listened to the lawyer and the woman talking at the same time.

". . . But he *is* going to have to realize, once he gets this extortion-blackmail bullshit out of his head, that I charge a fee, and if he's not willing to pay it he *will*, indeed, have to go somewhere else." She seemed to smile, though it was a bland expression. "We can play our games, but it still has to be within the context of the jobs we're paid to do. You can't expect me to give you information about my client, just as I don't expect you to shoot him down without provocation . . . Agreed?"

"I guess we are back where we started," Raymond said.

"Why? Where did you expect to be?"

He paused and said, "I don't know," as he got out of bed and then stood naked looking down at her. "But aside from all that, how was the fuck?"

"Let me put it this way," Carolyn said, her eyes moving up his body to his face, "it was about what I expected it to be."

18

MARY ALICE HAD SAID TO HIM, "You don't care about anybody else; you only think of yourself."

Bob Herzog had said to him, "You know what I admire about you? Your detachment. You don't let things bother you. You observe, you make judgments and you accept what you find."

Norb Bryl had said to him, "You spend two hundred and ten dollars on a *blue* suit?"

Wendell Robinson had said to him, "I don't mean to sound like I'm ass-kissing, but most of the time I don't think of you as being white."

Jerry Hunter had said to him, more than once, "What's the matter you're not talking?"

The girl from the *News* had said to him, "I think you're afraid of women. I think that's the root of the problem."

The woman, Carolyn Wilder, had said to him, "It was about what I expected it to be."

He had put on his blue suit and left her house because he couldn't think of anything to say. All the way home he had tried to think of something that would have nailed her to the antique headboard, her mouth open; but he couldn't think of anything. He went to bed and woke up during the night thinking of lines, but none of them had it. Until finally he said to himself, What're you doing? What difference does it make what she thinks?

He was working it out slowly, gradually eliminating personal feelings.

But it was not until morning, when he walked into his living room and again saw the broken glass, that he finally realized what he should have said to her and it amazed him that it had nothing to do with him, personally.

He should have told her flatly—not trying to be clever, not trying to upstage her with the last word—that if she continued to play games with Clement the time would come when Clement would kill her.

It was that clear now in his mind. He did not believe for a moment she had had any kind of a kickback scheme going with Guy. She had not denied it directly, because she would feel no need to, would not dignify it. Carolyn Wilder, of all the Recorder's Court defense lawyers he knew, would be the last one to ever get involved in backcourt deals. Especially with Guy.

He pried flattened chunks of lead from his living room wall and knew by looking at them they weren't from a P.38. When his landlady came in,

approaching the window as though something
might again come flying through the broken shards
of glass, he told her it was probably kids with a B-B
gun, over in the park. The landlady seemed to have
doubts, questions, but asked only if he'd reported it
to the police. Raymond reminded her he *was* the
police. She told him he would have to pay to have
the window replaced.

That morning, Raymond sat at his desk in a gray
tweed sportcoat he had not worn since spring—
since dieting and exercising—and the coat felt
loose, a size too large. He reviewed the Judicial
Tenure Commission's Report on the investigation
of Judge Guy, seeing familiar names, Carolyn
Wilder's appearing several times.

He did not tell his squad about the shooting—
whether it was an attempt on his life or a challenge—
not because he considered it a personal matter, but
because he didn't want to spend the morning
discussing it. He was quiet this morning, into himself, and they left him alone. They made phone
calls. They worked on other cases. They looked at
hard-core sex photos they had picked up during the
evidence-search of a victim's house: exclaiming,
whistling, Wendell pretending to be sick; Hunter
studying one of the photos and Norb Bryl saying to
him, "You go for that kinky stuff, huh?" Hunter

saying, "Jesus, Christ, what kind of pervert you think I am?" And Bryl saying, "Oh, one about six foot, sandy mustache, green-striped shirt . . ." At noon, Raymond told them he was going to skip lunch.

After they had left he took off his sportcoat, unlocked the plywood cabinet next to the GE battery charger and hung his .38 snub-nose with the rubber bands around the grip on a hook inside the cabinet. He brought out, then, a shoulder holster that held a 9-mm blue-steel Colt automatic with a hickory grip, slipped the rig on, adjusted it snugly beneath his left arm and put on his sportcoat again, now a perfect fit.

19

SANDY WOKE UP lying on her side, feeling Clement cuddled close to her and something hard pressing against her bare behind.

She said, "Is that for me, or you have to go to the bathroom?"

Clement didn't answer. She hadn't heard him come in last night. When she shifted to her back, turning her head to look at the Oklahoma Wildman, he made a face with his eyes still closed and said, "Get off me."

"Pardon me, did I touch you or something? . . . You have a big time last night?" No answer. "Well, I was somewhere, too, if you think I was sitting home."

Clement's little-boy face looked red and swollen; his breath smelled of sour-mash whiskey.

"The wildman all tuckered out? You big shit, where'd you go?"

Clement opened his eyes, blinked a few times to focus, seeing noon sunlight in the window and

Sandy's frizzy hair sticking out golden from the pillow. He said, "I went to that place out Wood'ard . . . took me back home it was so good." Clement's mouth was partly open against the pillow and he talked as though he had a toothache or had just eaten Mexican peppers.

Sandy said, "What? . . . What place?"

He worked his mouth to loosen the stickiness. "Line up your Albanian, I'm ready for him now," Clement said. "You all be sitting there when I walk in. You introduce us . . . we'll look into this business."

"*What* place?"

"Uncle Deano's."

"Jesus Christ," Sandy said, "he's Al*ban*ian, he doesn't like Country. He likes disco."

Clement stared at his little partner, waiting for what she said to make sense.

Finally he said, "Honey? . . . I want to talk to this man, I don't want to dance with him."

"Well, what if he doesn't want to go there?"

"Hey, aren't you with the good hands people?" Clement inched his own hand over as he said it and caught Sandy between her slender legs. "Aren't you?"

"Cut it out."

"Why, what's this?" Clement closed his eyes as he felt around. "Whiskers? You growing whiskers on me?"

"That hurts."

"Yeah, but hurts good, don't it? Huh? How 'bout right there? Feel pretty good?"

Sandy rolled toward him, pushing out her hips, then stopped. "I ain't gonna do it less you brush your teeth."

"Come on," Clement said, "we don't have to kiss. Let's just do it."

Clement laid around the rest of the day while he thought and stared out at Motor City. Sandy sat at the desk to write a letter to her mother in French Lick, Indiana, that began "Dear Mom, The weather has been very warm for October, but I don't mind it a bit as I hate cold weather. Brrrr." And stopped there. She rattled the ballpoint pen between her front teeth until Clement told her to, goddamn-it, cut it out.

She went over and turned on the TV and said, "Hey, *Nashville on the Road* . . . my God, anybody ever tell you you look like Marty Robbins? You and him could be twin brothers." Clement didn't answer. Sandy turned to him again after a few minutes and said, "That doesn't make any sense, does it? Marty goes, 'Would you like to sing another song for us?' And Donna Fargo—you hear her?— she goes, 'I can't hardly pass up an offer like that.' What offer? Marty didn't offer her nothing."

Clement was staring at her, hard. Sandy got dressed and left the apartment without saying another word.

What Clement thought about was a hundred thousand dollars and the possibility of prying it out of Carolyn Wilder. He heard himself saying to her, "Here's how it is. You give me the hunnert or else I send the cops this notebook, has your phone number written in the judge's hand, the initials of your company . . . Wilder, Sultan and Fine . . . I tear a few pages out of the book so on the lefthand page facing your number and all're these amounts of money, payments, dates and arrows pointing over to you. What do you think?" She had hung up the phone. That's what she thought. She was a tough lady. She didn't get wimpy or act scared for no good reason. She listened and then hung up the phone.

Sandy came back after a couple of hours and glanced at him as she turned on the television. He didn't even look at her, just continued to stare out the window.

Clement thought and thought and finally—with the sun going down and the tall glass stacks of the Renaissance Center turning silver—he said to himself, Jesus Christ, you think too much. *That's* the problem, you dumb shit. Thinking.

What was the quickest, surest way to get money off a person? Stick a gun in their mouth and ear back the hammer. Your money or your life, partner. Hell, that's the way it's always been done throughout history and around the world. Take it and git.

If Carolyn won't go for the con, shit, it was a dumb idea anyway, knock her on her ass, straddle her and let her look into the barrel of a Walther— except, shit, he'd gotten rid of it.

Well, some other gun then.

Which reminded him, he'd have to go shopping before meeting Sandy's Albanian. Go in some nigger bar and make a purchase. He thought of Marcus Sweeton and said to himself, no, stay away from Mr. Sweety for the time being. Sweety had hard bark on him, but he had been messing with dope lately and he wasn't sure where Sweety stood on matters of trust and not fucking an old buddy. Who *could* you trust these days? He looked over at Sandy curled up on the sofa watching Mike Douglas. Bless her heart. Clement told her to go ahead and watch her program, he'd fix supper.

They dug into fried steaks breaded country-style and served with Stove-Top Dressing and Miller High Life in the dining-L while the city outside turned dark and began to take on its evening glitter. It was Clement's favorite time of the day. He said, "All right, I'm paying full attention now. Tell me about Albanians."

Sandy said, "Okay, you know where like Italy is,

how it sticks down? Al*ban*ia is over on the other side of it."

Clement thought, Jesus Christ—But he had asked for this and he said, "Yeah?" shoveling Stove-Top into his mouth and sounding all ears.

"The Albanians that live *here*," Sandy said, "are mostly—you'll get a kick out of this—the really hardass ones that wouldn't live under the Turks or the Communists or somebody. See, so they came here."

"What's hardass about 'em?"

"Well, like Skender says, it's like if you do something to his brother you're doing it to him. I mean they really stick up for kin if anything happens to them. Like a husband beats up his wife? She goes home, tells her dad. The dad goes looking for his son-in-law and shoots him."

"Is that right?"

"But then the brother of the son-in-law shoots the dad and the dad's son, the brother of the guy's wife, shoots the brother of the husband. And sometimes they have to get somebody from Yugoslavia, where most of the hardass ones are, to come over and settle it, it gets so mixed up and confusing with everybody shooting each other."

"Where'n the hell are we," Clement said, "Detroit or East Tennessee?"

"A bunch of 'em live in Hamtramck mixed in

with all the Polacks," Sandy said. "Some others live out in the suburbs, Farmington Hills, all over. There're more Albanians here than any place in the United States, but they still have these old ways. Skender says it's called *besa*, like the Code of the West."

"The what?"

"*Besa*. It means like a promise. Like, I give you my word. Or sometimes he refers to it as 'the Custom.' "

"Shit," Clement said, "how come I never heard of 'em?"

"Skender says, 'If someone kills my brother and I do nothing, then I am nothing. I can never'—how'd he say it?—'put my face out among my people.' "

"That's the way he talks?"

"Listen, they're very serious. They get into one of these blood feuds, they have to hide out to stay alive. That's why Skender has the secret room. He built it himself four years ago."

"I think he's giving you a bunch of shit," Clement said, digging into his dressing.

"Really." Sandy was wide-eyed. "I saw the room again. It's hidden down in the basement behind a cinderblock wall that doesn't even have a door."

"Yeah? How you get into it?"

"He turns this switch that's like part of the furnace, up above it, and the wall—you hear this motor hum—and part of the wall comes open, real slow. That's where the safe is . . . with forty thousand dollars inside."

"He show it to you?"

"He told me it's in there."

"Uh-huh," Clement said. "Well, if it's a secret room, what'd he even let you in there for?"

Sandy got up and went into the kitchen. She came back with her purse. "I've been trying to tell you I went out with him last night, but you were into your thinking time. Who am *I*? I'm not important. Well, take a look at this, buddy." Sandy brought a small blue-felt box out of her purse, opened it and placed it next to Clement's beer glass—where the overhead light would reflect off the diamond in tiny glints of color.

"Skender wants to marry me."

Clement chewed, swallowed, took a sip of beer and sat back with the ring pinched between his fingers.

"What's it worth?"

"Almost four thousand."

"Bullshit."

"You a diamond expert now? I had it appraised over at the RenCen. That's where I went while you were thinking. It's worth three thousand seven hundred and fifty dollars. Plus tax."

"He *proposed* to you? . . . What'd you tell him?"

"I said I'd have to ask my brother."

* * *

Before he left the apartment Clement went into Del Weems' closet and picked out one of his sports jackets, the pink and yellow and green Lily Pulitzer model. He took it down to the lobby with him, handed it across the desk to Thomas Edison, the doorman, and said, "Hey, Tom, this is for you. Case I don't see you again."

The doorman, who had seen the coat on Del Weems throughout the past summer, said, "You leaving us?"

"Yeah, time to move on. Feel like I'm living in a fish bowl—people watching every move I make."

"Yeah, well, I don't know as I can take this coat."

"Don't be bashful," Clement said. "It's for letting me use your car . . . shit, for being a good guy. I'll tell you something. I know white people that've been personal friends of mine for years I couldn't count on like I have you. You wear it and watch all the colored girls' eyes light up."

It was nearly eight o'clock and Thomas Edison was going off duty. The night man was standing with him at the desk. They watched Clement walk over to the bank of elevators and get in, going down to the garage. As the door closed, Thomas Edison said to the night man, "What did he say to me?"

"What you think he said," the night man answered. "It was mighty white of you, boy."

Thomas Edison took the card out of his pocket that the black detective—Wendell Robinson was the name—had given him, picked up the phone and dialed the number on the card for Homicide, Squad Seven.

He said, "That redneck motherfucker you looking for's driving a '76 Mercury Montego, light blue, old beat up piece of shit . . . What? . . . Wait now, I'll tell you what. You ask me one question at a time, my man, and I'll see if I can give you the answers. How that be?"

20

RAYMOND CAME OUT of Sweety's Lounge and walked up to the house next door, 2925, the lower flat. Dull light showed in the windows; the porch was dark. He rang the bell. The black man in the velour bathrobe who opened the door said, "How you doing?" stepping aside. "Come on in."

Raymond wondered if the guy thought he was someone else. He walked in, smelled incense and turning saw clear plastic covers on the furniture, heard Motown music he couldn't identify coming from somewhere in back, saw a photograph in an illuminated frame of a young man with long light-brown hair parted in the middle and a full beard. Raymond came all the way around to face the black man, Mr. Sweety, standing now with the door closed behind him, Mr. Sweety raising a hand to rub his face thoughtfully and giving Raymond a flash of gold rings.

"You're not working tonight," Raymond said.

"Yeah, I'm working. I just ain't working *yet*."

He was studying Raymond, eye to eye with him, though Mr. Sweety was much heavier and when Raymond looked at the dark velour robe trimmed in beige and red he thought of draperies. Mr. Sweety said, "We ain't gonna bullshit each other, are we? You look like you might chew some plug, officer, but I doubt if you smoke what I got."

Raymond was showing his I.D. now. As he said his name his beeper went off.

Mr. Sweety said, "I like that. Got sound effects. You want to use the phone it's in the hall there."

When Raymond came back in the room Mr. Sweety was sitting at one end of the couch with his legs crossed, smoking a cigarette. He said, "I didn't think you was the dope squad. They come in, you should see the outfits, shirt open down to here, earrings, some of 'em . . ."

Raymond sat down across from him. He looked at the photo in the illuminated frame again.

"What kind of car you drive?"

"Eldorado. You want the license? S-W-E-E-T-Y."

"You own a '76 Montego?"

"No, never did."

"You know anybody who does?"

"Not offhand."

"How's your buddy Clement Mansell doing?"

"Oh, shit," Mr. Sweety said, tired, shaking his head. "I knew it."

"What's that?"

"I mean I was afraid we gonna get to him. I haven't seen the wildman in, I believe a year or so. Man runs too fast. I settle down, give up that craziness."

"You saw his girlfriend the other day."

"Oh, yeah, Sandy come in, Sandy like her weed. She come in time to time."

"Sandy tell you why he did the judge?"

"Sandy don't tell me nothing. Little jive chick run in run out."

"We can close you down," Raymond said.

"Man, I know that."

"Send you out to DeHoCo for a year. I thought you might want to trade."

"What am I gonna trade you? I don't have nothing to give's what I'm saying."

"The little jive chick ran in," Raymond said, "but she didn't run right out again, she stayed a while. Didn't she?"

"Sampling the goods. You know women, they like to shop."

Raymond hesitated, then took a chance. "How come she doesn't want Clement to know she was here?"

The question caught Sweety unprepared. Raymond saw it, the startled look in the man's eyes, there and then gone.

"You seem confused. What's the problem?"

"Ain't any problem."

"Why would Clement care if she came here?"

"I wouldn't know if he does or he don't, where his head's at these days."

Get off of it, Raymond thought. His gaze moved to the Scandinavian-looking guy in the photo and back to Mr. Sweety. "Why do you think he killed the judge?"

"I don't know as he did."

"Yeah, he did," Raymond said. "But he didn't have anybody driving for him. That make sense to you?"

"Man, come on, I don't know nothing, I don't *want* to know nothing."

"What reason would he have?"

Mr. Sweety sighed. "You have to ask him that."

"I did," Raymond said.

"Yeah? . . . What'd he say?"

"He said what difference does it make. Those were his words," Raymond said. "What difference does it make?"

"You talking to him like that, what you talking to me for?"

"Because you'd like to help me," Raymond said. "You'd like to get the wildman off your back, for good. But you're afraid if you give me something, Clement's liable to find out." Mr. Sweety didn't say anything. After a moment, Raymond got up. "Can I use your phone again?"

In the dark hallway the moving beat of the Motown sound was closer now, coming from a bed-room. Raymond held one of his cards toward the light to read a phone number written on the back, then dialed the number.

A male voice answered. "Lafayette East."

"Let me speak to Sergeant Robinson, please." Raymond waited. When he heard Wendell's voice he said, "Where are we?"

"Got a call out on the Montego," Wendell said. "Told 'em to get the number, see if it's on the sheet and tell MCMU where the car's at. But you see the problem?"

"Which one?" Raymond said. "That's all I see are problems."

"They spot him out in Oakland or Macomb County somewhere," Wendell said, "then the local people got the case. They pick him up for driving without a license, but they can't take a weapon out of the car less it's in plain sight. Say they do. Then he's out of our jurisdiction on some halfass gun charge. You understand what I'm saying?"

"Tell 'em—" Raymond paused. "I'm not wor-ried about jurisdiction right now. But we have to be sure it's admissible evidence. We find a gun on him, first it's got to be the right gun, then it's got to stand up in court the search was legal and the only sure way is if you take him in on the traffic charge and set a bond and he doesn't make it. Then you can go through the car when you list his possessions. Otherwise, you say you had reason to believe he was carrying a murder weapon—based on what? Shit," Raymond said. "I can see us losing him again on a technicality."

"He won't have the gun on him anyways," Wendell said.

"He probably won't, but what's he doing, driving around? Where did he get the car? . . . How about Sandy Stanton?"

"Went out, hasn't come back."

"What's your friend say about letting us in the apartment?"

"Yeah, Mr. Edison says fine. Wants to know if we have a search warrant, I told him you're handling that."

"Everybody's into legal rights," Raymond said. "We see something we want we'll get a warrant and go back. How about the Buick?"

"Hasn't moved. Nobody's gone near it."

"Okay, call a truck, have it picked up. I'll be leaving here shortly."

"I hear the Commodores now," Wendell said. "You and Mr. Sweety spinning records?"

Raymond was thinking. He said, "Listen, let's not worry about Clement, I mean picking him up. Tell 'em just try and locate him and stay close. I'll see you in a few minutes."

He walked back into the living room, looking again at the illuminated photo of the man with the brown beard and long hair.

"Who's that, a friend of yours?"

Mr. Sweety glanced over. He said, "This picture here?" and sounded surprised. "It's Jesus. Who you think it was?"

"It's a photograph," Raymond said.

Mr. Sweety said, "Yeah, it's a good likeness, ain't it?"

Raymond sat down again, nodding, his gaze returning to the heavyset black man in the bathrobe.

"Are you saved?"

"Man, I hope so. I could use some saving."

"I know what you mean," Raymond said. "There's nothing like peace of mind. But I'm afraid I might've upset you. You're confused now. You don't know whether you should call Clement or not . . ."

"Wait now," Mr. Sweety said, with an expression of pain. "Why would I want to do that?"

"Well, to tell him I was here . . . tell him Sandy was here . . . But then you'd be getting involved, wouldn't you? If I wanted to remain saved," Raymond said, "especially if I was concerned about saving my ass, I think I'd keep quiet, figuring it's better to be a little confused than involved, right?"

"Lift my voice only to heaven," Mr. Sweety said.

"I'd even think twice about that," Raymond said. "You never know, somebody could have you bugged."

21

"YEAH, IT'S DARK IN HERE," Clement said, looking around Uncle Deano's, at the steer horns on the walls and the mirrors framed with horse collars. "Darker'n most places that play Country, but it's intimate. You know it? I thought if we was gonna have a intimate talk why not have it at a intimate place?" Clement straightened, looking up. "Except for that goddamn pinball machine; sounds like a monkey playing a 'lectric organ." He settled down again. "I'll tell you something else. If our mom hadn't been carried away by a tornado last spring, we'd be holding this meeting in Lawton."

Sandy said to Skender Lulgjaraj, "He means Lawton, Oklahoma."

"Well, hell, he's heard of Lawton, hasn't he? If he hasn't, he's sure heard of Fort Sill . . . Here," Clement said, "make you feel at home."

He took off his K-mart cowboy hat, reached across the table and placed it on Skender Lulgjaraj's thick head of black hair. The hat sat high and

Skender tried to pull it down tighter as he turned to Sandy.

"Hey," Sandy said, "you look like a regular cowpoke."

"I don't think it fit me," Skender said, holding onto the brim with both hands.

"It looks cute," Sandy told him. "Goes with your outfit nice." She reached over to brush a kernel of popcorn from the lapel of Skender's black suit, then picked another one from the hair that showed in the open V of his silky beige sportshirt.

Clement was reaching out, stopping their waitress with his extended arm. He said, "Hey, I like your T-shirt. Honey, bring us another round, will you, please? And some more popcorn and go on over and ask Larry if he'll do 'You Picked a Fine Time to Leave Me, Lucille' the next set? Okay? Thank you, hon." He turned to Skender and said, "Our mom loved that song. She'd listen to it and get real mad and say, 'That woman's just trash, leave four children, *hungry* children, like that.' I believe she loved that song, I'd say just a smidge behind Luckenback, Texas. I *know* you heard that one."

Skender said, "Luke . . . what?"

"He's putting me on," Clement said to Sandy. "You putting me on, Skenny? You mean to tell me you never heard Waylon do 'Luckenback, Texas'? Time we got back to the basics of life?"

Sandy said, "It's 'Time we got back to the basics of love' . . . not life."

Clement squinted at her. "You sure?"

Sandy glanced over at the bandstand in the corner where Larry Lee Adkins and the Hanging Tree—three guitars and a set of drums—were getting ready for the next set. "He just played it," Sandy said. "Ask him."

Clement was thoughtful. "He says let's sell your diamond ring, get some boots and faded jeans . . ."

"And he says we got a four-car garage and we're still building on," Sandy said. "So maybe it's time we got back to the basics of love."

"That doesn't rhyme."

"I never said it did. But it's *love*, not life."

Skender, with his cowboy hat sitting on top of his head, would look from one to the other.

Clement grinned at him. "Well, it don't matter. We're here to talk about the basics of love anyway, aren't we, partner?" He paused, cocking his head. "Listen. Hear what they're playing? 'Everybody Loves a Winner,' " Clement half singing, half saying it. "That's a old Dalaney and Bonnie number."

"You're sure full of platter chatter this evening," Sandy said. "You ought to get a job at CXI and get paid for it."

"Well, I got nothing against work. I come a piece from the oil fields to the world of speculation,"

Clement said, seeing Sandy rolling her eyes as he tightroped along the edge of truth. "But I'd rather see my investments do the work than me, if you know what I mean and I think you do." He looked over at Skender and gave him a wink. "I understand you're in the restaurant business."

"Coney Island red-hot places," Skender said. "I start out, I save eighty-three dollars and thirty-four cents a month. The end of a year I have one thousand dollars. I buy a HUD house, fix it up and rent it to people. I keep saving eighty-three dollars and thirty-four cents a month. I buy another house, fix it up. Then I sell the first house and buy a Coney Island. I buy another house, more houses, fix them up, sell some of them, buy an apartment, buy another Coney Island. In twelve years I have two apartments now I keep for rent and four Coney Island red-hot places."

Sandy reached over to touch Skender's arm, looking at Clement. "Hasn't he got a cute accent?"

Clement said, "Yeah, I 'magine you're paying Uncle Sam a chunk, too."

Skender shrugged. "Yes, I pay. But I have money."

"You ever been married?"

"No, thirty-four years old, I never marry. My cousin Toma and my grandfather, the houseman, the head of the family, they try to get me to marry someone from Tuzi, in Yugoslavia, bring her over here to marry. But I say no and make them very angry, because I want to marry an American girl."

Clement was listening intently, leaning over the table on his arms. He said, "I know what you mean, partner. Nice American girl . . . knows how to fix herself up, shaves under her arms . . . uses a nice perfume, various deodorants and flavors"— winking at Skender—"if you know what I mean. See," Clement said, "I don't mean to get personal with you, but I got to look out for sis here or I swear our mom'll come storming back from wherever she's at and give me the dickens. I said to her, Sandy—didn't I?—it's entirely up to you. But if this fella is sincere he won't mind satisfying some of my natural curiousity and concern. I said, after all, if you're gonna be Mrs. Lulgurri . . ."

Sandy rolled her eyes.

Skender said, "Lulgjaraj. It's a very common name. When I look in the telephone book I see there are more Lulgjaraj than Mansell. I look hard, I don't see your name. Another question I have, you don't mind, if you sister and brother, why do you have different names?"

"One thing," Clement said, "you can look at us and tell we both got shook out of the same tree, can't you? Well, it's a pretty interesting story how Sandy come to change her name . . . while she was out in Hollywood, was right after the Miss Universe contest . . ."

Skender was nodding, smiling. "Yes?" Sandy was sitting back in her chair, rolling her eyes.

Clement stopped. "I'll tell you, I sure like a man with a natural smile like you got. It shows good character traits." Clement stared hard at Skender, nodding slowly, thoughtfully, as Skender smiled, the smile becoming fixed in an awkward, almost pained expression.

"I'll tell you something else," Clement said. "I've been all over this country, coast to coast wherever my work as a speculator takes me, but believe it or not, you're my first Albanian . . . Where you living now, Skenny?"

Skender went to the Men's as they got ready to leave. Clement said to Sandy, "I wasn't able to get a gun."

She seemed nervous now, which surprised Clement, and said, "Be nice. You don't have to do it tonight."

Clement said, "Hell I don't. I got seven dollars to my name and no place to sleep."

Clement stayed close behind Skender's black Cadillac, not letting any traffic get between them:

straight down Woodward from Royal Oak into Detroit, east on the Davison Freeway to Joseph Campau and a ride down Hamtramck's main drag, then
a right at Caniff to head west, back toward Woodward, Clement thinking, This bird doesn't even
know how to get home. He turned a corner and
parked behind the Cadillac in front of a U-shaped,
three-story apartment building, 2781 Cardoni.

Skender told them he had been in this place four
years. He had moved in right after his brother was
shot and killed. Clement paid attention, looking
away from the street signs in the light on the corner,
and followed Skender and Sandy into the building.

Say he was shot? Clement asked and found out,
yes, by a member of another family. It was a long
boring story that Clement didn't understand, something about an argument in a bar leading to the
shooting of the brother, then a cousin and two from
the other family were killed before some guy came
over from Yugoslavia and settled the matter.

On the stairway Clement asked Skender if he
had shot the two from the other family. But Skender
didn't hear him or else ignored the question, telling
Sandy, yes, he still lived on the first floor. Sandy
wanted to know why they were going up to the second floor then. Skender said wait and see.

Clement couldn't picture this skinny camel-
jockey-looking guy shooting anybody anyway.

He seemed to make a ceremony of unlocking the

front apartment on the right and stepping back for them to enter. It was a big apartment. Clement was struck by the newness of everything. He thought it looked like a store display and found out he wasn't far wrong.

"For my new bride," Skender said, smiling, showing white teeth and gold caps in the light—Clement getting a good look at him for the first time—Skender sweeping the cowboy hat from his head to present the room, "Decorated with the Mediterranean suit by Lasky Furniture on Joe Campau"—Skender, Clement judged, going about five-nine, a hundred and thirty, maybe shorter, his hair giving him height—Skender showing them the master bedroom then, the other bedroom that would be a sewing room—Clement giving Sandy a nudge—the pink and green bathroom, the fully-equipped kitchen, ice-maker in the refrigerator, two bottles of slivovitz chilled for the surprise celebration . . .

Sandy looked surprised all right. She said, "Gee, it's really nice."

Clement wasn't in any hurry. He let her walk around the apartment touching wild-animal figurines and the petals of the plastic tulip lamps, looking at the twin stardust-upholstered recliner chairs, looking at the painting of the big-eyed little girl and what looked like a real tear coming down her cheek, while Skender opened a bottle of slivovitz and brought it out to them with his fingers stuck in three stem glasses and the cowboy hat on the back of his head.

Clement kept calling Sandy sis. Saying, "Hey, you're gonna love this place, aren't you, sis?" Or, "How 'bout that sewing room, sis? God darn but he's a thoughtful fella, isn't he?" He said, "Man, this is choice stuff," and got Skender to open the second bottle, Clement deciding it tasted something like bitter mule piss, but he wanted the Albanian good and relaxed. Near the bottom of the second bottle he said, "Now what's this about a secret room somewhere? I hope it ain't for locking sis in when she's pouty or mean . . ." Sandy appeared to sigh with relief.

It was about the cleanest basement Clement had ever seen, with separate locked stalls for each of the building's twelve tenants, a big furnace that was like a ship's boiler with aluminum ducts coming out of it and running along the ceiling, cinderblock walls painted light green . . .

Skender said, "Now watch, please."

As though Clement was going to look anywhere else—as Skender reached up to what looked like a metal fuse box mounted high on the wall by the furnace, opened it and snapped a switch to the "up" position. Clement heard a motor begin to hum; he located it in the overhead and followed an insulated wire over to a section of cinderblock wall. About three feet of the wall, from cement floor to unfinished ceiling, was groaning on unseen metal hinges, coming open right before his eyes, the motor high-pitched now, straining to actuate the massive load. Son of a gun . . .

The room inside was about ten-by-twelve. Clement stepped inside saying out loud, "I'll be a son of a gun." He saw the floor safe right away. About two feet high, with a telephone and a phone book sitting on top. There was an office-model refrigerator that contained a two-burner range, a record player on a stand, a half-dozen folded-up canvas chairs, a pile of sleeping bags, a table with a sugar bowl on it, prints on the wall of a white seaside village, one of Jesus showing his Sacred Heart and one with a lot of funny looking words Clement couldn't read. Behind a folding door was a smaller room with a sink and toilet and shelves stocked with canned goods.

As Clement looked around, Skender turned on the record player. In a moment Donna Summer was coming on loud, filling the cinderblock room with disco music from one of her Greatest Hits.

Clement tried to ignore the sound. He said, "My oh my oh my. You play house down here or you hide for real?"

Skender, smiling, said, "I'm sorry. What?"

"I heard of Eye-talians going to the mattresses—how come I never heard of you people?"

"Specially since you read so much," Sandy said.

Clement grinned at her. Little bugger, she was loosening up. That was good; they'd have some fun. He had said to her many times, as he did now, "If it ain't fun, it ain't worth doing, is it?"

She said, "You want me to leave?"

"Hell no, I don't want you to leave. Do we?" Looking over at Skender and seeing him kneeling down at the safe now, opening it—the safe wasn't even locked—and shoving a window envelope inside he had taken out of his inside coat pocket.

Right before your very eyes, Clement thought. You believe it? He would love to be able to tell this later on. Maybe to Sweety. Watch his old nigger face . . .

He said, "Hey, brother-in-law"—feeling a nice glow from the plum brandy and the bourbon he'd had before—"what you got in that box there?" The music wasn't too bad . . .

"I keep some money, some things." Skender drew an automatic out of the safe, held it up for Clement to see. Clement stepped over hesitantly, reached out and let Skender hand the gun to him. He felt Sandy watching, gave her a quick glance.

"This here's a Browning."

"Yes, and this one is a Czech seven-six-five. This little one is a Mauser. This one, I think, yes, is a

Smith and Wesson. This one . . . I don't know what it is." Skender was laying the pistols on the floor next to the safe.

Clement released the clip from the Browning, looked at it and punched it back into the grip. "You keep 'em all loaded?"

"Yes, of course," Skender said.

"What else you got in there?"

"No more guns. I keep some money . . ."

"How much?"

Skender looked up at him now, for a moment hesitant, then reached up quickly to keep the cowboy hat from falling down his back. "I put some in last week. I think now . . . four hundred, a little more."

"Four hundred," Clement said. He waited. "Four hundred, huh?"

"A little more."

"How much more?"

"Maybe fifty dollars."

Clement frowned. "You keep money in the bank?"

Skender hesitated again.

Sandy said, "It's okay, he won't tell nobody."

"In a saving certificate," Skender said, taking the envelope out again and opening it to look at a pink deposit receipt, "forty thousand three hundred and forty-three dollars."

Clement said, "That's where your forty grand is, in *savings?*"

"Yes, of course."

"I thought you didn't trust banks."

Skender looked at him. "Yes, I trust the bank. They loan me money when I need it."

Clement glared at Sandy. "Turn that goddamn goat-tit music off!" As she hesitated, startled, he stepped over to the record player and swept the arm scratching across Donna Summer's Greatest Hits. "That disco shit just ricochets off my mind!"

There was a silence.

Sandy said quietly, very slowly, "I think somebody ought to calm down and quit acting like a spoiled brat. You'll live longer."

Skender seemed glad to look at Sandy as she spoke. He said, "I don't understand why he did that."

"Little misunderstanding," Sandy said. "Everything's okay now."

Clement said, calm again, "How much you got in your checking account?"

Sandy grinned and shook her head as Skender looked up at Clement.

"I don't keep much there. This time of the month maybe a few hundred." Skender seemed to prepare himself then and said, "Why do you want to know this?" Hesitant, as though the question might be out of line, an affront to Clement.

"You have a little sister," Clement said, "you want to be sure she's taken care of." He was looking around the room now, hands on his hips.

"You don't have to worry about that," Skender said. "Can I have the gun back now? I put them away."

Sandy was watching Skender. She saw his serious, almost-sad expression now. Disappointed. Or finally getting suspicious.

Clement, still looking around, wasn't paying any attention to him, not even looking at him as he said, "When you're hiding in here and the door's closed, can you open it if you want?"

"Yes, there's a switch." Skender nodded. "There."

Clement walked over to the metal switch housing mounted on the side wall, turned the Browning automatic in his hand to hold it by the barrel and whacked at the housing with the gun butt until it hung loose and he heard some excited words in Albanian. Clement turned and put the Browning on Skender, who was pushing himself up from the floor. "Stay right there, Skenny. Be a good boy." He tore the switch from the wall, threw it out into the basement, then paused and reconsidered what he was about to do. Locking the guy in wasn't going to teach him anything. Introduce him to reality. Clement stepped toward the Albanian.

"You got the EMS number handy?"

Skender was staring hard at him, black eyes glowing. Yes, Albanians could get sore at you,

Clement decided. He heard Skender say, "I want you to leave here, now."

"We're going, partner, but first I want to call the Emergency Medical Service."

Skender frowned, taking his time. "Why do you need them?"

Yes, they could get pissed at you, but my Lord, they were innocent about things. Place a level on this boy, up one side and down the other and get a true square.

"I don't need the EMS," Clement said. "You do."

He heard Sandy say something like, Oh God, as he lifted the K-mart cowboy hat off the Albanian's head and placed the nose of the Browning against the man's hairline, the man's forehead creasing in furrows as he tried to raise his eyes. "Now edge over to the door," Clement said.

The Albanian tried to look at Sandy and Clement wrist-flicked the gun, giving him a back-hand whack across the head. Skender came to attention. He began moving on his knees toward the opening in the wall, Clement prodding him along.

"Go on out, then turn around and sit down."

Sandy said, "What're you gonna do to him?"

"Just bring the phone out, hon. There's enough cord. Tell the operator you want the Emergency Medical Service. When they answer, tell 'em to send a van over here to twenty-seven eighty-one Cardoni, corner of Caniff." He looked at Skender, sitting outside the opening in the wall, and said, "Hold on, partner, I'll be right with you."

Sandy hurried out of there with the phone, edging past Skender. Clement followed, roughing Skender's hair with his hand as he came out.

Skender was swallowing. He said something in a language Clement didn't understand, then said, "You are crazy . . ."

"Lay back and stick your leg in the opening," Clement said. "Either one, I don't care." He walked over to the furnace, reached up, and looked over his shoulder as he flicked the switch. With the hum of the motor the wall began to swing slowly closed. He saw Skender, twisted around watching him, draw his leg away from the wall and Clement switched the motor off. He said, "It's up to you, partner"—walking over to him and placing the muzzle of the Browning against Skender's head—"put your leg down or get your fur-cap head all over the basement."

Sandy was saying into the phone, "Hi, we're gonna need an ambulance. I mean we *do* need one, right now . . ."

Clement walked back to the furnace, reached up, flicked the switch on again and watched the wall moving in again, touching Skender's leg now and pushing it up against the stationary section of wall—Skender staring, not believing it was happening to him—and Clement pulled the switch down. As the hum of the motor stopped, Skender looked around, eyes wide with fright and perhaps a little hope.

Clement said, "I want to impress something on you, partner. I'm disappointed, but I ain't really mad at you, else I'd be pulling the trigger by now. See, but when you're laying in the hospital with your leg in a cast, I don't want you to have any bad thoughts like wanting to tell the police or the FBI or anybody. You do, I'll come visit you again and stick your head in there 'stead of your leg. You hear me? Nod your head."

Sandy was saying, "No, the person didn't have a heart attack . . ."

Clement flicked up the switch and let his hand come down.

Sandy was saying, "Course it's serious . . ."

With the hum of the motor Skender began to cry out. He sucked in his breath, holding it, his face straining, then let the sound come out, his eyes closed tightly now and his face upturned, the sound rising, building to a prolonged scream.

Sandy said into the phone, "Hey, does that sound serious enough for you? You dumb shit . . ."

22

RAYMOND HAD A VISION. Or what he imagined a vision might be like. Herzog told him the Albanian was in the hospital and Raymond saw clearly, in the next few moments, what was happening and very possibly what was going to happen.

He saw the Albanians going after Clement.

He saw Clement running to get his gun, to defend himself.

He saw Mr. Sweety, *yes*, with the gun, the Walther P.38.

He saw Clement holding the gun, the Guy-Simpson murder weapon, and saw himself extending the Colt 9-mm in two hands and saw . . . the clarity of the vision began to fade. He wasn't sure if visions were always accurate. He told himself to back up, look at it again, carefully, beginning at his desk in the squadroom. He remembered . . .

* * *

Wendell on the phone saying to someone, "What you know for a fact and what you believe, that could be two different things. I want to know what you *know*."

Norb Bryl saying to a middle-aged woman sitting at his desk, "We can help her, I give you my word as a man." And the woman saying something and Bryl saying, "Well, I hope somebody doesn't kill her."

Hunter saying to Maureen, imitating a voice out of Amos and Andy, " 'Yeah, she come up to me and says she wants to pet my puppy.' I'm thinking, ah-*ha*, he got it on with her, before he killed her, right? Isn't that what it sounds like?" Maureen grinning expectantly. "No, the guy's got a *dog* in his car and she wants to pet the dog."

Inspector Herzog coming in, approaching Raymond's desk: "You mentioned, wasn't Mansell's girlfriend—what's her name, Sandy Stanton—going with one of the Albanians?"

This was where the prevision began, Raymond feeling the jab in his stomach, realizing he had forgotten to talk to Skender, to warn him, be careful . . .

Saying "Skender Lulgjaraj," and feeling his stomach knotting.

Herzog saying, "Yeah, Skender. Art Blaney was over at Hutzel visiting his wife. He's going past a room, sees a familiar face. It's Toma. Art looks in,

Skender's in traction with a fractured leg. Art wants to know what happened and Toma says, 'He fell down the stairs.' "

Raymond remembered feeling worn out, even with the thing in his stomach, and saying, "Oh, shit . . ."

And Herzog saying, "Let's go in my office."

It was while walking from the squadroom to the office with the view of the river and the highrise that Raymond had his vision.

"I was gonna call him," Raymond said. "I don't know what I was thinking. I know the guy's being set up and I didn't call him."

"Toma says it was an accident," Herzog said. "Maybe it was."

Raymond shook his head. "No—I'm gonna find out what happened, but it wasn't an accident."

"Well, you have hunches," Herzog said, "and most of them turn out to be nothing, so you don't follow up on some." Herzog looked over at a wallboard of newspaper clippings covering the Guy-Simpson murders. "Half those news stories are hunches, speculation. Who killed the judge? . . . Who gives a shit? You notice, there's hardly any mention of Adele Simpson, she's a minor figure. It's all about the judge, what a prick he was. We give them a few facts and, for the most part, they're satisfied, leave us alone and write interviews with people who say, 'Oh, yes, I knew the judge intimately, it doesn't surprise me at all.' They don't care if we ever solve it, they've got so much to write about."

Raymond, reviewing his vision, seemed patient, attentive.

Herzog said, "That girl from the *News*, Sylvia Marcus, she's the only one asks about Mansell. If he's a suspect, where is he? Why isn't he upstairs?"

"I haven't seen her around," Raymond said.

"She's here every day. She picked up on him somehow, maybe getting a little here and there, sees a case folder open on somebody's desk—Sylvia's a very bright girl."

"You think so?" Raymond said.

"Well, she asks good questions," Herzog said. "I have a few myself I've been wondering about. Like the car, the Buick. We seem to be taking this one kinda leisurely."

"I know what you mean," Raymond said. "But you know how long we've been on it? Seventy-two hours. That's all. Since Sandy got back from visiting Mr. Sweety the car hasn't moved—till last night, we took it in, had it vacuumed, dusted. It's like the car's been driven twelve thousand miles with gloves on. Clement's driving a '76 Montego now. He went out last night, but nobody could find him. Didn't come back this morning. Sandy went out, came back early this morning in a cab. We went in the apartment over there last night while they're both out. No gun under the underwear or in the toilet tank. Nothing of the judge's."

"So he got rid of the gun," Herzog said.

Raymond didn't say anything.

"You've been holding back, not wanting to break down the doors too soon," Herzog said. "Meanwhile the guy's riding around in a Montego, you tell me, and might've broken somebody's leg. If you can't get Mansell with the gun, how're you gonna get him?"

"Maybe the gun's still around," Raymond said. "But you're right, I think I've been holding back, being a little too polite, expecting people—you might say—to be reasonable and forgetting a very important principle of police work."

Herzog nodded. "When you got 'em by the balls . . ."

"Right," Raymond said, ". . . the head and the heart soon follow."

Someone in the family had died recently and that's why the Albanians were in black. Coming down the hospital corridor and seeing the figures, Raymond thought at first they were priests. A nurse was trying to remove them from the room, with their packages and paper sacks, telling them only two at a time, please, and to wait in the visitor's lounge. He saw Toma Sinistaj.

Then Toma said something as he saw Raymond Cruz and the delegation in black move down the hall.

Raymond thought of Toma as a face on a foreign coin. Or he thought of him as a Balkan diplomat or a distance runner. He wore a blue shirt with his narrow black suit and tie. He was about thirty-eight but seemed older; his full mustache was black; his eyes were almost black and never wandered when they looked at you. Raymond remembered this; he knew Toma from several times in the past when Albanians had tried to kill each other and sometimes succeeded. He remembered that Toma owned restaurants, that he carried a Beretta, with license, and a beeper.

Attached to the hospital bed was a frame with an elaborate system of wires that hoisted Skender's plaster-covered leg in the air: like a white sculpture that would be entitled *Leg*. Skender's eyes remained closed. When Raymond asked how he was, Toma said, "He'll be like that a long time and then he'll be a cripple. You know why? Because he wanted to marry a girl he met at a disco place. She tells him okay, but first he has to meet her brother."

"He's not her brother," Raymond said.

"No, I don't think so either. They planned this a long time."

"How much did they get?"

"What difference does it make?" Toma said. "We don't look at it, was it a misdemeanor or felony? You know that. He did it to Skender, he did it to me, it's the same thing. I'm going to look at this Mansell in the eyes . . ."

"It's not that simple," Raymond said.

"Why not?" Toma said. "The only thing makes it difficult, you worried you have to arrest me." He shrugged. "All right, if you prove I kill him. You do what you have to do, I do what I have to do."

"No, it isn't that simple, because I want him too," Raymond said. "You're gonna have to get in line. After we're done you can have him charged with felonies, assault, but it isn't gonna mean much if he's doing life. You understand what I'm saying?"

"I understand you want him for killing the judge," Toma said. "I spend some time up on that fifth floor, I talk to people, different ones I know. I understand why you want this man. But if you don't care personally that he killed the judge, then why do you care who kills him? You see the way I look at it? You tell me to get in line. I tell you, you want him you better get him quick, or he'll be dead."

Raymond said, "You always look in their eyes?"

Toma seemed to smile. "If there's time."

"He's killed nine people."

Toma said, "Yes? If you know he kills people, why do you let him? Before I come to this country when I was sixteen I have already kill nine people, maybe a few more—most of them Soviet, but some Albanian, *Ghegs*, my own people. Before the Soviets—before my time, were the Turks; but before the Turks, *always*, we have the Custom. If you don't know about it you don't know anything about me."

"I think of us as friends," Raymond said, wanting the man to know that he understood.

"Yes, you give your word and keep it," Toma said. "I think you know about honor because it doesn't seem to bother you to talk about it. It isn't an old thing in books to you. But maybe honor goes so far with you and stops. Say a policeman is killed. Then I think you want to kill the person who killed him."

"Yes," Raymond said. Basically it was true.

"But you don't understand the honor that even if a man who's smoking my tobacco—he doesn't have to be my brother, but a man I bring into my house—if he's offended in some way then I'm offended. And if he's killed then I kill the person who killed him, because this goes back to before policemen and courts of law. Now—wait, don't say anything, please. A man breaks the leg of your cousin who is like a brother—a very trusting, very nice person—and steals his money. What does your honor tell you to do?"

"My honor tells me," Raymond said, the word sounding strange to him, saying it out loud, "to take the guy's head off."

"You see?" Toma said. "Your honor stops. It tells you something, yes. But you can't say, simply, 'Kill him,' and mean to do it. You say what you *feel* like doing, something more than killing him. But what you would actually do is . . . what?"

"Arrest him," Raymond said.

"There," Toma said. "Well, we're able to talk about it even if we don't see it the same. You don't call me a crazy Albanian."

Raymond said, "How're you gonna find him?"

"We have people looking, some others helping, friends. Some of your own people, some with the Hamtramck police, they tell us a few things they hear. We know what kind of car he has, where the girl lives. We find him, all right."

"What if he leaves town?"

Toma shrugged. "We wait. Why does he live here? He likes it? People are easy to rob? If he leaves we wait for him to come back, or, we go after him. Either way."

Raymond looked at the man lying in traction. "How'd he break Skender's leg?"

Toma hesitated, then said, "He broke it very deliberately. You see the Medical Service report?"

"It said he fell down the basement stairs and they found him on the floor. One of the tenants did and called EMS."

"Yes, that was the girlfriend who called," Toma said. "As soon as you came in here—see, I know you're after this Mansell and you figure out he did this; so I'm not going to lie to you, say Skender fell down the stairs. You want that person for murder, but you don't have him. So I know you don't have evidence, and if you don't find some he remains free, even though he's killed two people—no, nine, you say."

"It takes time," Raymond said.

Toma shook his head. "No, it doesn't. Tell me where to find him. It takes only a few minutes."

Raymond didn't say anything.

"For the sake of honor," Toma said.

"Well, it would take care of yours," Raymond said, "but it wouldn't do much for mine, would it?"

Toma studied him with his direct gaze, curious now. "There's more to it than I know about." He paused and then said, "Maybe you *would* take his head off."

"Maybe," Raymond said.

Toma continued to stare, thoughtful. "If he resists, yes. I can see that. Or if they tell you, all right, you can shoot him on sight. But if he gives himself up, then what do you do?"

"Turn it around," Raymond said. "You open the door and he's just sitting there. What would *you* do?"

"I'd kill him," Toma said. "What have we been talking about?"

"I know, but I mean if he was unarmed."

"Yes, and I say I'd kill him. What does his being armed or not have to do with it? Are you saying there are certain conditions, rules, like a game?" Toma emphasized with his eyes, showing surprise, bewilderment, overacting a little but with style, letting his expression fade to a smile, that remained in his eyes. "This is a strange kind of honor, you only feel it if he has a gun. What if he shoots you first? Then you die with your honor?" Toma paused. "They call us the crazy Albanians . . ."

It was time to leave. Raymond got ready, looking at Skender again. "Tell me how the leg was broken."

"He tried with a heavy object at first," Toma said. "It was very painful, but it didn't seem to injure him enough. So he raised Skender's foot up on a case, a box, with Skender lying on the floor and struck the leg at the knee with a metal pipe until the leg was bent the other way. He says he remembers the sound of the girl crying out, saying something, then the sound of the ambulance as he was riding in it, going to Detroit General, and that's all he remembers. This morning," Toma said, "I had him brought here to a doctor I know."

"You say he heard Sandy?"

"The girl? Yes, she cried out something."

"He remember what she said?"

Toma looked at Skender, asleep, then back to Raymond and shrugged. "Does it make any difference?"

"I don't know," Raymond said. "It might."

Hunter was in the blue Plymouth standing at the hospital entrance. He turned the key as Raymond got in . . . held the key, his foot pressing the accelerator, but the car wouldn't start. It gave them an eager, relentless, annoying sound, as though it was trying, but the engine refused to fire.

"Toma was there. He wants to do Clement himself."

"Who doesn't?" Hunter said. "Fucking car . . ."

"He was talking about his code of honor. Says he's gonna look Clement in the eye and blow him away."

"Tell him, go ahead."

"I said, what if he's unarmed? He says, what's that got to do with it?"

"Drive this piece of shit, you know why they're fucking going out of business." The engine caught and Hunter said, "I don't believe it."

"See, what he couldn't understand, we'd only shoot him if he was resisting."

"Yeah? . . . Where we going?"

"Sweety's Lounge, over on Kercheval. But his point was . . ." Raymond paused. "Well, he didn't understand."

"He didn't understand what?"

"I told him the guy's killed nine people and very calmly he says, 'Yes? If you know he kills people, why do you let him?'"

"What'd you tell him?"

"I don't know—we started talking about honor then."

"The Custom," Hunter said. "Fucking Albanians are crazy."

Raymond looked over at him. He said, "You sure?"

A young woman with a full Afro and worried eyes, a scowl, holding a floral housecoat tightly about her, opened the door and told them Mr. Sweety was working. Raymond said, "You mind if we just look in? I want to show him something. That picture over the couch."

The woman said, "What picture?" half turning, and Raymond moved Hunter into the doorway. He waited as Hunter peered in and then came around to look at him as if expecting a punch line. They went down the steps to the sidewalk.

"You see it?"

"Yeah. Picture of some guy."

"You know who it is?"

"I don't know—some rock star? Leon Russell."

"It's Jesus."

Hunter said, "Yeah?" Not very surprised.

"It's a *photo*graph."

"Yeah, I don't think it looks much like him."

Walking next door to Sweety's Lounge Raymond didn't say anything else. He was wondering why things amazed him that didn't amaze other people.

There were white voices in the black bar. Two women in serious, dramatic conversation.

It was dark in here in the afternoon. Mr. Sweety looked like a pirate in his black sportshirt hanging open and a nylon stocking knotted tightly over his hair, coming along the duckboards to the front bend in the bar. The place smelled of beer, an old place with a high ceiling made of tin. Two women and a man sat at the far end of the bar. They looked this way as Raymond and Hunter came in and took stools, then turned back to the voices coming from the television set mounted above the bar. A soap opera.

Raymond said, "I thought you worked nights."

"I work all the time," Mr. Sweety said. "What can I get you?"

"You want to talk here or at your house?" Raymond asked. him. "I don't want to get into anything might embarrass you in front of your customers."

"Don't do it then," Mr. Sweety said.

"No, it's up to you," Raymond said.

"How 'bout if I serve you something?"

"There's only one thing you can give us we want," Raymond said and held up his two index fingers about seven inches apart. "It's this big. It's blue steel. And it's got P.38 stamped on the side."

"Hey, shit, come on . . ."

"Sandy told me she gave it to you."

Mr. Sweety leaned on his hands spaced wide apart on the bar so that he was eye-level with Raymond and Hunter seated on stools. Mr. Sweety looked down toward the end of the bar, seemed to wipe his mouth on his shoulder and looked back at Raymond again.

"Sandy told you what?"

"She said she gave you a Walther P.38 that Clement wanted you to hold for him."

"Wait," Hunter said, "let me read him his rights."

"Read me for what? I ain't signing no rights."

"You don't have to," Hunter said. "Those people down there're witnesses. Then we'll serve you with the search warrant."

As he said this Raymond took a thick number ten envelope out of his inside coat pocket and placed it facedown on the bar. His hand remained on it, at rest.

Mr. Sweety turned his head back and forth as though he had a stiff neck. "Hey, come on now, man. I don't know shit about nothing. I told him that last night."

"I'll tell you something," Raymond said. "I believe you. I think you got caught in the middle of something and you're naturally a little confused. I would be too."

"I'm not talking to you," Mr. Sweety said.

"I can understand your position," Raymond said, "sitting on a hot gun and here we are coming down on you." Raymond raised his hand from the envelope, palm up. "Wait now. I also see you're still more confused than involved. Sandy laid this on you and you don't know what's going on. She comes in the other day, she tells you Clement wants you to hold the gun for him. But wait a minute. We come to find out Clement doesn't know anything about it. That's straight—listen to me. Hear the whole thing. I told you last night Sandy doesn't want Clement to know she came here. And what do you do? You act very surprised. So I think about it—why would you be surprised? Well, because she *said* it was from Clement. But if Clement doesn't know she was here then he doesn't know she delivered anything. Right? . . . You with me?"

"You losing me on the turns," Mr. Sweety said.

"I know you've got some questions," Raymond said, "but how much do you really want to know? See, all we want is the gun. Now. Listen very carefully. If we have to *look* for the gun, then what we're gonna find is a murder weapon in your possession. Then, you not only get your rights read, you get to see a warrant for your arrest on the charge of murder in the first degree, which carries mandatory life. On the other hand . . . you listening?"

"I'm listening," Mr. Sweety said. "What's the other hand?"

"If you tell us of your own free will some person gave you the gun but you don't know anything about it, whose it is, how it was used, *any*thing; then what we have here is still another example of citizen cooperation and alert police work combining their efforts to solve a brutal crime . . . You like it?"

Mr. Sweety was silent, thinking.

He said, "He don't know she gave this piece to anybody. I mean Clement. That what you saying?"

"That's correct."

"Where does he think it is?"

"Well, I don't think she lifted it off him," Raymond said. "Do you?"

"No way."

"So I think he gave it to her to get rid of and she laid it off on you. It isn't as easy as it sounds, throwing a gun in the river. Maybe she was coming here anyway, you know? Or maybe she told *you* to get rid of it. I'm not gonna ask you that. But if she did, that puts a burden on you. You got to take it out in your car somewhere . . . somebody finds the gun, remembers seeing you . . . the way it always happens. You been around, you know these things. Who wants to be associated with a hot gun. No, I don't blame you." Raymond waited a moment. "You coming to a decision?"

Mr. Sweety didn't answer.

"Where's the gun, at your house?"

"Down the basement."

"Let's go get it."

"I got to call Anita, have her come over here."

Raymond and Hunter looked at each other but didn't say anything. They waited for Mr. Sweety to come back from the phone that was halfway down the bar, by the cash register.

Raymond said, "You feel better now?"

Mr. Sweety said, "Shit . . ."

They got back into the blue Plymouth, Raymond carrying a brown paper bag. He said, "It's work, you know it? It wears you out."

Hunter said, "That's why they pay you all that money. Now where?"

"Let's go see Sandy. No, drop me off and get this

to the lab. But don't tag it yet, I mean with any names on it."

Hunter held the key turned, his foot mashing the accelerator. "Fucking car . . ."

Raymond waited patiently. He thought back, reviewing the conversation with Mr. Sweety, pleased. Then said, "I think I left the envelope on the bar," and patted his breast pocket. "Yeah, I did."

"You need it?"

"From Oral Roberts," Raymond said. "No, I'll probably be hearing from him again."

23

A HAMTRAMCK POLICE DETECTIVE by the name of Frank Kochanski picked up his phone and said to Toma, "Where you been?"

"I'm still at the hospital."

"This character you're looking for's at the Eagle. We saw his car by there and I give Harry a call. Harry says yeah, he's in there having a few pops, making phone calls."

"The Eagle?" Toma said, surprised that the man was still in the vicinity of Skender's apartment, little more than a mile from it.

"The Eagle, on Campau," Kochanski said. "How many Eagles you know?"

Toma called the bar. Harry said, "Yeah . . . no, wait a minute, he's picking up his change . . ."

Toma walked down the hall to the third-floor visitor's lounge where the male members of the Lulgjaraj family were waiting. They watched him unfold a city map, study it for a few moments, then place it on the coffeetable and draw a circle with his finger to take in, roughly, Hamtramck and the near east side of Detroit. He said, "He's somewhere in here. But he stays most of the time downtown; I think he'll go there. If he knows how, he'll take the Chrysler. If he doesn't, he may take McDougall." Toma paused. His finger began tracing the line that indicated East Grand Boulevard. "But he could go this way, too, from Joseph Campau. We don't know him, so we have to look for him all these places."

About forty minutes later Skender opened his eyes to the beeping sound. It stopped and Toma was standing close to him, touching his face.

"Go back to sleep."

At the public phone Toma called his service, was given a number and dialed it.

"Where is he?"

"In a house on Van Dyke Place. We're at the corner of Van Dyke and Jefferson," the voice said in Albanian.

"Wait for me," Toma said.

"But if he comes out . . ." the voice began.

"Kill him," Toma said.

"I think what happens to niggers is they come up here and find out they can talk back to you," Clement said, "so all they do then's argue. I tole your nigger woman I *know* she's upstairs. I called her office enough times they finally told me she's home. So what're you arguing with me for?"

"I'm never home to clients," Carolyn said. "I'll see you in my office or, more likely, the Wayne County Jail, but not here. So, Clement, you're going to have to leave."

"All you're doing's reading. You sick? I see a person in their bathrobe the middle of the day I figure they work nights or they're sick."

Carolyn took off her glasses, brought her bare feet down from the hassock and placed the glasses inside the book as she closed it on her lap. "I'm going to argue with you, too, if you don't leave," Carolyn said, "and I promise you'll lose."

Clement didn't seem to hear her. He was looking around the room, at the abstract paintings, at the bar, his gaze moving past Carolyn sitting in the bamboo chair in a beige and white striped caftan, to the beige couch that was covered with pillows in shades of blue. He walked over and let himself fall back into it, his boots levering up and then down, hitting hard on the Sarouk carpet. He pulled a pillow out from behind him, getting comfortable.

"Shit, I'm tired. You know it?"

Carolyn watched him, curiosity soothing impatience, calming her as she studied the man half-reclined on her couch, his head bent against the backrest cushion, fingers shoved into tight pockets now. The Oklahoma Wildman. Born somewhere between fifty and one hundred years too late.

Or a little boy she could hear saying, "I don't have nothing to do." Kicking at the Sarouk, at the ripple, with the heel of his boot, trying to flatten it.

"That carpet you seem determined to destroy," Carolyn said, "cost fifteen thousand dollars."

"No shit?" He looked down at the blue oriental pattern.

"No shit," Carolyn said. "It's worth much more than that now."

"Why don't you sell it, get the money?"

"I enjoy it. I didn't buy it as an investment."

"How much you make a year?"

"Enough to live the way I want."

"Come on, how much you make?"

"Why do you want to know?"

"You don't keep any money in the house, do you?" Clement grinned at her. "*I* know, it's all in VISA cards. That shit's ruining me, you know it?"

"Am I supposed to feel sorry for you?"

"No, but you could write me a check."

"Why would I do that?"

"You know why."

"Clement, you're a terrible extortionist."

"I know. But there was that chicken-fat judge dead and nothing to come of it. Seemed a shame. Then I see your phone number in his book and I commenced to scheme." Clement squinted. "How come he had your number?"

"He called a few times, wanted me to go out with him."

"Jesus, you didn't, did you?"

"No, Clement, I didn't."

"You ain't a young girl, but I *know* you can do better'n that."

Carolyn said, "This chat's costing you money, Clement. If we're getting into your situation there's a twenty-five-hundred-dollar retainer to think about. If we go to trial, I'll need another seventy-five, in advance."

Clement blinked and squinted. Carolyn watched his act indifferently—Clement shaking his head now.

"First thing you must learn in school, I mean lawyers, is how to turn things around. I come up here to get a check and you tell me you want ten thousand dollars."

"If I'm going to represent you."

"For what? Shit, they're dickin' around, they're never gonna have a case. I'm pulling out, going down to Tampa, Florida, for the winter. But I don't have the stake I thought I was gonna. That's why I need you to write me a check."

Carolyn sat low in the chair studying Clement, her elbow on the arm, her cheek resting against her hand.

"You never cease to amaze me."

"I don't?"

"Always seem so calm. Never upset. How do you manage that?"

"Thinking good thoughts," Clement said. "Go get your checkbook."

"What do you need, a couple hundred?"

Clement squinted at her again. "Couple *hun-nert?*" He had come seeking no particular amount. She had mentioned a ten-thousand-dollar fee and that didn't sound too bad. Nice round number. But now—shit, looking at him like he was the janitor, waiting for him to leave so she could open her book again—he doubled the amount and said, "Twenty thousand oughta do it."

Carolyn didn't say anything. She didn't move until he said, "You're pretty calm yourself." Then watched as she came out of the chair, laying the book on the hassock, and went to the desk in the bay of front windows.

With her profile to him, leaning over the desk, she said, "I'm doing this against my better judgment," opening a business-size checkbook and writing now.

Clement was surprised. He'd expected her to give him an argument. He could see the curve of her fanny against the robe. She tore a check from the book and walked across the room, right past him, not looking at him until she was standing in the doorway that opened on the upstairs hall. Clement could see the railing behind her and now she was offering him the check.

"Here. Take it."

Something wasn't right. Clement stared and watched her move out into the hallway now and hold the check over the railing.

"All right, then pick it up on your way out," Carolyn said. "But if you take it, please don't expect me to ever help you again, in or out of court. Understood?"

Clement got up and crossed toward Carolyn. Her extended arm looked pale and naked sticking out of the robe. As he reached her she handed him the check. Clement looked at it.

"This says two hunnert."

Carolyn called over the railing, downstairs, "Marcie?"

"I said twenty thousand. You left out some oughts."

Carolyn turned to look at him. "Even if I could write a check in that amount, do you really think I would?"

"Yes, I do," Clement said. " 'Stead of me rolling up your rug or taking your jewelry—sure, I do."

"But a check—you know I could stop payment as soon as you leave."

"Then I'd come back, wouldn't I?"

"I don't believe this," Carolyn said. "All I have to do is call the police."

"Man, it's hard to get through to some people," Clement said. "Where's your bathroom?"

Carolyn hesitated, then gestured with her hand, a vague motion. "Right there. The first door." She turned with her back to the railing for Clement to go past, then tried to pull away as he took her by the arm.

"Let's me and you go toidy."

"Now wait a minute—" Clement's fingers dug into her upper arm and she called out, "Marcie!"

"She's locked in the pantry." Clement was moving Carolyn along now. "I told you she was arguing with me. People argue—you're a lawyer—you got to make your point or shut 'em up, huh?" He pushed Carolyn into the bathroom and swung the door closed behind them, looking around. "Man, this is some biffy; you could have a party in here . . . big stall shower . . . I like a tub-bath myself, but this'll do fine. Take your robe off."

"Clement?" Carolyn began.

"What?"

"Whatever you're doing . . ." She tried a sincere expression with a slight smile. "Can I offer you a little advice?"

"How much's the retainer?"

"No, this is free. Whatever you have in mind"—

slowly, with a soft lilt to her voice—"I think you should consider very carefully the position you're in." Clement hooked a finger in the ring of the caftan's zipper. "Clement, be nice, okay?"

"You'd stop payment, huh?" The caftan opened as he pulled down. She tried to hold it closed. He took her two hands and brought them away, standing close, looking into her face.

"I don't have anywhere *near* that much," Carolyn said, still sincere, "so what difference does it make?"

"How much you got?"

"Let's go look in the checkbook."

"Take off the robe first." He let go of her hands.

"Clement, really, if you'll stop and think for a minute . . ." His hands slipped inside the rough-cotton garment, moved up her body and felt her elbows come in tightly, her eyes staring into his.

"What you think I'm gonna do to you? . . . Huh? Tell me." He moved his thumbs across her breasts. "Hey, your nobs're sticking out . . . That feel pretty good? Juuuust brush 'em a little, huh? . . . They get hard as little rocks." His right hand moved lightly down her side to her hip, their eyes still holding. "Now what am I gonna do? . . . That your belly button right there? . . . My, we don't have no panties on, do we?" His voice drowsy. "Tell what you think I'm gonna do to you . . . Huh? Come on . . ."

Clement drew his right hand out of the caftan, bringing it down past his own hip, curled the hand into a fist and grunted, going up on his toes, as he drove the fist into Carolyn's stomach.

Once he got her into the shower, the caftan off her shoulders, pinning her arms, Clement gave Carolyn a working over with a few kidney punches and body hooks, a couple of stinging jabs to the face before a right cross drew blood from her nose and mouth and he turned the shower on her. The job was trying to keep her on her feet, glassy-eyed and moaning, Clement doubting she had much air left in her. He gave Carolyn a towel and guided her back to the desk in the window bay, bright with afternoon sunlight. Opening the checkbook, Clement said, "Let's see now how much you want to give me."

He looked at himself in the mirrored walls of the first floor, grinned a little at the hotshot grinning back at him and walked out of there with a check for six thousand five hundred dollars in the pocket of his denim jacket, thinking: I believe you stumbled onto something, boy.

It was sure nice out.

There was a guy standing across the street. A young guy in a dark suit.

It was sure easier than going in with a gun. Pick

out the right party, impress on the party why they should not call the police, then go to a downtown bank at once and cash the check. See, then if the bank calls the party to verify the check, the party is still seeing life through pain and fear and would say, you bet it's good—fast.

There were three guys over there now, standing, talking.

Carolyn was probably upstairs looking out the window. Man, but it was a big place. Weird. High picket fence, like spears, all around and a blacktop parking area in the side yard—no grass—like the place had once been a residence, then a commercial establishment of some kind, with its big kitchen and bathroom, then a residence again. His car sat over there all by itself, up against the iron fence.

The three guys across the street, he realized now—looking through the fence at them as he approached his car—were wearing black suits. Dark-haired guys with mustaches and black suits . . .

Jesus Christ, he had never even *seen* an Albanian before yesterday. He said to himself, Oh shit—wanting to run for the Montego, but making himself walk, not wanting to get anybody excited just yet, least not until he was behind the car on the driver's side and could open the door and reach under the seat.

The three guys were coming across the street.

They looked like undertakers. They were opening their black suitcoats and reaching inside . . .

Clement was still five long strides from the car when they drew pistols and began firing at him. He couldn't believe it. Right out on the street, three guys he'd never seen before in his life shooting at him through the fence, not asking him to wait-up there, find out if he was the party they wanted—Christ, just blazing away at him! Clement got his door open and saw the windows drilled and patterns form at the same time, the windows shattered but held together. He got the Browning from under the seat, edged to the rear curve of the Montego, extended the Browning over the edge of the trunk and, as he saw them through the widely spaced pickets, the three of them coming toward the drive, he began squeezing the trigger, feeling the gun jump, hearing that hard report in his ears, and saw them scatter, running along the fence on the other side of the drive. Clement got in the Montego, backed up, headed toward the rear of the house and almost braked when he saw the chain across the exit drive—thought, What, you don't want to scratch up your new car?—kept going and tore through those links without even feeling a tug—sailed out hanging a right into the alley and faced another split moment of decision as he saw the end of the alley coming up fast. Turn left, away from the boys in black? Or hang another right and have to drive past the front of the house, where they were presently swarming? To hell with them. He cranked a right . . . saw the black suits back in the street again, looking this way, then all three of them aiming with both arms extended, like they knew what they were doing. The sound of the shots came as *pops*, far away, but the windshield blossomed at once in fragmenting circles. Clement floored it right at them. Saw them run for the sidewalk and veered over to jump the curb and sweep along close to the fence. Two of them ducked into the drive, out of the way, while the third set a fence-climbing record, just pulling his legs up as Clement scraped the Montego against the metal pickets, swerved back onto the street and took a couple of more shots in the rear end before he got to Jefferson and turned without stopping into the westbound traffic.

He couldn't believe he had never heard of Albanians.

24

SANDY WAS WEARING her Bert Parks T-shirt with tight faded jeans. She let go of the door, resigned, walked ahead of Raymond into the living room.

"We alone?"

"You mean is Clement here? No. But Del called. He's coming back this weekend."

"What's that do to your arrangement?"

"It doesn't do nothing. I move out."

"Clement find another place?"

Sandy seemed worn-out. She didn't answer, she moved in a circle, indecisive, before dragging herself over to the couch and curling a leg beneath her as she sunk down.

"Tired?"

"Yeah, a little."

"Out late last night, huh?"

"Pretty late."

Raymond came over and sat at the other end of the couch, playing with a folded piece of notepaper now, rolling it in one hand the way you might roll a cigarette.

"I'm tired too," Raymond said. "You want to know where I've been?"

"Not partic'larly."

"First I went to Hutzel . . ."

"What's Hutzel?"

"It's a hospital. Up at the Medical Center."

Sandy held her hands close to her face, idly concentrating on a fingernail, putting it between her front teeth then, holding the nail with her teeth as she twisted the finger.

"I saw Skender."

"Then where'd you go?"

"Skender's in traction. He's gonna be crippled the rest of his life. You can say, oh, what happened? And we can throw that back and forth a while, or you can tell me how you feel about it."

"I don't have to talk to you," Sandy said, "so I don't think I will."

"You know the kind of person Skender is— quiet, very nice guy—"

"Hey, come on." Sandy got up abruptly. She went over to the windows and stood with her back to Raymond, who rolled and unrolled the piece of notepaper between his thumb and fingers.

"What'd Clement call him, the chicken-fat Albanian?" Sandy didn't answer. "You don't have a typewriter, do you? I mean Del Weems."

Sandy shrugged. "I don't know."

He handed her the piece of notepaper.

"What's this?"

"Read it."

Sandy unrolled it, saw:

SURPRISE
CHICKEN FAT!!!

and let the paper curl up again. Raymond took it. He left her standing at the window and returned to the couch.

"He leaves the note and shoots up my apartment with a .22. The question is, was he trying to kill me, or was he just having some fun?"

Sandy turned to the television set that was in the corner between the banks of windows, dialed the knob through the channels, back and forth, stood looking at the screen a moment, then came back to her end of the couch and sat down on her leg, her gaze holding on Bob Eubanks talking to a panel of newlywed wives, asking them what film star will their husbands say "*you* would most like to make whoopee with."

"Who would you?" Raymond said.

"Robert Redford," Sandy answered, watching the television screen. An oriental-looking newlywed wife also said Robert Redford. The other three said John Travolta.

"One time," Sandy said, with a little more life in her now, "Bob Eubanks asked them what was the most *unusual* place they ever made whoopee? And this girl goes—it's bleeped out, but you can read her lips. She goes, 'In the ass.' And Bob Eubanks goes, '*No!* I mean a place like a location.' I thought he was gonna die."

"You ever married?" Raymond asked.

"Yeah, once. This shithead from Bedford. His big ambition was to move to Indianapolis."

"I guess you've seen some sights."

"Not a whole lot worth remembering."

"How old are you?"

"I'm twenty-*three*." Giving the number an edge of panic in her tone.

"I don't mean to sound square," Raymond said, "but you might consider a different way of life."

Sandy was still gazing at the television screen. "Look at that"—amazed—"all four of the husbands said John Travolta. Jesus. You know how many John Travoltas there are around? If I had my choice, who I'd pick, you know who it'd be?"

"You said Robert Redford."

"No, he's the one I'd like to make whoopee with. No, I mean the one, like somebody I wouldn't mind being married to."

"Who's that?"

"Don't laugh, but Gregory Peck."

"Is that right?"

"I mean a young Gregory Peck."

"Yeah, I've always liked him."

"He's so . . . calm. You want to know something? When you first came here, the first time, you reminded me of him. A younger Gregory Peck—that's what I thought of."

Raymond smiled. "Were you smoking?"

"*No.* I didn't have nothing but seeds and stems. I told you that, didn't I? Didn't we discuss that one time?"

"You've been smoking today though."

"Some, but I don't feel it. God, I wish I did."

"I know what you mean," Raymond said. "Mr. Sweety told us about the gun."

Sandy sighed and seemed tired again. "Here we go."

"A Walther P.38 HP model, made in Germany about 1940," Raymond said. "It's probably been to war, killed some people. But the only ones we know for sure it's killed are Alvin Guy and Adele Simpson. Mr. Sweety says you're the one gave it to him."

"He said that?"

"It's true, isn't it?"

"I don't know—I thought Gregory Peck was cool," Sandy said, "but I think you could give him some lessons. I've been seeing it coming and, I'll tell you the truth, I don't know what to do. If you think I'm gonna testify against Clement—I mean even if he was paralyzed from the neck down and had to be fed with a spoon—even if you *swear* you're gonna put him away forever, like the last time, make me all these promises if I'll say he had the gun, whatever it was that time, and I wouldn't do it and thank *God*, Christ, I didn't, cause he walked out of the courtroom, didn't he?"

"He isn't gonna walk this time," Raymond said, not even convincing himself.

Sandy said, "Bull *shit, you* don't know. Practically everybody he knows made him in that house—where was it, on St. Marys—with that fucking gun and he *walked*. The only way in the world—I'll tell you right now—I'd ever testify against Clement is if he's dead and buried with a stake through his heart and even then I'd be nervous." Sandy got up. "You can send me to jail you want, but I swear I'm not saying one fucking word." She went over to the front windows again and stood motionless, looking out.

Bob Eubanks was saying, "Now, gentlemen, listen carefully. Who will your wife say, of all your friends, is the most oversexed? First names only, please."

Raymond got up. He walked over to the set thinking, Jerry. Turned it off and stood next to Sandy looking down at the city . . . cars coming off the Chrysler Freeway and turning onto Jefferson, the Renaissance Center, people in there coming out of work, conventions, meeting for drinks . . .

"Have you seen him today?"

"No."

"You talk to him?"

"No."

"Why do you stay with him?"

He didn't think she was going to answer; but she said, after a moment, "I don't know." Listless again. "He's fun . . ."

"He kills people."

"*I* don't know that." She started to turn from the windows and Raymond put his hand on her shoulder, lightly, feeling small bones.

"You wish he'd disappear, leave you alone," Raymond said. "You won't make the move because you're afraid to. He scares you to death. So you pretend he's a normal person, maybe just a little wild, and say he's fun. Was he fun when he put Skender's leg up and took the pipe? . . ."

"I'm not saying one fucking word to you!" She tried to turn and pull free, but Raymond put both hands on her shoulders now and held her facing the pane of glass, the view.

"All I want you to do is listen," Raymond said. "Okay?" Relaxing his grip, his hands moving gently over her shoulders before coming to rest. "I wondered, why didn't he kill Skender? He killed the judge, he killed the woman with the judge. You see, I don't think Clement planned it or anybody paid him to do it. He kills in the line of business, or when he feels like it. I think he came out of the racetrack looking for you and Skender—I know you were setting the poor guy up—and I think the judge got in Clement's way, that's all, and one thing led to another and . . . what does Clement do when he gets mad at somebody? Well, he might shoot you. Or, if he halfway likes you or feels sorry for you, he might only break your leg, let you off with a warning. You see what I mean?"

"You answer your own question," Sandy said.

"What question's that?"

"Will I testify against him. You admit he kills people he gets mad at. Or breaks their leg. What do you think he'd do to *me*?"

"I'm not asking you to testify. Have I said anything about testifying?" Raymond paused. "Are you thinking about something else?"

"Are you kidding—something *else?*"

"I think you're missing the point here," Raymond said. "What happens, say in the next day or so, before we pick him up, Clement finds out Sweety has the gun?"

"Oh, Jesus—"

"He'd want to know how he got it, wouldn't he?"

Sandy came around and was looking up at him

with a terrible fear in her eyes that seemed almost a yearning. "*Why?* I mean he doesn't have to know that, does he?"

Raymond's hands moved gently on her shoulders. "What were you supposed to do with the gun, get rid of it?"

"Throw it in the river."

There it was. Not something he could use; still, it was nice to hear, verifying what he had put together in small pieces.

"So why'd you take it to Sweety?"

"Because I was going there." She was a little girl again, pouting, resentment in her tone. "I'm not gonna walk out on the Belle Isle Bridge. What am I suppose to be doing if somebody sees me? Standing there on the bridge . . ."

"I know, it sounds easy," Raymond said, "but it isn't. What'd you tell Sweety to do with it?"

"Anything he wanted. Just get rid of it."

"And he looked at it the same way you did. So he hid it down the basement. But weren't you afraid he might call Clement?"

"Why would he?" Her tone changed as she said, "Listen, I'm not making a statement—if you think you're being clever."

"I told you, I'm not asking you to snitch," Raymond said. "But how come you didn't tell Clement you took the gun over there?"

"God, I don't know." Weary again. "He gets so

picky and irritated sometimes . . ." She turned to
the window and Raymond kept quiet, letting her
stare at her reflection against the fading light. Almost at once the T-shirt image on the window
changed to white and she was looking up at him
again. "Wait a minute—if you know where the gun
is then you already picked it up, huh? You're not
gonna *leave* it there."

"Sandy," Raymond said, "what difference does
it make where the gun is? What's that got to do
with *you?*"

"He'll find out—"

"Wait. Let me suggest something," Raymond
said, "before he finds out *any*thing, tell him you
took the gun over there. That's all. You're off the
hook."

"But I didn't do anything to get him in trouble—
I *didn't*. Will you just, God, explain it to him?" In
desperate need of help, but not listening.

"Sandy, look, all you have to do is tell him the
truth. You gave the gun to Mr. Sweety. Tell him, because you were afraid. Isn't that right? I don't think
Clement was very smart to give it to you in the first
place, but that's not your fault. At the time, I can
understand him being a little nervous. What is this?
He's hardly out of bed, reading about the judge in
the paper and we're banging on the door. The gun's
down in the Buick or somewhere—he just wants to

get rid of it, quick." Raymond paused. "Sandy? Look at me. You listening?"

"Yes . . ."

"Do you see any reason to tell him anything else? Maybe get him excited, as you say, picky and irritated? No, just say, 'Honey, I think I ought to tell you something. I was afraid to throw the gun in the river, so I gave it to your friend Mr. Sweety.' You can say, you know, looking at him very innocently, 'Was that all right, honey?' And he'll say sure, fine. See, keep it simple. But you're gonna have to do it pretty quick. Next time you see him, or if he calls."

"God, I don't know," Sandy said, "I got a feeling I'm in awful deep trouble."

"Well, you go with a guy like Clement you're gonna have some close ones," Raymond said. "What I'd do, if you want my advice, I'd tell him and then split. Go find you a young Gregory Peck somewhere. Twenty-three, Sandy, you're not getting any younger."

"Thanks a lot," Sandy said.

"On the other hand you stick with Clement, you have a good chance of not getting any older," Raymond said. "So there you are."

25

RAYMOND SAID, "What're we having, a telethon or something?"

Hunter was on the phone. He raised his eyes and one hand, motioning to Raymond, but didn't catch him in time. Raymond was moving from the squad-room door to the coffeemaker.

Norb Bryl was on the phone. He was saying it wasn't the tires, it was the wheel alignment; he said you pay thirty-four hundred dollars for an automobile you expect it to go in a straight line, was that right or wrong?

Wendell Robinson was on the phone, sounding pleasant but in mild pain, saying he had been taking cold showers to keep himself civil; but if someone's old man didn't go back on nights pretty soon, then maybe it wasn't meant to be.

Maureen Downey was on the phone, saying okay, fine, swivelling around from her desk as she hung up to watch Raymond pour a cup of coffee.

"There was a shooting, three o'clock this afternoon. On Van Dyke Place."

Raymond stopped pouring.

"MCMU told us about it, so I called the precinct, just now," Maureen said, "and the sergeant read me the PCR. Three unidentified males, all in dark clothes, dark hair, shooting at an unidentified male driving a light blue older-model car that might be a big Ford or a Lincoln."

"Or a Mercury Montego," Raymond said. "Did he shoot back?"

"They think so, but no reported injuries or fatalities. MCMU's checking the hospitals."

"How was it reported?"

"The call came from the woman next door to two-oh-one, where the shooting took place—in the driveway and out on the street—and we know who lives at two-oh-one, don't we?"

"They talk to Carolyn Wilder?"

"They said they talked to the maid. She said Ms. Wilder wasn't home. But then—"

Hunter, off the phone, said, "We got him by the ass!" and Raymond looked over. "It's the gun, man. Absolutely no question. I'm gonna go pick it up."

Maureen waited for Raymond to turn back to her. He said, "I'm sorry. What?"

"Carolyn Wilder phoned almost an hour ago. She wants you to call."

"Okay." He picked up his coffee mug and started to move away.

"At home," Maureen said.

Raymond stopped and looked at Maureen again, appreciating her timing. "You ask her if she heard the shots?"

"No, but I'll bet you she did."

Raymond went to the unofficial lieutenant's desk beneath the window and dialed Carolyn's number.

"I hear you had some excitement."

"I'd like to see you," Carolyn said.

"Fine. I'll be leaving here pretty soon. You sound different."

"I'll bet I do."

Now he was puzzled. Her voice was low, yet colder than he had ever heard it. "Marcie see what happened?"

"No, but I did."

Raymond didn't say anything.

"Who are they?" Carolyn said.

And now he wasn't sure how much to tell her. "Clement picked on the wrong one this time and it snapped back at him. Why, you want to file his complaint?"

"I would like to laugh," Carolyn said, "but my mouth hurts. Before this sounds even more like farce, why don't we save it until you get here."

Raymond hung up, still puzzled. He said to Norb Bryl, who was standing now, clipping several pens into his shirt pocket, "What exactly is farce?"

"It's a used car that's supposed to drive in a straight line," Bryl said, "but pulls to the left. If you don't need me I've got something to do."

The door closed behind Bryl, then opened again as Hunter came in with a brown paper bag that was grease-stained and could be a bag of doughnuts. He placed it on the lieutenant's desk, pleased. "No prints, but this is the little mother that did it. Absolutely no question."

Raymond looked across the squadroom. He said, "Maureen, if you want to go, you can, it's pretty late; but if you want to stay, lock the door. Okay?"

Wendell said, "How 'bout me?"

"Same thing. You want to leave, go ahead."

Hunter said, "Shit, you got his interest now. Afraid he might miss something."

Maureen came over, hesitantly, and sat at Bryl's desk.

Hunter said, "How come you don't ask me if I want to leave?"

"You're already in it," Raymond said. He looked at Maureen and then Wendell. "We took the gun off this guy Sweety without a search warrant. I'm not worrying it's gonna kick back at us, that's not what I'm getting to. I wanted to find out, you know, without typing up all the papers and pleading with some judge, if this is really the gun or not. All right, we find out it is. No question about it—our friend up in the lab checks it out without entering any names and numbers in the book—we have a murder weapon. Now . . . if we take it to the prosecutor at this point he says, fine, but how do we prove it's Mansell's gun? We say, well, if we're very persuasive we can get this guy by the name of Sweety to cop. The prosecutor says, who's Sweety? We tell him he's a guy that used to run with Mansell, he's done time and now he's dealing drugs. The prosecutor says, Jesus Christ, *that's* my witness? We say, well, we can't help the kind of people we have to associate with in this business; he's all we got."

"Sandy," Maureen said.

"Right, we've also got Sandy," Raymond said, "but you can pull all her fingernails out, which she hasn't got much of anyway, and she'll still never say a word. Not out of loyalty, but because Clement scares the shit out of her."

"How about if I talked to her?" Maureen said.

"Sure, why not? I'm open to suggestions. But let me review what we've got. An arm that could be Clement's sticking out of a car at Hazel Park. Possibly the same car at the scene, which Sandy has the keys to and we say she gave to Clement. Clement's lawyer, Miss Wilder, looks at us and says, 'Yeah? Prove it.' We can put Clement at another scene, three years ago, where slugs were dug out of a wall from a Walther P.38"—Raymond picked up the paper bag—"right here, our murder weapon. But how do we show it belongs to Clement?"

There was a silence.

Maureen said, "Wow. I think I know what you're gonna do."

Again a silence. Raymond was aware of the four of them sitting in an old-fashioned police office under fluorescent lights, plotting.

Hunter said, "I don't see no other way."

Wendell said, "You want me to talk to the brother, Mr. Sweety?"

"No, it's my responsibility if anybody gets blamed. I'm gonna do it," Raymond said. "At least try to arrange it. Wendell, you know Toma pretty well, the Albanians. Have a talk with him, like we're thinking about busting him for the attempt, we're watching him, you know, so he better not do anything dumb for the next couple days . . . Maureen, you want to take a shot at Sandy, go ahead. I think she wants somebody to talk to and, who knows . . ."

The phone rang.

"Jerry, let's see about putting MCMU on Sweety around the clock now."

The phone rang. Raymond laid his hand on it.

"Put a couple guys in the bar—if they can hang around without getting smashed."

The phone rang.

Raymond picked it up. He said, "Squad Seven, Lieutenant Cruz."

Clement's voice said, "Hey, partner. I got a complaint I want to make. Some crazy fuckers're trying to kill me."

He parked behind Piper's Alley on St. Antoine, a few blocks south of 1300, came through the kitchen with the paper bag and Charlie Meyer, the owner, said, "Raymond," almost sadly, "you don't bring your lunch here. This is a restaurant."

Raymond smiled, gave him a wave and continued out into the main room, looking past plastic fern and Tiffany lamps at the booths of after-work drinkers, a swarm of them at the bar, guys and girls unwinding or winding up for the evening, either way unaware of the policeman with the paper bag who was wondering what it would be like to drop the bag on Clement's table—sitting there, next to one of the front windows in his denim jacket—say to Clement, Here, I got something for you, and as Clement's hand goes inside the bag say, loud enough to stop the room, DROP IT! and pull the Colt out of his sportcoat and blow him away.

Clement said, "There he is." Grinning. "You look like a man with pussy on his mind. See something here you like?"

Raymond sat down and placed the paper bag on the table, to one side. Clement had a drink in front of him—in his denims, someone off a freighter or a trail drive—sizing up the house.

"All these boogers come in here looking for quiff, you know it? Their badges and convention tags on, they end up looking at each other, I swear. What's in the bag, your lunch?"

"Yes, it's my lunch," Raymond said. "You owe me seventy-eight dollars for a new window."

Clement grinned. "Somebody shooting at you? Listen, partner, I got people shooting at me too. I see these fellas coming across the street, I'm thinking, what're they, undertakers? Wearing these black suits. What I don't understand is how come I never heard of Albanians."

"Well, they never heard of you either," Raymond said. "But now, it's a question of who gets you first. You want to turn yourself in, I think you'd live longer at Jackson than out on the street."

Clement was squinting at him. "You let those fellas loose like that, shoot at people?"

"You want to file a complaint, stop in the precinct. See, we don't get attempted or assault. Like what you did to Skender."

"Man, you keep on top."

"He'd have to file a charge, but they'd rather handle it themselves."

"And you let 'em?"

"If the man doesn't report you broke his leg, then we don't know about it, do we?"

"Jesus—" Clement shook his head. "You want a drink?"

"No, there's something I have to do yet."

He watched Clement drain his glass and look around for the waitress—not quite the leisurely, laid-back Clement this evening—half-turning and putting his arm on the table, his hand, Raymond judged, about eight inches away from the paper bag. Clement raised his other hand, motioned with it and looked at Raymond again.

"Reason I called you, I want you to understand something. I'm leaving town. I'm not leaving on account of the Albanians and I'm not leaving on account of you either. But I got no reason to sit around here with my thumb up my ass, so I'm moving on."

"When," Raymond asked, "tonight?"

"I *was*—send you a postcard from Cincinnati— till I got jacked around this afternoon and by the time I got to the bank it was closed. All three banks I went to. I just want you to know, partner, I'm not *running*, as you know the meaning of the word. But I'm not gonna wait while you dick around and I'm not gonna exchange unpleasantries with some people I don't even know who they are 'cept they wear black suits . . . Can you tell me why they dress like that?"

"One of them died," Raymond said.

"Well, some more of 'em are gonna if I hang around, so tell 'em it's just as well I'm leaving. I just don't want them thinking they run me off, cause they haven't. But shit, I get mixed up with those people—I got no incentive. You understand?" He looked up as the waitress took his glass. "Same way, hon." As she turned to Raymond, Clement said, "No, he don't want nothing. That's Jack Armstrong, the all-American Boy." Clement smiled at her and looked at Raymond again. "She don't know shit who I'm talking about, does she?"

"Sandy going with you?"

"I don't know, I suppose. She's cute, isn't she? 'Cept when she gets stoned. I tell her quit smoking that queer shit and drink liquor like a normal person."

"Some people," Raymond said, "you can't tell 'em anything."

"That's the truth."

"But long as they don't tell on *you* . . ." Raymond shrugged and let the words hang.

Clement stared at him.

Raymond was aware of the noise level in Piper's Alley. It surprised him that when he purposely listened to the sound of the place it was so loud. Everybody working at having fun. He said, "Well, I got to get going."

Clement stared at him. "You want me to think you know something I don't."

"You're nervous this evening," Raymond said. "But long as you trust your friends, what're you worried about?"

Clement stared at him. His head turned a little and he stared at the paper sack. He said, "That ain't your lunch, is it?"

"No, it isn't my lunch. Isn't a bag of fry cakes, either," Raymond said. "You want it?"

"Oh, my," Clement said, beginning to grin just a little. "We getting tricky, are we? Want to hand me somebody else's murder gun?" His eyes raised, his expression changing abruptly as Raymond got up from the table. "Where you going? I ain't done yet."

Raymond said, "Yes, you are," and walked out with the sack. He used the telephone in the kitchen, noise all around him, to call Hunter, told him not to move, he'd be right there.

A few minutes later Raymond walked into the squadroom.

"Maureen leave yet?"

"Right after you did. I put MCMU on Sweety's place, told 'em to get somebody in the bar and the rest out of sight."

"Good." Raymond opened his address book to "S" and began dialing a number. "Clement made an announcement. He's leaving town tomorrow."

Hunter said, "We better have the party tonight then."

Raymond nodded. "I think we should try." He said into the phone then, "Sandy? This is Lieutenant Cruz. How you doing? . . . Yeah, I know, some are better than others. You having a nice talk with Maureen? . . . Yeah, well, let me speak to her a minute." He put his hand over the phone as he looked at Hunter. "She says it isn't her day." Taking his hand away, Raymond said, "Maureen? . . . listen, tell her Clement'll probably call or be over in a little while. In fact, any time now, so you better get out of there. Explain to her—she can say we questioned her about the gun, even leaned on her a little, tried to scare her, if she wants. But tell her to keep it simple. She took the gun over to Sweety's, period. That's all she knows. Was she crying? . . . Uh-huh, well, tell her if she feels like she's going to save it for Clement, just in case . . . Hey, Maureen? Tell her you wish you were twenty-three again."

"You're all heart," Hunter said.

"I can sympathize with Sandy a little," Raymond said, "I can. But I'm not too worried about her. I mean, if she can hang around with Clement three, four years and she's still in one piece . . ."

"She knows how to cover her ass," Hunter said.

"If anything's bothering me at the moment,

that I feel a certain responsibility . . ." Raymond paused, thoughtful, and looked over at Hunter. "You got Sweety's number?"

Hunter dialed it and stayed on the phone. Raymond picked up his phone and sat back, crossing his loafers on the corner of the gray metal desk. He said, "Mr. Sweety, how you doing? This is Lieutenant Cruz . . . What I was wondering, has Clement called you yet?"

"Has *Clement* called me!"

Both Raymond and Hunter moved the receivers away from their ears, looking at each other with expressions of pain.

"Where are you?" Raymond asked. "You at home or at work?"

"I'm home. What you mean has Clement called me?"

"Anita working?"

"Yeah, she's over there."

"Why don't you go help her," Raymond said.

"Why?"

"I think you're gonna be busy tonight."

There was a silence before Mr. Sweety said, "Why is Clement gonna call me?"

"When he does," Raymond said, "tell him you're glad he called, you've been wanting to get in touch with him. In fact, you want to see him."

"I want to *see* him? For what?"

"To give him back his gun."

"You *took* the gun! . . . I *gave* it to you!"

Hunter had his eyes and mouth open wide, miming Mr. Sweety's emotional state.

"No, you told us it's in the basement," Raymond said, solemn, straight-faced. "We assume it's still there."

There was a silence again. Mr. Sweety said, "I don't want no parts of that man. I'm getting dumped on—whole big load of shit coming down on me."

"No, you're all right. You have my word," Raymond said. "He comes for the gun, tell him where it is. In fact, how about this? Tell him he'll have to go get it himself, you're busy."

Silence. "I'd have to let him in the house."

"Not if you put the key under the mat," Raymond said and had to smile now, looking at Hunter. A couple of kids getting away with something.

There were tales of heroics and tales of tricky nonprocedural moves, old-pro stunts, told in the Athens Bar on Monroe in Greektown, two short blocks from 1300 Beaubien. Raymond wondered if, not so much the heroes, the tricky movers ever looked ahead and saw replays, recountings: a twenty-year pro, an insider, telling appreciative someday pros that it wasn't to go beyond this table:

"So he cons the guy into handing over the gun, has ballistics fire it to make sure it's the murder weapon, then—here's the part—he puts it *back* in the guy's basement, inside the furnace where it was, and has the guy tell the shooter to come get his gun, he doesn't want any part of it. You follow? He's got to make the shooter with the gun or he doesn't make him. He's got to set him up . . ." And the someday pros at the table wait with expectant grins, gleams in their eyes. Yeah? . . .

Then what? Raymond was thinking, riding in the blue Plymouth police car with Hunter.

Go on . . .

Well, the way it should happen: With Mr. Sweety's place under surveillance Mansell walks in, comes out with the gun in his pocket and they shine lights on him and that's it. If he stays inside they ask him to come out and eventually he does, after trying to hide the gun again or pound it apart with a hammer; but they would still have him with the gun, be able to make a case.

But maybe another way it could happen and be told about later in the Athens Bar: For some reason the surveillance is called off . . . There could be a reason.

Clement comes out with the gun, the gun loaded, the way it was found. He comes out on the porch and stops dead as he hears, "That's far enough—" He sees Cruz on the sidewalk beneath the streetlight. Cruz with his sportcoat open, hands at his sides . . .

You're weird, Raymond said to himself.

But he continued to picture the scene as they drove over East Jefferson, hearing, "That's far enough—" and trying to think of what Clement might say then. Yeah, Clement would say something and then he would say something else, something short and to the point and then . . .

Hunter said, "We both going in?"

Raymond, holding the paper bag on his lap, said, "No, I'm gonna do it." He was silent for about a block and then said, "He's got another gun. If he was shooting at the Albanians he got another gun somewhere."

26

MAUREEN LET SANDY PACE the living room in her Bert Parks T-shirt and satin shorts, Sandy shredding a Kleenex tissue, dropping tiny pieces of it but leaving no pattern of a trail. Maybe she had to wear herself out before she'd sit down.

"You jog?" Maureen asked her.

Sandy paused to look at the lady homicide sergeant on the couch in her little schoolteacher navy blazer and gray skirt—like a nun in street clothes except for the gun, Sandy suspected, in the worn brown handbag.

"You kidding? *Jog* . . . no, I don't go sailing either, or play golf. Jesus Christ, do I jog . . ."

"You have a nice trim figure," Maureen said, "I thought maybe you exercised."

"I've been running to the bathroom every ten minutes since your buddy Lieutenant Cruz was here. I don't *need* any more exercise, I'll tell you." She paced over to the dining-L and back to the desk in the living room before stopping again to look at Maureen. "How would you tell him?"

"Just the way Lieutenant Cruz suggested," Maureen said. "You gave the gun to Mr. Sweety because you were afraid to throw it away yourself."

"It's true."

"So you have nothing to worry about."

"He's gonna ask me if the cops were here, I know he is."

"Well, I'm here," Maureen said. "I asked you if you saw a gun in Clement Mansell's possession, here or anywhere else and you told me no. That's all you have to say. Don't complicate it."

"You don't know him."

"I'll bet I've known a few like him though." Maureen watched Sandy move to the windows and look out toward the river. "There's one guy we sent to Jackson keeps writing to me. He says we're pen pals. I think when he gets out in about seven years he wants to get together."

"Clement's only been to prison once," Sandy said. "He's been to *jail* plenty of times, but he's only spent like a year in a regular prison. He says he won't ever go back again and I believe him. God, he makes up his mind to something . . . but he's so un-pre*dic*table. One time we're out at Pine Knob, the Allman Brothers were there. Everybody, you know, they're drinking beer and acting crazy, rolling joints on their coolers. This boy turns around and offers Clement a toke? Clement slaps it out of his hand like he was the boy's dad or something, gives him this real mean look. All while the Allman Brothers're playing Clement's waving his arms around to make the smoke go away. Sometimes, I swear, he's like a little old man."

"You must like him a lot," Maureen said.

Sandy turned from the window. "Shit, I'm scared not to." She stared off, mouth partly open, then gradually began to grin, though not giving it much. "He's cute, though, you know it? God, in bed . . . I think that's where he got his nickname, the Wildman? I swear, he gets it up, like he says, you got to hit it with a stick to make it go down." Sandy's grin broadened as her gaze moved to Maureen and she said, "What're you smiling at?"

"I've had some experience there, too," Maureen said. "I was assigned to Sex Crimes for nine years. I think I saw everything there is to see. I mean, you know, funny things."

"God," Sandy said, "that must've been interesting. Like rapists and degenerates and all? Perverts?"

"Uh-huh, lot of perverts. People you'd least expect."

"Isn't that the way? Like schoolteachers . . . preachers?"

"Uh-huh. A lot of flashers."

"Yeah? Guys with raincoats and nothing under-neath?"

"The pros cut the whole front out of their pants," Maureen said. "One of the weirdest ones—we got a rape report. Right over in the City-County Building, one of the secretaries was dragged into the stairway and raped, had her clothes torn off. We asked her to describe the guy, if he had any un-usual marks or characteristics. The girl said yes, come to think of it, he had an infantile penis."

"God," Sandy said, "a rapist." She sounded a lit-tle sad. "Did you get him?"

"We rounded up suspects, repeat offenders," Maureen said, "but first we had to qualify them, if you understand what I mean."

Sandy's face brightened. "Yeah, to see who had an infantile one." She frowned. "How little is in-fantile?"

"Wait," Maureen said. "A suspect would be brought in, then one of the guys in the squad would tell him to drop his pants."

"Didn't you see any of 'em?"

"Well, a few. But during the investigation I think something like a hundred and fifty-seven penises were inspected."

"Wow," Sandy said, with something like awe. "A hundred and fifty-seven. God . . ." She paused then with a puzzled expression. "Wait a minute. This girl said the guy's joint was infantile, but compared to *what?* I mean her old man could've had a shlong that hung down to his knees. You know it?"

"We thought of that," Maureen said. "Compared to what? We never did get the guy."

"That's really something," Sandy said. "At least you get to meet a lot of interesting people."

"Well, I'm never bored," Maureen said.

When Sandy was alone again she let the silence and dismal evening sky work on her. It was the best time of the day to be depressed. She was able to cry for a few minutes, shredding another Kleenex, made moaning sounds as she went into the bedroom, stood in front of the full-length mirror and studied her image hiding there puffy-eyed behind Bert Parks' big grin.

She said out loud, "You poor thing." She curled her lower lip down and got her chin to quiver and studied the expression. Then parted her lips slightly and opened her eyes wide in a look of surprised innocence. "Well, *I* didn't know. God, I thought you'd be *glad*"—pouty again—" 'stead of being an old meany." Sandy stared at her slumped shoulders, her pitiful expression. She stared for a long silent moment and then said, "Fuck it." She took off the T-shirt and jeans and tried it again, looking at a bra-less image now, hooked her thumbs into the narrow band of her white panties and cocked a hip . . . turned sideways and stared past her shoulder, letting her eyelids become heavy . . . turned full front again and stared with her bare feet apart, hands moving to her narrow hips.

She said, "Hey, are you Sandy Stanton?" and cocked her head slightly. "Yeah, I thought you were. You've got a dynamite body, you know it? I mean anybody can see you've got it together. *Look* at you. You are a fucking groovy chick, you know it? Yeah, I know it. Then what's the problem? What problem? I don't have a problem, you have a problem? . . ."

When Clement came in he said, "Where you think you're at, a nudist camp?" Without a bit of fun in his voice. "Jesus, turn that boresome music off—"

"We a little irritable this evening?"

With a foot-dragging funky step and two whole joints working in her, Sandy got over to the hi-fi just ahead of Clement and saved the Bee Gees from being scratched to death. She said, "What on *earth* is the *matter* with you?"

He walked over to the windows and stood looking out at the downtown lights.

Sandy tried again. "This your thinking time?"

He didn't answer.

"I've been worried about you—sitting here all day. There's such a thing as telephones, you know." Yeah, get a little pissed at him.

Early this morning Sandy had let the EMS attendants into Skender's apartment building, told them "Down the basement" and got out of there fast. They drove over to Woodward Avenue, pulled up alongside Blessed Sacrament Cathedral and Clement told her to get out, take a cab home. She'd said, "What am I suppose to do, stand out on the street like a hooker?" He gave her a shove. She asked him where he was going to stay and he said, "Don't worry about it." In one of his moods.

Evidently still in it. Good. She could think about standing on that Woodward Avenue street corner with all the colored guys slowing up to look her over and get really pissed at him.

She said, "Don't worry about *me*, just think about yourself."

Still looking out the window Clement said, "I *was* thinking about you. Come on over here. You ever been up the top of the RenCen?"

"Course I have. I used to work there."

He put his arm around her bare waist, pulling her in close. "Seven-hundred feet up in the air. You sit there with your cocktail and it turns. It turns reeeeeal slow. You look at Canada a while. You look downriver at the Ambassador Bridge. You look over De-troit then as you turn real real slow, giving yourself time to wonder and think about things."

"I didn't throw the gun in the river," Sandy said. "I gave it to Mr. Sweety."

"I know you did."

"You want to know why?"

"I know why."

"How do you know?"

"I talked to him."

"Are you mad?"

"No . . ." He didn't sound too sure about it. "See, when I was up there thinking about you? . . ."

"Yeah?"

"I called you up and the line was busy."

Sandy held on, not making a sound.

"I thought, who could she be talking to? Not the Albanian."

"Uh-unh . . ." Sandy said, thinking, Please, God—

"And then it come to me. You were talking to Sweety."

"God, are you smart." She felt herself shaking a little and slipped her arm around Clement. "I know you don't like me to smoke weed, but it's sure good when I'm nervous."

"Tell me what you're nervous about."

"Well, I thought you'd be mad that I didn't, you know, throw the gun away. But I really thought Mr. Sweety would know how better."

"I understand that," Clement said. "But see, then another person knows my business."

"Yeah, but he doesn't really *know* anything. I mean, it's just a gun."

"Well, how come he's nervous and wants me to come get it then? I told him, chuck it in the river you don't want it. He goes, 'I ain't fooling with no hot gun. It's yours, you take care of it.' See, why would he think the gun's hot?"

"Well, maybe the police talked to him." Right away, Sandy knew she had made a mistake, said too much.

"That's a thought," Clement said, giving her a squeeze. "Like they talked to you, huh?"

Even with miles of nighttime lights outside reaching way way off, Sandy felt walls around her, no more room than inside a box, a coffin. It was a terrible feeling. She said, "I was so worried about you today, I didn't know where you were or if anything happened to you or *any*thing."

"They come see you today?"

"Well, this lady cop stopped by. Asked if I knew anything about a gun. But she was real nice about it."

"Tricking you," Clement said.

"Yeah, but I didn't tell her nothing. I *didn't*."

Clement patted her. He said, "I know you didn't, hon. It's just their chicken-fat ways . . . You been smoking a little?"

"Few tokes is all, now and then." She was surprised, he was making it sound so simple.

"When'd you get it?"

"The other day."

"When you give Sweety the gun?"

"Uh-huh. I just got a little bit."

"Oh my," Clement said with a sigh. "Life can sure play a tune on you you let it."

"I didn't *do* anything wrong."

"I know you didn't, hon. But see what's happened? They got to Sweety and I 'magine made a deal with him. He sets me up or they shut him down, put him on the trailer. I come get the gun, walk out of there and twenty squad cars converge on my ass out of nowhere. 'Throw up your hands, motherfucker!' They'd have to empty their weapons," Clement said, "cause I sure ain't doing hard time. Never have and never will."

"Let's go to Tampa, Florida," Sandy said, "right now."

"I'd like to, hon, but we got some problems. Those goddamn Albanian undertakers shot your Montego all to hell—no, that's something I'll tell you about after," Clement said, Sandy frowning up at him. "First thing, we got to get shuck of the gun."

"Why? Why not just walk away from it?" Sandy was still frowning. This was not turning out simple at all.

"Cause I don't leave behind anything might catch up with me later," Clement said. "If I don't get rid of the gun then I got to be rid of anybody could take the stand against me. I don't think you'd care for that."

"Yeah, but you *know* I wouldn't testify."

"Hon, I know it but I *don't* know it. People change their mind. The only thing perfectly clear in *my* mind, I ain't gonna do time. So the gun goes or you and Marcus Sweeton go. Which'd you rather?"

"I thought everything was gonna be good now." Sandy's voice was faint, sounding as far away as her gaze, the little girl wishing she was out there somewhere, even out beyond the lights of Canada.

"We'll make her," Clement said. "I'm gonna call Sweety back, tell him the arrangements."

"But you said if you picked the gun up—"

"Trust the good hands people," Clement said. "You feel that good hand on you there? Here comes another good hand—close your eyes. Here comes another good hand . . . closer . . . closer . . . Where is it going to land? . . ."

Doing was more fun than thinking. But sometimes thinking made the doing more worthwhile. Like if he had known he was going to do the judge he would have thought something up to make it pay more and the doing would have been more satisfying. When he tried to explain this to Sandy, she said she would just as soon not know what he was thinking, if it was all the same. She turned on the television set and he turned it off.

"What am I saying?"

"I don't *know* what you're saying, or want to."

"I'm saying like in this deal here," Clement said, "there are ways to skin by. Shit, lay in the weeds and let it pass over. Like that Grand Trunk railroad train passed over me. But there also ways of doing it with some style, so you let the other party know what you think of their chicken-fat scheme. You follow me?"

"No," Sandy said.

"Then keep your eyes open," Clement said, "and see if your old dad ain't a thinker as well as a doer."

27

RAYMOND THOUGHT OF Madeline de Beaubien, the girl who overheard the plot and warned the garrison Pontiac and his braves were coming to the parley with sawed-off muskets under their blankets and saved Detroit from the Ottawas.

The house could have belonged to one of her early descendants, an exhibit at Greenfield Village that people walked through looking into 19th-century rooms with velvet ropes across the doorways, a cold house despite amber reflections in the hall chandelier and a rose cast to the mirrored walls. The house was too serious.

That was it, Raymond decided. The house didn't see anything funny going on or hear people laugh. Marcie told him solemnly, a funeral-home greeter, Ms. Wilder was waiting for him in her sitting room.

An audience with the queen. No more, Raymond thought, mounting the stairway, not surprised to find her in semidarkness, track lighting turned low, directed toward squares of abstract colors, Carolyn lying on the couch away from the lights. She told him he was late and he asked, For what?

He let himself relax and said, "Let's start over."

"You were going to leave in a few minutes," Carolyn said. "That's what you told me."

"I know, and then we got into something. What's the matter with your voice?"

He did not see her face clearly until he turned on the lamp at the end of the couch away from her and saw the bruise marks and swelling, her mouth puffed and slightly open. Carolyn's eyes held his with a quiet expression, her eyes blinking once, staring at him, blinking again, waiting for him to speak.

"I told you," Raymond said.

Her expression began to turn cold.

"Didn't I tell you? No, you can handle him, no problem."

"I knew you'd have to say it," Carolyn said, "but I didn't think you'd overdo it."

"You didn't? Listen, I'm not through yet," Raymond said. "If I can think of some more ways to say it I'm going to, every way I know how."

She said, "You're serious . . ."

"You bet I am. I told you, don't fool with Clement, but you did anyway."

"I misjudged him a little."

"A *little* . . ."

She began to smile and said, "Do you feel better now?"

He said, "Do you?" Then surprised both of them.

He went to one knee to get close to her and very gently touched her face, her mouth, with the tips of his fingers. He said, "You don't want to be a tough broad." She said, "No . . ." and slipped her arms around him and brought him against her. The faint sound that came from her might have been pain, but he didn't think so.

He said, "I want to tell you something. Then we'll see if we're still friends, or whatever we are. I didn't plan this. As a matter of fact, I came here I was a little on the muscle. I was gonna listen, try to be civil and get out."

"What happened?" Carolyn said.

He liked the subdued sound of her voice.

"I don't know. I think you've changed. Or I've changed. Maybe I have. But what I want to tell you, I think you're too serious."

She didn't expect that, or didn't understand what he meant. "He beat *hell* out of me . . ."

"I know he did," touching her face again, soothing her with his voice and his fingers. "I'm not gonna say it any more, you know who he is . . . Tell me why he's going to the bank tomorrow."

"He made me give him a check. All the money I had in the account."

"How much is that?"

"Over six thousand."

"What did you say one time, he's fascinating? I'm sorry, I've got to quit that . . . Did you stop payment?"

"No, I'm going to file on three counts and get him for assault, extortion and probably larceny from a person. He took more than a hundred in cash."

"Hold off on it," Raymond said. "Let me bring him up on the homicides, then you can file all the charges you want."

"You'll never convict him," Carolyn said, "unless you have more than I know about."

"Did he have a gun?"

"Not when he was here; at least he didn't show it. But when I heard shots and looked out the bathroom window—I thought it was the police and I remember thinking, Wait, as I went to the window, I want to see him killed."

"Really?"

"It was in my mind."

"Did he have a gun then?"

"Yes, shooting back at them. It was an automatic, a fairly good size. But who are they?"

He told her about Skender, Toma. She knew something about Albanian blood feuds and now wasn't surprised. "On the phone you thought I wanted to file against them on behalf of Clement, while I'm thinking of all the ways I want to see him convicted."

"Let me do it," Raymond said. "I'm close. In fact, it could happen tonight, as soon as I hear something." Looking at her, thinking of Clement, he said, "Did he . . . molest you?"

Carolyn began to smile again, her eyes appreciating him. "Did he *molest* me? . . .

"Come on—did he?"

Her mood became quiet. "Not really."

"What does that mean, not really?"

"He touched me . . ."

"Make you take your clothes off?"

"He opened my robe—" Carolyn stopped, she seemed mildly surprised. "You know what I'm doing? I'm being coy. I've never been coy in my life."

"No, you've been too busy impressing yourself," Raymond said. "Tell me what he did."

"What're you trying to do, analyze me? He felt me up, but we didn't go all the way." Now Raymond smiled and she said, "You think you have insights, is that it?"

"Maybe, if that's the word. I don't expect to see something and then look and say, uh-huh, there it is. I try to look without expecting and see what's actually there. Is that insight?"

"You're sly," Carolyn said. "I think I have you down and you slip away."

He said, "You have me down . . . where? It's like

filling out an Interrogation Record of an Information for Arraignment, you know what I mean?
Sometimes the form isn't big enough, or it doesn't
ask the right questions."

"You think I presume too much," Carolyn said,
"see only what I expect to see. Is that it?"

"I don't know, we can talk about it sometime."
He was tired and wasn't sure if he should close his
eyes.

"If I make presumptions," Carolyn said, "what
about you?"

"What about me?"

"We were making love and you said, 'I know
you . . . ' "

"I didn't think you heard me."

"What did you mean?"

"Well, it was like I saw *you*. Not what you do or
who you believe you are, just you. Does that make
sense?"

"I don't know . . ."

"But you didn't say anything, did you? I think
you changed back after that and I didn't know you
anymore. You became the woman lawyer again
who thinks she has to be a tough broad. But look
what happens to tough broads." Raymond was
silent a moment. "Let me take care of him, Carolyn."

*   *   *

When Hunter called Raymond was sitting on the couch with Carolyn's legs across his lap, both tired of words, on safer ground now but still intimately aware of one another. Carolyn asked if he had always lived here, trying to picture him in another life, when he wasn't a policeman. And Raymond said, "In Detroit? No, I was born in McAllen, Texas. We lived in San Antonio, Dallas. We came here when I was ten." She asked, almost hesitantly, if his father was a farmer and Raymond looked at her and smiled. "You mean, was he a migrant? No, he was a barber. He was a dude, the way he dressed, wore pointed patent-leather shoes." The phone rang then, Raymond waiting for it. He lifted Carolyn's legs and got up. "My dad was fifty-seven when he died."

Hunter said, "Mansell called back, just now. He wants Sweety to bring him the gun."

"Where?"

"It got complicated. Sweety told him he was going to a family thing at his mother's—trying to hurry Clement up, get it over with. Clement tells him to take the gun along with him. Sweety says he isn't gonna touch it. If Clement wants the gun tonight he has to come in the next half hour."

Raymond said, "What difference does it make? The key's under the mat."

"Yeah, he told Clement that," Hunter said. "But what he did was confuse the issue with this going to see his mother and Clement says, okay, he'd just as soon get it tomorrow anyway, sometime in the afternoon." Hunter waited. "You still there?"

"You're gonna have to get Sweety out of there for a while," Raymond said, "keep the story straight. Clement could check, he could still come tonight."

"I don't think he will. It's something he has to do, but it's the kind of thing you put off," Hunter said. "Wendell get hold of you?"

"Not yet."

"He talked to Toma. Toma says he'll kill the guy if he sees him. In other words, fuck you. But he slipped and gave us one. Skender's Cadillac's missing and Toma thinks Mansell's got it."

"Where're you?"

"In the bar."

"He could go in there tonight. I don't mean with the key. He could come in the alley, through the yard, go in a back window."

"Is that right?" Hunter said, very patiently for Hunter. "It turns out the flat next to Sweety's is vacant, so MCMU's spending the night there. Is that close enough? What's the matter, you got a guilty conscience—I'm out here working my ass off, you're with a broad?"

When Raymond returned to the couch he stood looking down at her, uncertain, removed from where he had been only a few minutes before. He said, "My mother's name was Mary Frances Connolly."

He saw Carolyn's face against a blue pillow, composed, looking up at him. She said, "Really?" a little surprised.

"You want to know what she did?"

"She was a schoolteacher," Carolyn said.

"No, she was called Franny and operated a beauty shop in the Statler Hotel, when it was still there."

Carolyn said, "Do you know what my mother did? Nothing. Why don't you sit down?"

He lifted her legs and got under them, sitting low in the couch, his head against the cushion.

"You want to go to bed, I'll get out of your way."

"No, stay here. You've watched me, but I haven't watched you," Carolyn said. "You like your work, don't you?"

"Yeah, I do," Raymond said.

"You don't get tired of the same thing every day?"

"Well, nobody likes surveillance; but outside of that it's usually, well, each one's different."

"There's surveillance and there's lying in wait," Carolyn said quietly. "I think you're setting Clement up."

He was touching her bare toes, feeling them relaxed, pliable. "You're not ticklish, huh?"

"A little."

"That's the way you are in court, very cool. All the pros make it look easy."

"I said, I have a feeling you're setting Clement up."

"And I have a feeling he knows it," Raymond said, "so it's up to him, isn't it?"

"But you seem fairly certain he's going to come."

"He's gonna do *some*thing, I know that."

"How do you know?"

"We looked each other in the eye," Raymond said.

He smiled and Carolyn said, "My God, you haven't grown up either."

Raymond worked his head against the cushion, getting comfortable. "I was kidding."

She saw him against lamplight, his eyes closed, simply himself now. She said, "No, you weren't."

28

AT EIGHT O'CLOCK the next morning Raymond phoned Inspector Herzog to report on the surveillance. Herzog, he was told, had left a day early on his vacation. Raymond felt relief. Then tensed up again as he had the call transferred to Commander Lionel Hearn, who was a good police officer, quiet, reasonable, but did not smile easily and this bothered Raymond. Commander Hearn was black. Raymond told him about the surveillance of Sweety's Lounge and residence and the purpose, without offering details. Commander Hearn said fine, and then asked Raymond where he had stationed himself.

Raymond said, "As a matter of fact I'm at Mansell's lawyer's place. It's only about three or four minutes away." Silence. "I want Ms. Wilder to be there if an arrest is made. I don't want us thrown out of court on any surprise technicalities. We're gonna do it absolutely straight." Silence—while Raymond imagined Commander Hearn putting bits and pieces together in his mind and getting a picture of Raymond in his shirtsleeves, tie off but freshly shaved, a breakfast tray on the desk next to his holstered Colt automatic. The commander said he had never heard of this type of precaution before; was it necessary? Raymond said, "Well, actually Ms. Wilder's not representing Mansell and won't be if we bring him to trial. He hasn't retained her and she's willing to go along; so I think she could serve as a very valuable witness." Silence again.

The commander said, "Well, if you think you know what you're doing, good luck."

Raymond turned to Carolyn and said, "I'm not this casual, not at all."

"You convinced me," she said.

Hunter had gone home at seven and returned just before noon. He kept in contact with Raymond using a phone that MCMU had taken out of Sweety's residence and connected to a jack in the recently vacated flat next door. Along with Hunter there were six MCMU officers in the flat, three armed with shotguns, watching front and rear. There were no automobiles on the street that could be identified as police cars. Hunter called every hour.

At noon he said, "Everything's cool. Sweety's in the bar, the key's under the mat."

At 12:50 Hunter said, "Where'd you sleep, on the couch? . . . Yeah, how come you're changing the subject?"

At 1:55 Hunter said, "I'm gonna have Herzog put you in for a citation. 'Without regard for his own personal safety' . . . You getting much?"

At 2:25 Hunter said, "Black Cadillac went past, turned around up the street, coming back. Here we go. Parking right in front."

"I'm on my way," Raymond said.

"Shit," Hunter said.

"What's wrong?"

"It's not Mansell. It's his dizzy girlfriend."

She was supposed to walk through it, no problem, nothing to get excited about. Fine. Except it took forever to get the front door open while she danced around, dying to go to the bathroom. She couldn't find the basement light switch. She tried to open the hot water heater before she realized it wasn't the furnace. She found the gun, the Walther, and dropped it in the brown leather shoulder bag she'd brought along. Upstairs again when she went to use the phone, it wasn't there. Hey, come on. She found a phone in the kitchen, dialed and said, "The way it's going, I almost forgot why I fucking came in here. It just isn't my day . . . Yeah, I got it . . . No, I haven't seen a soul." She listened to his voice that was almost a whisper and said, "Hang around for what? You want me to bring it or not?" She looked outside, studying the cars on the street as she was supposed to, and came out looking up and down, dragging the shoulderbag along by the straps, got in the Cadillac and drove off.

Raymond crossed over from Carolyn's gray Mercedes as Hunter and the MCMU officers came out of the flat next to Sweety's.

Hunter said, "You see her? She's so stoned I bet she don't even know she was here."

When Toma looked out and saw the car, he thought of a time when he was sixteen and had sighted down the barrel of a Mauser on a Russian soldier who had got out of his truck to relieve himself—the same distance from the apartment window to the car across the street—and had killed the man with one shot. He had waited three days for a Russian truck. He had been in Skender's apartment perhaps three minutes, getting some books to take to the hospital, and had not looked out the window with the hope or intention of seeing something of interest. But there it was, Skender's black Cadillac.

Sometimes you had to work hard and sometimes it was handed to you. Toma put the books on the windowsill and took out his .32-caliber Beretta. Then saw that he wasn't being handed everything.

The person in the car was a young girl with funny looking golden hair. Smoking a cigarette. Taking her time.

Toma watched for several minutes. Finally the girl got out of the car and slammed the door. Then opened it again and bent over to reach inside, held this pose for nearly a minute, then came out again with a brown leather bag that appeared worn and soft. The girl held it at her side by the shoulder strap as she crossed the street, the bottom of the bag brushing the pavement, and entered the building's courtyard. Toma stepped back from the window. She passed along the walk to the front entrance. Now she stood there. She didn't go into the vestibule, she stood outside, waiting, not more than thirty feet from Toma, who was looking at her back now. She seemed relaxed but didn't move. Toma turned, looking toward the street again.

A gray Mercedes passed slowly. A black Ford passed . . . another one.

He's here, Toma thought.

But how could he be?

Then knew—as he turned to look at the girl again and saw the glass door open and Mansell step outside—*in the basement*. In the room made for hiding.

Or in the apartment upstairs Skender was preparing, furnishing.

Jesus, the man had nerve. Toma went to his knees to raise the window, slowly. The screen was still in place; he'd fire through it. Men with nerve died like anyone else if shot in the right place. But the girl was in the way. He could see only a small part of Mansell. The girl was holding up the big leather purse. Mansell, yes, had a gun in his hand. Toma aimed carefully. But Mansell would move, lean to look past the girl toward the street. Now he was reaching into the purse—Toma thinking, What is this? Is it a show? For a moment he thought he saw a different gun in Mansell's hand.

Why doesn't he hurry?

Now he was going inside, the glass door closing, the girl turning away but taking her time.

It was in Toma's mind to run, *now*, meet him in the hall . . .

But something strange was going on. The girl was walking out of the courtyard with the same uncertain but uncaring stride . . . then stepping out of the way, onto the grass, and Toma saw familiar faces, Raymond Cruz, Hunter, homicide people, and some not familiar, a woman with them—coming quickly along the entrance walk, past his front-row seat.

Yes, like a show, Toma thought.

Raymond Cruz was looking at the girl. He seemed to hesitate. The girl nodded, once. Not nodding hello, but saying something with the nod. Cruz kept going with the others. All of them eager. Of course—because they know Mansell's inside.

It *is* a show, Toma thought.

They were in the vestibule now. He could hear someone buzzing the door open for them.

The girl with the strange blond hair was still in the courtyard, forgotten—looking inside her big purse now, feeling in there like she was looking for her keys as she walked out to the street—past a uniformed policeman getting out of a squad car—and across the street to Skender's Cadillac.

If she had given Mansell a gun and was leaving him here, of all places—*No,* not of all places, the *only* place!

Toma ran from Skender's apartment down the hall to the back stairs, hearing others on the stairs above him. He turned off the light and started down, as quietly as he could, still not certain what the show was about, even though he had thought of a way to end it.

29

STANDING IN THE FIRST-FLOOR HALLWAY, the MCMU people hurrying past them, Carolyn said, "Does this happen often?"

They had searched every apartment, every room, every closet in the building and were still going up and down halls past each other. Around in circles, Raymond thought. There was no way Mansell could have gotten out, nowhere between the roof and the basement he could be hiding.

He said to her, "We'll find him."

"But he's not here."

"Yes, he is," Raymond said, with nothing to lose.

Hunter came up to them. He said, "Well?"

Raymond pictured again what he had seen from the car, going past slowly in Carolyn's Mercedes: Sandy at the door, Clement coming out. Going past again . . . going in then as Sandy came out, seeing her nod, accepting it because he was anxious, evidently too anxious . . .

He said, "Where's Sandy?" Hunter looked at him. He looked at Hunter.

Carolyn said, "I don't believe this." She watched Hunter walk off toward the front of the building. "What do you do now?"

"Wait," Raymond said.

"For what?"

Hunter turned and started back. "Hey, you see Toma yet? He's here."

As Carolyn watched, Raymond began to smile.

Toma left the apartment door open; he sat reading one of the books he would bring Skender, a book about the cultivation and care of house plants. When Raymond Cruz and a woman and Hunter appeared in the doorway Toma said, "Well, how are you?"

Raymond said, "Toma Sinistaj, Carolyn Wilder. Ms. Wilder does criminal work, she's one of the best defense attorneys in town. I mention it in case you want to retain her right now and get that out of the way."

Toma said, "You don't want to talk to me alone?"

"I want you to tell me where he is. Right here's fine."

"I'm giving you something, Raymond; but you don't want all your people watching. I could have

killed him. You understand that? I came very close.
Then I said no."

"Why?"

"You'll see. Or you won't; it's up to you. But I
think you better get rid of your people."

A door closed down the hall.

It was quiet in the building now. Toma took
them to the basement where he turned on fluorescent lights and let them stand looking around for a
moment, preparing his audience.

"He had a gun," Toma said. "This one," opening his suitcoat and drawing an automatic from his
waistband. "You see it? It's a Browning. It belongs
to this family and has killed no one."

"Where is he?" Raymond said.

Toma nodded. "Watch the wall there." He
walked over to the furnace, where Raymond was
standing, Raymond stepping out of his way,
reached up, stretching to his tiptoes, and pulled the
switch down.

With the humming sound the wall began to come
apart, the three-foot section of cement blocks opening toward them, gradually revealing the room, the
record player, the safe . . . Clement Mansell seated
in a canvas chair with his legs crossed.

He said, "Hey, shit, what is going *on?* I come
down here to put back something Sandy give me

she says her friend Skender loaned her for protection and this undertaker sticks a pistol in my back, locks me in here."

"He had the wall already open," Toma said, "waiting in there for you to find him."

"With the Browning?" Raymond said.

Toma nodded. "He wants you to believe he got it from the blond girl with the hair."

"You searched him good?"

"Of course."

"What about in the room?"

"I made sure." Toma hefted the Browning. "This is the only gun he had. There were some in there, but I took them out yesterday."

Clement said, "Are you looking for a gun, it's got P.38 stamped on the side and some other numbers and kinda looks like a German Luger? . . . I haven't seen it."

Pull him out, Raymond thought. No, go in there with him. Tell Toma to close the wall.

"We got Sandy," Hunter was saying to Clement. "Saw her hand you the gun and you hand it back, thinking you're foxing somebody."

"Hey, bullshit," Clement said. "You had Sandy you wouldn't be standing there with that egg smeared all over your face."

Raymond wanted to pull him up out of the chair—where he sat low with one knee sticking out at an angle, his boot resting on the other knee, elbows on the chair arms, hands clasped in front of him—and hit Clement as hard as he could.

The man's eyes danced from Hunter to Raymond, then to Carolyn. He said, "How you doing, lady?" Frowning then. "Jesus, what'd you do to your face, run into something?" His gaze moved back to Raymond. "What the undertaker says, that's my story. I come down here to return a weapon Sandy was given or swiped off her boyfriend. If you think you saw something different or you don't like what you see now, tough titty, I'm sticking to it. There ain't any way in the world you're gonna lay the judge on me, partner, or anybody else. And I'll tell you something, you never will." His gaze moved to Carolyn and he winked. "Have I got 'em by the gonads, counselor, or haven't I? I want to thank you very much for that loan." He patted his jacket pocket. "I got the check right here. Gonna cash her as I leave here for Tampa, Florida, never to return. Which I bet chokes you all up some." With his half-grin he looked at Raymond again. "What do you say, partner, you give up?"

Raymond said nothing. He reached up with his right hand, felt the switch mounted on the wall and flicked it on.

As the wall began to close Clement said, "Hey—" He didn't move right away, he said, "My lawyer's standing right there, shithead." They saw him rise out of the chair now, saying, "Hey, come on, goddamn-it—" They could see his fingers in the opening before he pulled them in. They could see a line of light inside and hear him scream, "Goddamn-it, open this goddamn—" And that was all.

Raymond reached up again. The humming motor sound stopped. There was a silence. Carolyn turned, started for the stairs, and Raymond looked over.

"Carolyn?"

She didn't pause or look back. "I'll be in the car."

He watched her go up the stairs—no objections from her, no emotion—and again there was silence. Hunter approached the cinderblock wall almost cautiously and ran his hand over it. He looked at Raymond and said, straightfaced, "Where'd he go?"

Toma said to Raymond, "You see why I didn't kill him. This way satisfies both of us. For me, it's like Skender doing it to him, which is much better. For you, it seems the only way you're going to get this man who kills people."

Hunter said, "You sure he can't open it?"

"He broke the switch himself when he was here before," Toma said.

Raymond listened as they spoke in low tones, almost reverently, Toma saying, "He prepared his own tomb. There's water, a little food for his last meals, a toilet. He could last—I don't know—fifty, sixty days maybe. But eventually he dies." Hunter saying now, "We had the place covered, but somehow he slipped out. I don't see any problem, do you? Man disappeared." Toma saying, "It's also soundproof." Then Hunter wondering if after a while there might be an odor and Toma saying, "One of the tenants complains we open the wall and say, 'Oh, so that's where he was hiding. Oh, that's too bad.'"

It's done, Raymond thought. Walk away.

30

THEY HAD SEVERAL DRINKS at the Athens Bar, quiet drinks, Raymond and Hunter alone at a table, with little to talk about until Hunter leaned in to tell what worried him. Like Carolyn Wilder. Would she blow it or not? Raymond said he didn't think so. She had walked out (her car was gone when they left the apartment building) and it was like saying to them, do what you want. Without saying it. He believed she could handle it. Carolyn had learned to be realistic about Clement: she could send him away for assault and robbery, but knew he would come back if she did.

Hunter said, "You want to know exactly what it's like? It's like the first time I ever went to a whorehouse. I was sixteen years old, these guys took me to a place corner of Seward and Second. After, you're all clutched up, you don't know whether to feel proud of yourself or guilty. You know what I mean? And after a while you don't

think of it either way; it's something you did."
Hunter went home to bed.

Raymond walked back to 1300 Beaubien. The
snack counter in the lobby was closed and he
looked at his watch: 5:40. The squadroom was
locked, empty. He went in and sat at his desk beneath the window. It was dismal outside, a gray
cast to the sky; somber, semidark inside, but he
didn't bother to turn on lights.

He had felt relief as the wall closed and Mansell
disappeared; but the relief was an absence of pres-
sure, not something in itself. He tried to analyze
what he was feeling now. He didn't feel good, he
didn't feel bad. He called Carolyn. She said, "Are
you worried I'm going to tell on you?" He said,
"No." She said, "Then why talk about it. I'm aw-
fully tired. Why don't you call me tomorrow,
maybe go out to dinner, get a little high? How does
that sound?"

A little after six Raymond looked up at the
sound of the door opening. He saw the figure in the
doorway backlighted from the hall.

Sandy said, "Anybody home? . . . What're you
doing sitting in the dark?" She came in, letting the
door swing closed. "God, am I whacked out." She
dropped her shoulderbag on Hunter's desk, sunk
into his swivel chair and put her boots up on the
corner of the desk.

Raymond could see her in faint light from the window. He didn't move because he felt no reason to. He had not been thinking of Sandy Stanton. He had obvious questions but did not feel like asking them. He did not feel like getting himself into the role, being the policeman right now.

"I pulled in the garage downstairs, a guy goes, hey, you can't park here. I told him it's okay, it's a stolen car, I'm returning it. The guy at the desk downstairs—what is that place?"

"First Precinct," Raymond said.

"He goes, hey, where you going? I tell him I'm going up to five. He goes, you can't go up there. I'm thinking, try and get out of here, shit, you can't even get *in* . . . I thought you'd be looking for me. I sat in the apartment not knowing what's going on, finally the phone rang. It was Del. He isn't coming home, he's going to Acapulco. You ready for this? And he wants me to fly out to L.A. and go with him . . . and bring his pink and green flowered sportcoat that asshole gave to the doorman. How am I gonna get it back?"

Raymond said, "Is that what you came to ask me?"

"No, I wanted to know if it's okay to go or if you're gonna arrest me or what. I'm so fucking whacked I want to go *some*where, I'm telling you, and sleep for about a week." She made fists, holding them out, and said, "My nerves are like *that*."

"You left Skender's car?"

"Yeah, I told the guy it really wasn't stolen it was *sort* of stolen and that you know all about it."

"What about the gun?"

Sandy dug into her bag. She brought out the Walther and laid it on Hunter's desk.

She said, "Do we have to get into it again? I haven't seen shitbird at all, he hasn't called, thank God, I don't know where he is, if he's in jail or what and I don't want to know. I'm twenty-three and I got to get my ass in gear and I think going to Acapulco could be very good for me. What do you think?"

"I think you ought to go," Raymond said.

"Really?"

Raymond didn't say any more. Sandy got up with her bag. "I'll just leave the gun here." Raymond nodded. She said, "Listen, I'm not mad at you, I think you've been a pretty neat guy, considering. I know you have a job to do and, you know—so maybe I'll see you again sometime . . ."

Raymond raised his hand to her. As the door swung in, closing off the light from the hall, he brought his hand down and got up. He went over to Hunter's desk and picked up the Walther, hefting it, feeling its weight. He shifted the gun to his left hand and brought out his Colt 9-mm from the shoulder holster, feeling both of the guns now, judging the Colt to be a good half-pound heavier.

Two-gun Cruz. In a dark room all by himself. Two-gun Cruz, shit. Sneaky Cruz . . . Dead-ass Cruz . . . Or how do you like Chicken-fat Cruz, chicken fat?

After a couple of hours Clement put Donna Summer's "Love To Love You, Baby" on the record player to hear the sound of a human voice. He inventoried the canned goods, found all kinds of mashed chick peas and pressed meat and not one goddamn thing he liked to eat. There was nothing to drink except water and two cans of Tab and he expected they'd be turning the water off when they thought of it—if the plan was to leave him here. He had thought the wall would open again within a minute or so after it closed. All right, five minutes. Well, give 'em ten. Okay, play the game with 'em, maybe a half hour, which was supposed to give him a good scare. No—what they'd do, he realized after an hour or so, sure, they'd open it up and ask him if he wanted to confess, telling him if he didn't they'd close it up again and take out the motor. The dumb fucks. He'd look scared and say, yes, Jesus, just get me out of here, I'll confess to anything you want. Then come up for the exam and tell 'em to get fucked, the confession was signed under duress and he was not only walking, he was filing suit against the police department. A hundred thousand dollars for fucking up his nervous system. Look how he was shaking . . .

He had been glancing at his gold watch since the wall closed on him at a little after three and he had never seen time go so slow. He'd sit down, he'd get up and pace around a little to the music, then began picturing disco dancers and moved to the beat some more, seeing if he could do it—shit, it was easy—he could *feel* it and wished there was a mirror so he could see himself doing it—shit, dancing all by himself to the nigger girl singing in a secret basement room. Nobody in the world would believe it.

He looked at his gold watch at 6:50, 7:15, 7:35, 8:02, 8:20, 9:05 after some dancing, 9:32 turning off the record player for a rest and at 9:42. It was right after that he heard the sound, the wall moving.

Clement got in the canvas chair facing the opening as it widened, seeing the clean basement a little at a time, the light reflecting off the cement floor it was so clean.

If it was the Albanian, he was dead.

It could be Carolyn, her heart bleeding for him. But she'd be too scared—unless it was somebody she sent. No, it would have to be the cops, come back to make their threatening offer. Clement told himself to get ready to look scared.

He waited. The humming sound of the motor continued. No one appeared. Clement got up out of the chair and approached the opening, inched his head out, looking over at the furnace. Nobody there. Nobody jumped on him when he walked out. He went over to the switch, reached up and flicked it off.

Who?

See—it ran through Clement's mind—if it was a friend, the friend would be standing here. And if he wanted to run through his current list of friends, that could only be one person. So it wasn't Sandy. Unless she wanted to help him, but not be associated with him anymore—ran like hell. Or it was somebody like the Albanians who wanted to take him outside, which didn't make sense. Or it was somebody with a guilty conscience, which *could* make sense even though it was hard to imagine.

Clement went up the stairs to the first-floor hall and followed it to the front entrance. He might as well keep going. Anyone meaning to get him would have considered his slipping out the back, so there was no point in getting tricky. Go on out. And he did, walked out to the street, and what did he see sitting there but Skender's black Cadillac.

Now, was it a coincidence, the car was picked up and returned? Or had Sandy left it here this afternoon and took off on foot? Or was somebody tempting him again? Or—wait now—was the gun in there and they'd stop him, arrest him with it?

No. He could be stopped for stealing a car—number two hundred and sixty something—but if there was a gun in it somewhere it would belong to the owner, not him. No prints anyway. Clement opened the driver-side door and felt under the seat. No gun. Just the keys. Did he want to think about this a while or did he want to haul ass?

Clement took the Cadillac south to downtown, got off at the Lafayette exit, just past the giant red Strohs Beer sign giving warmth to the night sky, and ten minutes later was in the elevator going up to 2504. He hoped Sandy was home and would be able to explain some of these weird things going on.

31

CLEMENT STILL HAD A KEY to the apartment that Sandy had given him. He went in and saw lights glittering outside the windows but not one was on in the apartment. He listened a moment and called out, "Hon?"

It was about 10:30; she could be asleep, she had probably smoked enough reefers to send her off early. Clement turned on the light in the hallway as he walked into the bedroom. "Hon bun?"

Nope. The bed wasn't made. That was par—but there weren't any of her clothes lying around. Clement turned the bedroom light on and went over to the closet. It looked like only Del Weems' stuff hanging inside. He went to the dresser, was about to bend down to open one of the drawers she used, but never got there.

He saw the Walther P.38 lying on the dresser about ten inches from his eyes.

She *still* hadn't dumped the goddamn thing. He could hear himself saying, with pain in his voice,

"Hon, I don't believe it. Twice now. Are you intentionally trying to fuck me or what?" He had a mind to throw the goddamn thing out the window, man, just to be *rid* of it. Like the goddamn thing had stickum on it. He picked up the gun.

It felt good though. Fired straight and true. He checked the clip, pushed the spring down, saw it was loaded but lacking about two rounds, and punched it back into the grip with the palm of his hand.

He walked into the living room trying to recall something. Fired five at the judge, three at the woman. He had reloaded when he got back to the garage, before he hid it. He seemed to recall he had fully reloaded it. Hadn't he? . . . He turned on the desk lamp. A note written on pale-green paper lay squarely in position before the chair. Clement sat down without touching it, spreading his elbows to get low, close to the note, and laid the Walther to one side.

Dear Clement:-

If you read this then you don't know yet I have left. I am not telling you where I'm going for I am leaving you for good as my nerves can't stand any more of your kind of life and I'm getting too old for it. One thing I guess I have to tell you I did not throw the gun away

again and I'll tell you why. There was some-
body every place I went. I would start to get
out of the car and somebody would be there
watching. I don't know why but it is not easy
to throw away a gun. I have had enough so
goodbye.

> *Yours,*
> *Sandy*

P.S. I think you better run!!!
P.P.S. IT'S TOO LATE.

Clement frowned, staring at the note. Something
here was weird. The second postscript was bigger
and in a different handwriting. If she scribbled it
quick, maybe—but it wasn't like that. It was in big
printed letters. Clement felt goosebumps crawl up
his arms, over his shoulders and neck, up under his
hair. He stared at the notepaper in the soft glow of
the lamp, the rest of the living room dark, almost
dark, wanting to look up, wanting to look out past
the green-shaded glow of light. He had not heard a
sound, but he could feel it. Someone else was in the
room, watching him.

There was a button switch attached to a light cord
that ran along the floor by the front windows. It

was behind Clement's chair, so that he had to turn half around and reach over with the toe of his boot. He punched the button and a chrome lamp beamed on, its light rising through the branches of a ficus tree.

Raymond Cruz sat only a few feet away from the tree, in a chair by the side windows.

"Jesus," Clement said, his hand gathering the note, squeezing it into a ball.

"I've read it," Raymond said. "In fact, I wrote part of it."

Clement was still half turned; the desk, with the Walther lying on it, to his left now. "Was it you let me out?" He saw Raymond nod. "Go have some dinner and think better of it, did you?"

"Yeah, I gave it some thought," Raymond said. "That wasn't the way to do it."

"I hope to tell you," Clement said. "I thought what you'd do, open it up and tell mc to sign a statement else you'd shut me in there for good."

"I don't want a statement," Raymond said.

Clement cocked his head, looking at him warily. "Yeah? What's this party about then?"

Raymond got up. As he came over to the desk Clement turned in his chair to get both Raymond and the Walther lined up in front of him. "I got something here," Raymond said. His hand went into his coat. "Now don't get excited." The hand came out again holding the Colt 9-mm automatic.

Clement sat rigid. Raymond moved the lamp aside and laid the Colt on the desk.

"Pick up yours and I'll pick up mine. How's that sound?"

Clement was squinting but starting to smile a little. "You serious?"

"Stand up."

"What for?"

"You'll feel better. Come on."

Clement wasn't sure. He sensed he should be laying back, not moving too much yet. It was true though, he'd have more choices on his feet. He rose, moving the chair back away from him. They stood now directly across the desk from one another.

"Put your hands on the edge of the desk," Raymond said, "like this . . . Okay, now whenever you're ready, pick up your gun. Or, whenever I'm ready."

Clement said, "You think I'm fucking crazy or something? I don't even know this piece's loaded."

"You checked it in the bedroom," Raymond said, "I heard you. You want to check it again, go ahead. You're short two rounds we fired in ballistics, that's all."

Clement stared, amazed. "You took the gun from Sweety, tested it and put it *back?*"

"With the same live rounds," Raymond said.

"You don't trust me we'll trade. You use mine, I'll use yours, I don't care."

Clement's expression seemed bland, open, as though he might be listening or might be off somewhere in his mind.

Raymond said, "This was your idea. Remember?"

"I don't think you're serious," Clement said. "Right *here?* It's too close."

"We can go outside, or up on the roof," Raymond said. "You want to go outside?"

"Fuck no, I don't want to go outside. You got some scheme—I don't know what, but you're pulling something, aren't you? Trying to spook me into signing a statement. Man, you're going way around to do it."

"I don't want a statement," Raymond said. "I told you that. You sign a confession, we come up in court you say it was under duress, coercion, some chickenshit thing. This is fair, isn't it? You said, why don't we have a shooting match. Okay, we're doing it."

"Just grab for the guns, huh?"

"Wait a minute," Raymond said. "No, I think the way we ought to do it—pick up the gun and hold it at your side. Go ahead. I think that'll be better." Raymond brought the Colt toward him and held it pointing down, the barrel extending below the edge of the desk. "Yeah, that's better. See, then when you bring it up you have to clear the desk and there's less chance of getting shot in the balls."

"Come on," Clement said, "cut the shit."

"All right, then you reach for yours and I raise mine," Raymond said, "it's up to you." He waited.

Clement's right hand edged over to the Walther, touched it, hesitated, then covered the grip and brought it toward him, off the table. He said, "I don't believe this."

"Okay, you ready?" Raymond said. "Any time you want, do it."

"Wait just a minute," Clement said.

They stared, face to face, three feet apart. There was no sound in the room.

"I SAID WAIT!"

There was a silence again before Raymond said, "What's the matter, Wildman?"

Clement put the Walther on the desk and walked away. He said, "You're fucking crazy, you know it?"

Raymond turned, his gaze following Clement as he went around the couch and through the dining-L. He heard Clement say from the kitchen, "You know we could *both* kill each other? You realize that?"

The kitchen was back of the wall that was a few feet behind the couch. Clement could come out again through the dining-L, to Raymond's right, or he could come out from the front hall, to Raymond's left.

Either way, it didn't seem to make much difference.

Raymond moved from the desk over to the front windows, glancing out at the spectacle of lights and reflecting glass, before turning to stand with his back to it. The apartment looked more comfortable at night with the lamps on; Raymond still didn't like the colors though, green and gray.

Clement was saying from the kitchen, "That was interesting, that talk we had in your office. I never done that before with a cop . . . like seeing where each other's coming from. You know it? . . ."

He'll have something in his hand, Raymond thought.

". . . Yeah, that was interesting. Getting down to the basics of life, you might say. I mean our kind of life. You want a drink? . . ."

Here we go, Raymond thought. He didn't answer.

". . . Don't say I didn't ask you. We got some Chivas . . . No, that's it for the Chivas, aaaall gone. How 'bout a beer? Got some cold Miller's . . . That mean no? How come you're not talking?"

It's his turn, Raymond thought, holding the Colt 9-mm at his side, looking at the dining-L, then moving his gaze slowly across the wall that was behind the couch to the entrance hall.

Clement was saying now, "See, what I got out of that talk we had—me and you are on different sides, but we're alike in a lot of ways . . ."

He's trying to put you to sleep, Raymond thought.

". . . You know it? I figured you were a real serious type, but I see you got a sense of humor."

Clement appeared, coming out of the front hall with a bottle of beer in each hand and walked over to the desk. "It might be a little weird, your sense of humor, but then each person's got their own style, way of doing things."

Raymond watched him place the bottle in his right hand on the desk, then, maybe twelve inches from the Walther. The hand remained there.

"I brought you a beer just in case," Clement said.

The hand came slowly, carefully, away from the desk to the front of his denim jacket.

"I got a opener here someplace, stuck it in my jeans. Okay, partner? I'm just going in here to get the opener." He glanced down.

The hand moved inside the denim jacket.

Raymond raised the Colt 9-mm, extended.

As Clement looked up, Raymond shot him three times. He fired seeing Clement's eyes and fired again in the roomful of sound, still seeing the man's eyes, and fired again as Clement was slammed against the couch and almost went over it with the momentum but collapsed into cushions and lay there, denim legs stretching to the beer bottle on the floor with foam oozing out of it, his hands holding his chest and stomach now as though he were holding his life in, not wanting it to escape, his eyes open in stunned surprise.

He said, "You shot me . . . Jesus Christ, you *shot* me . . ."

Raymond approached him. He reached down, gently moving Clement's hands aside, felt a handle and drew it from Clement's belt. Raymond looked at it in his hand as he straightened. A curved handle that was fashioned from bone or the horn of an animal, attached to a stainless steel bottle opener.

Raymond went to the desk. He placed the opener next to the Walther, picked up the phone and dialed a number he had known for fifteen years. As he waited he reholstered the Colt. When a voice came on Raymond identified himself, gave the address and hung up.

Clement was staring at him, eyes glazed, clouding over. "You call EMS?"

"I called the Wayne County Morgue."

Clement continued to stare, dazed, eyes unblinking.

Raymond could hear street sounds very faintly, far away.

Clement said, "I don't believe it . . . what did you kill me for?"

Raymond didn't answer. Maybe tomorrow he'd think of something he might have said. After a little while Raymond picked up the opener from the desk and began paring the nail of his right index finger with the sharply pointed hooked edge.

THE UNDISPUTED MASTER
OF THE CRIME NOVEL

DJIBOUTI
A Novel

978-0-06-173521-9 (trade paperback)

Elmore Leonard brings his trademark wit and inimitable style to this twisting, gripping—and sometimes playful— tale of modern-day piracy.

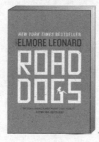

ROAD DOGS
A Novel

978-0-06-198570-6 (trade paperback)

The further adventures of Jack Foley, out of prison but right back into trouble.

PRONTO

978-0-06-212033-5 (trade paperback)

A brilliant combination of suspense and black humor featuring Raylan Givens, the inspiration behind the FX series *Justified*.

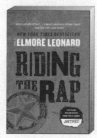

RIDING THE RAP

978-0-06-212247-6 (trade paperback)

Raylan Givens returns to bust open a kidnapping ring in the sequel to *Pronto*.

FIRE IN THE HOLE
Stories

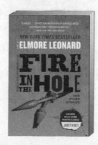

978-0-06-212034-2 (trade paperback)

This short fiction collection features a few beloved Elmore Leonard characters, including Raylan Givens in the title story that was the basis for the pilot of the hit FX series *Justified*.

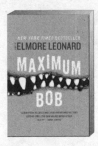

MAXIMUM BOB

978-0-06-200940-1 (trade paperback)

Florida Judge "Maximum" Bob Gibbs has thrown the
book at so many felons, it's beginning to look
as if one of them is throwing it back at him.

TISHOMINGO BLUES

978-0-06-200939-5 (trade paperback)

The Dixie Mafia is aiming to shoot high-diver Dennis
Lenahan from the top of his 80-foot ladder.

RUM PUNCH
A Novel

978-0-06-211982-7 (trade paperback)

Cops try to use Jackie Burke to get at the gunrunner she's
been bringing cash into the country for, but she hatches a
plan to keep the money for herself.

FREAKY DEAKY
A Novel

978-0-06-212035-9 (trade paperback)

It's only after he transfers out of the bomb squad that
Chris Mankowski begins playing with dynamite.

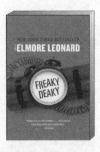

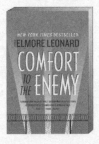

COMFORT TO THE ENEMY AND OTHER CARL WEBSTER STORIES

978-0-06-173515-8 (trade paperback)

First time in print in the U.S.
A collection of 3 stories about the legendary lawman
Carl Webster.

GET SHORTY
A Novel

978-0-06-212025-0 (trade paperback)

A Miami shylock, Chili Palmer, goes to Hollywood and becomes a movie producer. Why not?

BANDITS

978-0-06-212032-8 (trade paperback)

An unlikely trio targeting millions of dollars is sure to make out like bandits—if they survive.

KILLSHOT
A Novel

978-0-06-212159-2 (trade paperback)

After witnessing a scam, Carmen and her husband must outrun the thugs bent on eliminating any living evidence.

MR. PARADISE
A Novel

978-0-06-211905-6 (trade paperback)

Elmore Leonard presents a whole new cast of characters—the kind that only he can create—in this Detroit homicide book.

GLITZ
A Novel

978-0-06-212158-5 (trade paperback)

A classic Elmore Leonard novel, spinning from the lazy beaches of Puerto Rico to the mean streets of Miami to the non-stop jangle of Atlantic City's one-armed bandits.

BIG BOUNCE
A Novel

978-0-06-218428-3 (trade paperback)

Razor-sharp and wholly unpredictable, this Elmore Leonard classic is a sly, beguiling story of a man, a woman, and a nasty little crime.

CUBA LIBRE

978-0-06-218429-0 (trade paperback)

This spellbinding journey into the heart and soul of the Cuban revolution of a hundred years ago showcases an explosive mix of high adventure, history brought to life, and a honey of a love story.

STICK
A Novel

978-0-06-218435-1 (trade paperback)

An ex–con trying to go straight finds himself tempted by a high stakes, sweet–revenge scam . . . and targeted by a psycho killer with a score to settle.

CITY PRIMEVAL
A Novel

978-0-06-219135-9 (trade paperback)

City Primeval is classic Elmore Leonard: an erratic killer, a city going about its business, and suspense that won't quit.

SPLIT IMAGES
A Novel

978-0-06-212251-3 (trade paperback)

When homicide cop Bryan Hurd takes a vacation, he lands in Palm Beach and finds murder in the Sunshine State.